Run-away love

Run-away love

USA TODAY BESTSELLING AUTHOR

Melanie Harlow

Melanie Harlow

Entangled Publishing, LLC
644 Shrewsbury Commons Ave., STE 181
Shrewsbury, PA 17361
rights@entangledpublishing.com

Amara is an imprint of Entangled Publishing, LLC.

Visit our website at www.entangledpublishing.com.

Edited by Nancy Smay and Julia Griffis
Cover art/illustration and design by Hang Le
Stock art by Anastasia Pechnikova/Gettyimages, Tanya Shulga/Gettyimages,
Preto_perola/Gettyimages
Map Illustration by Francesca Weber
Interior design by Britt Marczak

ISBN 978-1-64937-766-1

Manufactured in the United States of America

First Edition July 2024

10 9 8 7 6 5 4 3 2 1

ALSO BY MELANIE HARLOW

CHERRY TREE HARBOR SERIES

Runaway Love
Hideaway Heart
Make-Believe Match
Small Town Swoon

1. Cherry Blossom Inn
2. Harbor Lights Salon & Spa
3. Bayview Service Station
4. The Pier Inn
5. Lush Wine Bar
6. Main Street Coffee
7. Larry's Barber Shop
8. George Buckley's House
9. Ari DeLuca's House
10. Moe's Diner
11. The Sweet Shoppe
12. Waterfront Park
13. The Lighthouse
14. Farmer's Market
15. Chapel by the Sea
16. Buckley's Pub
17. Austin Buckley's House

For Cori
Thanks for sharing stories, friendship, wine,
and the last fourteen years!

At Entangled, we want our readers to be well-informed. If you would like to know if this book contains any elements that might be of concern for you, please check the back of the book for details.

Chapter 1

VERONICA

*S*ometimes, when the universe wants you to change the course of your life, it sends you a sign.

Perhaps a recurring dream. Or you keep seeing the same numbers everywhere. Or hearing the same song over and over again.

Me?

I got a sext.

I had very little experience with sexting—none at all, really—but in my opinion, this one wasn't bad.

It was from my fiancé, Cornelius "Neil" Vanderhoof V.

> Hey Valerie. I can't stop thinking about your naked body in my bed last night. Your sexy mouth. Those hands all over me. The way I licked every inch of your skin.

There were even some emojis. An eggplant. A cat. Some raindrops.

While I was taking it all in, another text arrived.

Suddenly I was subjected to an up-close and personal pic of the Vanderhoof family jewels, making it *very* clear that Neil was eager to repeat last night's activities, right now if possible.

> Look how bad I want you right now. Think we have time for an afternoon delight?

An afternoon delight?

Today?

There were a few obvious problems with this.

First, my name wasn't Valerie.

Second, I hadn't been in his bed last night.

Finally, we were going to be busy this afternoon.

GETTING MARRIED.

In fact, I was already tucked away in the little "bride's room" off the vestibule of Cherry Tree Harbor's charming little Chapel by the Sea. I was wearing the big white strapless dress Neil had liked best. My veil was pinned above the elegant chignon he had suggested. My makeup had been professionally done, and it was understated and classic—just like Neil had requested. He'd even sent me a photo from Pinterest so I could get the look just right.

A natural eye. A faint blush on the cheeks. A demure, nude lip.

"But I like a red lip," I said.

"I know you do, teacup, but that's more of a showy thing, isn't it? Like stage makeup?"

My shoulders stiffened. Was that a dig at my past? When Neil and I met, I was a Radio City Rockette. He was in the audience one night, and he said when the curtain went up, he took one look at me and knew in an instant he had to have me. He waited with flowers at the stage door every night for a week before I finally gave in and had dinner with him.

"It's just that Mother would prefer we keep things toned down," he went on.

"Things like my personality?"

"Don't make such a fuss, teacup. It's just lipstick. And you know how she is."

Did I ever.

I'd been putting up with Bootsy Vanderhoof's subtle judgment and criticism for a solid year. She handed out her opinions like they were gold coins, about everything from my wardrobe (too black) to my job (too splashy) to my complexion (too pale) to my laugh (too loud).

"Yes," I said through my teeth.

"Good." Neil had given me a patronizing kiss on the cheek—he'd perfected that move—and moved on to how he'd prefer me to wear flats with my wedding dress instead of heels. He wasn't short, but I was a solid five-foot-ten, and two-inch heels made us about even in stature.

This was not in keeping with the way Neil saw the world.

"But Neil," I said, "I wore heels when I had my final fitting. If I wear flats with my dress, it will be too long."

"No need to fuss, the shop will hem it for you," he said confidently. "We've still got two weeks, and we're certainly good enough customers. All three of my sisters bought their wedding gowns there." His voice took on the haughty tone of someone who'd done a massive favor for you that you didn't properly appreciate. "The Vanderhoof family has practically kept that shop in business."

I pressed my lips together. I knew alllll about his three older sisters' weddings—where they bought their gowns and what flowers they carried and what foods were served at dinner and what music was played at the yacht club receptions. Every one of them had done practically the same exact thing, as if the same June wedding was on repeat three years in a row—ours would be the fourth. The guests had to feel like they were in the movie *Groundhog Day* at this point.

But if I'd learned anything in the last year, it was that the Vanderhoofs of Chicago's Gold Coast believed in tradition. Tradition ruled the day. You did not ignore it, buck it, or break it. You didn't dare criticize it. You embraced it, reverently, eagerly, yet nonchalantly—no one likes a fuss—and then the Vanderhoofs would approve of you.

And the crazy thing was, I'd wanted that approval. I'd worked so hard to earn it, to be treated like I fit in to their family. *Twelve months* of allowing myself to be shaped into a different person. Of trying to distract myself from grief. Of doing my best to keep a promise I never should have made in the first place. I'd been so desperate to belong.

But as I stared at those texts, it was like a fog began to lift.

This was all wrong.

I didn't want to marry him.

And he didn't really want to marry me—not the real me, anyway.

I glanced at my phone again, certain that this wasn't the first time he'd cheated and would not be the last.

There had been several times over the last year that I'd suspected Neil wasn't entirely faithful—the smell of a strange perfume on his clothes, a flirtatious wink at a pub waitress, a knowing look exchanged among his male co-workers at the office Christmas party.

He always brushed aside my worries or had a decent enough excuse, but doubt lingered at the back of my mind. His father was a notorious cheat—a *philanderer*, whispered the ladies at tennis— and Neil had been groomed his entire life to step into his father's polished wing tips.

Like father, like son, was what everyone said about them.

"I don't want to marry him," I said out loud. "I don't want his name or his money or his Lake Shore Drive high-rise or his family connections. I don't need to be Veronica Vanderhoof—I'll be plain old Roni Sutton, and I'm fine with that."

"Are you okay, dear?"

I jumped at the sound of the voice behind me.

It was Irene, the church's wedding coordinator, who'd entered the room so quietly I hadn't heard her.

"Yes." I was surprised at how calm I sounded. "I'm actually okay."

Irene moved closer to me with tentative steps, hugging her clipboard to her chest. "Are you sure?" She glanced around the empty room. "Where are your friends? I thought you had…" She checked her notes. "Three bridesmaids?"

"I do, but they're not my friends. They're the groom's sisters. I think they're with the family, greeting guests."

"Oh. I see." Her eyes moved down the page. "No maid of honor?"

"She had a baby two days ago, so she couldn't make it." I felt a pang of longing for Morgan, who'd been so loyal to me.

"And no father of the bride, correct? You'll be unescorted down the aisle?"

I wasn't going to walk down the aisle, escorted or otherwise, but Irene didn't need to know that yet.

"That's the plan," I said.

Suddenly I was grateful for the sneakers hidden beneath the ballgown skirt of my newly hemmed dress, rather than the ivory Chanel ballet flats Neil had gifted me last week. It had felt like a monumental act of defiance to wear them, even if they couldn't be seen—I saw it now as a little sign that not all of my spirit had been snuffed out.

Also, I might have to make a hasty exit.

"Well, try to relax." Irene smiled without showing any teeth. "Guests are starting to arrive, but you've got about thirty more minutes."

"Actually, could you send Neil in here?"

Irene looked aghast and steepled her fingers above her pearls. "Neil? The *groom*?"

"Yes, please."

"But it's before the wedding! You can't see each other before the wedding."

"I know what the tradition is. Just send him in." Hopefully he didn't still have his hand in his pants when she found him.

Scandalized, she left the room. I glanced at my phone again, rereading the words he'd sent Valerie, his assistant. She'd worked for him for about six months, a pretty young blonde I'd heard Bootsy refer to behind one hand as a "social climber."

She must have stayed last night at the Vanderhoof's sprawling summer home overlooking the bay (they referred to it as a "cottage," but the place had eight bedrooms, a tennis court, and a name—they called it Rosethorn), although I found it hard to believe Bootsy had issued such an invitation. Maybe Neil had snuck her in.

I'd stayed at a quaint little inn just off Main Street that was walking distance from the salon and spa where Morgan and I had made hair and makeup appointments. After she'd called me sobbing that she wouldn't be able to come in from New York since she was going into early labor, Bootsy had suggested I keep the reservation since all the bedrooms at Rosethorn would be occupied by family. Neil hadn't argued.

More missed signs.

As I stuck my phone back into my bag, I remembered why I'd

been digging through it in the first place. After studying my classic and understated makeup in the full-length mirror bolted to one wall, I'd decided I looked so unlike myself that I'd started to panic.

Getting married shouldn't mean losing yourself completely, right? I knew marriage took patience, acceptance, and compromise, but did it have to take beige lipstick?

I'd decided to add a little bit of color to my look—I'd stuck my own makeup case in my bag—and was hunting for the tube of Don't F*ck With Me, my favorite shade of red, when I noticed the new text on my phone from Neil.

Pulling the head-turning color from the small, zippered bag now, I took out the tube and painted a bright, confident, badass red over the demure nude on my lips. I rubbed them together, puckered, and squared my shoulders.

"I'm calling it off," I promised the girl in the mirror. "I don't know where I go from here, but it won't be with him."

At the knock on the door, I jumped. "Come in!"

"Veronica, what is this?" Neil yelled through the door. "I'm not supposed to see you."

"Oh, just come in," I said crossly, shoving the lipstick back into my bag. "I'm not in the mood to play games."

"Mother said absolutely not."

I fumed, my nostrils flaring. "Fine. Then I'll come out."

"I don't think that's a good idea. Just stay where you belong, and we can talk later."

But I was done following his commands. I'd let him tell me what to do ever since he put a ring on my finger, as if the diamond gave him the right.

I flung open the door to see my fiancé standing there, looking handsome in his tux but undeniably perturbed. The famous slab-like Vanderhoof chin, identical to his father's and grandfather's, was thrust forward and rigid. He ran a hand over his impeccably styled dark blond hair without really touching it. "Is this necessary, teacup?" he asked.

"Yes," I said, glancing behind him at the guests entering the vestibule. "And I didn't want to do it out here, but I will if I must."

"Is this about the lipstick?" His eyes narrowed as he focused on my mouth. "Because I thought we agreed, no red."

"It's not about the lipstick. I got your texts."

"What texts?" Now his eyes shifted toward the church's double doors, which were propped open to the June sunshine. His family stood on the steps.

"Of course, you got my name wrong—it's Veronica, not Valerie—or maybe it's *me* who had it all wrong when I said yes to this wedding."

Neil's tanned complexion, golden from hours spent on the outdoor tennis courts or sailing on The Silver Spoon, his family's boat, suddenly went pallid. "What?"

"You texted the wrong woman, Neil. And you cheated on me."

Understanding of his error registered, and shock crossed his face. But he cleared his throat and composed himself quickly. "Veronica, please. Don't make a fuss. People can hear you."

"Well, if you'd have listened to me, we could be having this discussion behind closed doors. But you always think you know best."

People behind Neil were politely pretending nothing was wrong and making their way into the sanctuary. He glanced over his shoulder again and tried to take me by the arm, as if he wanted to steer me into the bride's room, but it was too late for that.

I shook off his hand. "I've had it, Neil. I can't believe I've wasted so much time trying to be someone I'm not."

"Veronica, what's come over you?"

"Do you even love me?"

"I'm marrying you, aren't I?"

"My god." I put the heels of my hands to my forehead. If the sext was a road sign, this conversation was like being knocked over the head with an iron skillet. "No. You are not marrying me."

"What are you talking about? The wedding is *today*." He adjusted his cuffs. "You are the bride, I am the groom, and we can deal with this *misunderstanding* tomorrow."

"This isn't a misunderstanding. It's a betrayal. And it's one I should have seen coming." I shook my head. "I've been a complete fool."

His eyes hardened. "On the contrary. Saying yes to me was the smartest thing you've ever done. I'm giving you a life you'd never be able to afford."

"I don't care about the money."

"Your mother did." Neil knew where to stick the knife. "On her deathbed, your mother asked me to take care of you, and I said I would give you everything you ever wanted, and you'd never have to worry about money again. All you had to do was say yes."

"And I did. Because I'd promised her I would at least give this life a chance. But your money can't give me what I want."

Neil laughed, a dismissive huff. "Of course it can. The only people who say money can't buy happiness are those who don't have any. Money can buy everything."

I lifted my chin. "I'm not for sale."

"Darling, everything—and everybody—is for sale. Now get back in that room before Mother sees you out here. And wipe off that lipstick."

I folded my arms over my chest. "No."

"We're getting married today," he said furiously, pointing a finger at the ground between us. "And that's final."

"And if I refuse to marry you?"

"You wouldn't dare. Because you realize, teacup," he said, a sneer on his lips, "that I own or control everything you have. Our apartment. Your job. Your credit cards. Your car. Your phone."

"You might as well add my friends and my clothes and my personality too," I told him. "You took everything I was and replaced it with who you wanted me to be. You made it impossible to leave."

"And you went along with it, because you knew it was in your best interest." He looked smug. "Face it. I'm the best thing that ever happened to you. You're *nothing* without me."

Fuck you was on the tip of my tongue, but since nothing I said seemed to be sinking in, I kept my mouth shut. Clearly, I was going to have to get more dramatic if I wanted to make my point.

And if I know how to do anything, it's put on a show.

I adopted a serene expression, as if I'd given in. "Okay, Neil. You can have it your way."

Neil nodded. "That's more like it. I'll see you at the altar."

I watched him walk away and almost felt sorry for him.

He had no idea what was coming.

. . .

Twenty minutes later, I still wore the angelic smile as I glided up the aisle on my own, the pews on either side packed with Vanderhoof family and friends. Neil looked a bit put out that I hadn't wiped off the red lipstick, but he could hardly throw a fit about it now. The first half of the ceremony passed in a blur, the voice of the minister muffled and far away, my pulse quick and loud inside my head.

Then came the vows.

Neil and I faced each other. He looked sweaty and annoyed. I felt surprisingly cool and composed.

"Cornelius," said the minister, "do you take Veronica to be your wedded wife, to live together in marriage? Do you promise to love her, comfort her, honor and keep her for better or worse, for richer or poorer, in sickness and health, and forsaking all others, be faithful only to her, for as long as you both shall live?"

"I do," said Neil.

What a crock of shit, I thought.

"And Veronica, do you take Cornelius to be your wedded husband, to live together in marriage? Do you promise to love him, comfort him, honor and keep him for better or worse, for richer or poorer, in sickness and health and forsaking all others, be faithful only to him, for as long as you both shall live?"

I pretended to think it over, then shook my head. "Nah."

The minister's expression was confused, as if I'd spoken a foreign language. "I'm sorry?"

"I don't take him."

"Veronica." Neil spoke through his teeth, his eyes warning me to stick to the script. "Say the words."

"No way. You're not the boss of me."

His eyes hardened. "Stop this ridiculousness right now. You're acting like a silly little girl."

"I've *been* acting like a silly little girl for a year. Now I'm acting like a grown woman capable of making her own decisions. And I'm not going to marry you."

The minister looked completely baffled. The guests had started to get anxious, and I could hear tense murmurs echo throughout the sanctuary. Possibly a snicker or two.

"Goodbye, Neil." I started to walk back down the aisle and he grabbed my shoulder, spinning me around to face him again.

"You can't leave *me*," he said, his neck stretched forward like a goose. "I *chose* you. I *pursued* you. I *rescued* you from that tacky, low-class life and offered you a place in real society. I won't be dumped by a—a—two-bit, uneducated, red-lipped *showgirl*!"

The crowd gasped.

"Showgirl!" Shrinking back, I gathered up my dress in my hands, revealing my sneakers. "I am a motherfucking Radio City

Rockette, you two-timing, overgrown *frat boy*, and I've got more class in my pinkie toe than you'll ever have!"

And I let loose with a ball-change, *grande battement* that caught him squarely beneath the Vanderhoof chin.

"Ow!" Neil grabbed his jaw. "Veronica, what the hell are you doing?"

"I'm making a fuss!" I shouted joyfully. Then I threw the bouquet on the floor, pitched my engagement ring at his chest, hiked up the bottom of my dress, and took off running.

I was broke, I was stranded, and I was probably homeless.

But I was free.

Chapter 2

ONE DAY EARLIER

*T*hey say blood is thicker than water, and I've always believed it to be true.

Right up until this morning.

"A *dig*?" I stared at my sister, who'd just announced she could no longer nanny for me this summer. "Are you serious?"

"It's a very important dig!" Mabel protested, her eyes wide and serious behind her glasses.

"What exactly are you abandoning me to dig for?" I stacked the kids' cereal bowls and grabbed their juice cups with one hand.

"We never know—that's what makes it exciting!" Mabel followed me from the kitchen table to the sink. "They've found all kinds of things at this site. Bones, stoneware, coins, other artifacts.

This dig could really help us understand early life in the colonies!"

I frowned as I rinsed everything and loaded the dishwasher. "I don't think you understand my *current* life as a single father with seven-year-old twins."

"I *do*, Austin," Mabel insisted. "And I'm sorry to leave you high and dry. But it's a once-in-a-lifetime opportunity, and I am not throwing away my—shot!" She struck a dramatic pose, trigger finger pointing at the ceiling.

"Please. No more Hamilton. That will be the one good thing about having you gone—I won't have to listen to that soundtrack every day." I glared at her over one shoulder. "But couldn't you have told me about this sooner?"

"I'm *sorreeeeee*." Mabel laced her fingers and rested her chin on her knuckles. "It was a last-minute offer, and I was lucky to get it. Please don't be mad—this could help me get into a more prestigious PhD program. It's a dream for me."

"I'm not mad," I muttered. In fact, I was happy she was able to chase her academic dreams all the way to the finish line.

Of the five Buckley siblings, Mabel was the brainy one—she'd worked her ass off in school, earned tons of scholarships, and she deserved every accolade she'd ever gotten. It wasn't her fault my life had taken a sharp turn after our uncle died, leaving our dad without a business partner, or hit a major fork in the road when I unexpectedly discovered I was going to be a father of two at age twenty-five.

"Because if you're really mad, I can say no and stick around here this summer," Mabel went on solemnly. "I promised I'd help you out, and you know how much I love the kids. Plus, if you keep making that face, all those lines in your forehead might stay there."

I rolled my eyes, although I did try to relax my face a little. "I'd never make you stick around here for my sake. You need to go."

"Thank you!" She threw her arms around me, pinning my

arms to my sides and pressing her cheek against my back. "I'll totally help you find a replacement nanny before I leave!"

"Mabel, it's Friday. You said you had to be in Virginia on Sunday."

"It's Friday *morning*. That gives me practically two full days! I'm sure I can fit it in. You know I have a sixth sense about people."

"And it's June already. There are Help Wanted signs all over town. Anyone qualified already has a summer job." I started the dishwasher, wiped the counter where someone had spilled milk pouring their cereal (probably Owen, since Adelaide was a neat freak like me), and checked the chore charts on the fridge to make sure the kids were keeping up with the week's responsibilities. Adelaide's X's fit perfectly inside each box—not a single one missing. Owen's chart had a couple blanks, and he marked each completed task with different things, sometimes a sticker, sometimes a smiley face, sometimes a funny-looking shape I knew was supposed to be a guitar, which he was saving up for.

"Not necessarily." Mabel trailed me to the front of the house. "There must be *someone* still looking for work."

"Someone with childcare experience?" I checked my watch and yelled up the stairs to the kids that they had precisely five minutes until departure.

"Definitely."

"Who can cook?"

"For sure."

"With their own transportation?" I checked their backpacks to make sure they had everything they needed for camp—bathing suits, towels, sunscreen, goggles, flip flops, lunches.

"Of course."

"That the kids will like?" Owen's towel from yesterday was still wadded up in his bag, damp and reeking of chlorine, and I yanked it out.

"I mean, not as much as they like *me*…" she joked.

"And no criminal record?"

"Now you're just being picky." She met my dirty look with a cheeky grin. "You know, if you'd just be honest with Dad about wanting to quit Two Buckleys and make furniture, you wouldn't need a full-time nanny. You could work from home."

"You know I can't do that."

"Why not?"

"Because it would break Dad's heart. His father and grandfather started that business in 1945. He and his brother ran it for forty years. When Uncle Harry died—"

"I know the story," Mabel cut in. "I know you gave up going to college for him."

"That wasn't my point. College wasn't that big a deal to me anyway. I don't even know what I'd have studied," I said. *Architecture*, I thought. "And I never had grades like you. I probably would have flunked out."

"Bullshit." Mabel's tone was fierce. "I mean, *none* of you guys had grades like me, but in your case, I think it was because you were always working. School wasn't your priority."

"Dad was raising five kids on his own," I said. "I wanted to help out."

"You did help out, Austin." Mabel's voice softened, and she reached out to squeeze my forearm. "I'm pretty sure my kindergarten friends thought you were my dad because you were always there waiting for me after school."

I cocked one brow. "I was *fifteen*."

"Exactly. That was a long time ago." Her voice grew stronger as she lectured me. "Dad is sixty-five now, with a heart condition and bad hips. He can't work forever. When he retires, are you going to keep his business alive just to make him happy instead of doing what you love?"

"Doing what I love wouldn't support us," I said, evading the question. "Not for a while, anyway. I've got bills to pay, and I want the kids to be able to attend summer camps and play sports. Adelaide is talking about sailing lessons. Owen wants a guitar."

Sighing, she snatched the towel from my hands. "Here, I'll put this in the wash. You grab a clean one."

While she went down to the basement, I hustled upstairs and pulled a clean towel from the hall closet, double checking that it said *Buckley* on the tag so it wouldn't get lost. Adelaide was just coming out of her room.

"Did you make your bed?" I asked her, although it wasn't necessary. Adelaide always made her bed.

"Yes," she said. "Do I have time for Aunt Mabel to braid my hair?"

"If you hurry." I tipped up her chin and looked at her pink, freckled nose. "More sunscreen today, please. And you should probably wear a hat."

"Okay." She took off down the stairs and I poked my head into her room.

Bed made, light off, pajamas put away. A glance into her brother's room revealed the opposite—comforter hanging off the bed, pajamas on the floor, drawer open, light on. After tossing his Captain America PJ's into the hamper—he'd spilled juice on them this morning—I shook my head, switched off the light, and went into my bedroom across the hall.

Moving fast, I yanked up the covers on the only side of the king-sized bed that got used. I wasn't even sure why I'd bought such a big bed when we moved into this house two years ago—I'd been sleeping alone since the twins were born. Not that I'd been totally celibate for seven years, but I could definitely count the times I'd had sex on one hand.

And it wouldn't even take all my fingers.

For a moment I studied my hands, wide and rough and callused, the knuckles a little swollen, my fingernails trimmed but the cuticles raggedy. I had a cut across the back of my left hand from where I'd scraped it on a nail sticking out of an old deck board yesterday, and a blister had formed on my right thumb, thanks to a hole in my gloves. They were a working man's hands, and I couldn't even remember the last time they'd moved across soft feminine skin, or slid into long silky hair, or grabbed onto a curvy pair of hips.

Was that part of my life over for good? Most days I was so busy, I didn't even have time to miss it. But every now and then, after the lights were off and the house was dark and silent, I lay alone in my bed and wished I had someone to make a little noise with.

Not that there hadn't been offers over the years, both overt and subtle. But I didn't date. For one thing, I had no time. Aside from the week the twins spent with their mother out in California each summer, they were my responsibility twenty-four hours a day, seven days a week. And a good father puts his kids first.

Owen was still in the bathroom he shared with his sister, brushing his teeth. "You about ready, bud?" I asked.

"The lady said I had to brush for two full minutes," he said.

"What lady?" Tucking the towel under my arm, I put the cap back on the toothpaste.

"The lady at the dentist." He rinsed his toothbrush and whacked it a few times on the edge of the sink before placing it back in the holder.

"That's the hygienist. And she also said to floss every day, but I don't see you doing that." I frowned at his messy brown hair. "Good thing you guys have haircuts today. Did you brush this mop yet?"

"No."

I exhaled and grabbed the hairbrush from the top drawer, giving his thick waves a once-through. Leaning closer, I examined his head. "Is that peanut butter?"

"Maybe." Owen was unconcerned. "I had it with my banana this morning. Aunt Mabel said I needed some protein so I could get big muscles. Is it true that peanut butter gives you muscles?"

"Sure. If you eat it, instead of smearing it in your hair." I did the best I could to get it out, then gave up. "Come on, let's go."

Downstairs, Mabel was braiding Adelaide's long strawberry blond locks. Owen had the Buckley coloring—golden skin, chestnut hair, warm brown eyes—but Adelaide looked more like her mother, a fair-skinned, green-eyed redhead, every year. But that's where their similarities ended.

"I don't have to get too much cut off today, do I?" Adelaide looked up at me with worried eyes.

"Nope. Just a trim. But you need sunscreen on the part in your hair," I told her, stuffing the clean towel into Owen's backpack. "Don't forget."

"I can spray it before we get in the car." Mabel quickly wrapped an elastic around the second braid and gave it a tug. "Done."

"Mabel says we're getting a new nanny, because she's going on a dig," Adelaide said. "Is that true?"

"Yes." I pointed at two pairs of sneakers by the door. "Shoes on. Both of you."

"What's a dig?" Owen asked, standing still while his sister dropped down and tugged on her sneakers, then tied two perfect bows, making sure the ends of the shoelaces were even.

"It's where you forage in the dirt to find artifacts from the past," Mabel said dramatically. "It's like treasure hunting for a job!"

"Wait—that's a *job*? You can get *paid* to dig in the dirt?" Owen sounded interested in this kind of career path.

"Yes. But not much." Mabel laughed. "Archaeologists aren't really in it for the money."

"Who's going to be the new nanny?" Owen wondered.

"I don't know yet," I said. "We'll have to find one."

"Like Mary Poppins?" Adelaide's voice rose hopefully.

"We can't afford her."

"Is she going to live over the garage like Aunt Mabel?" Owen had his shoes on now, but still untied.

"I guess," I said, although I wasn't looking forward to having a stranger up in my business. I liked order. I liked routine. I liked things done a certain way—my way—and I didn't need someone coming in who'd ignore my instructions or, worse, try to take charge and make changes.

"Can you pick us up from camp today, Daddy?" Adelaide asked.

"Sorry, June bug." Guilt nicked at me. "I have to work. I'm putting in a new deck out on Lighthouse Point."

"Can't Grandpa put in the new deck?"

"He can help, but if I wasn't there, he'd try to do things he shouldn't, because he forgets he's old now."

"You're old too," Owen pointed out.

"Thanks." I bent down to tie his shoes, giving the bill of his cap a thump.

"Thirty-two isn't that old," Adelaide argued, and just when I was about to thank her, she added, "I mean, it's old, but not like *grandpa* old."

Mabel laughed, grabbing her bag from a chair near the front door and slinging it over her shoulder. "Okay, so I'm dropping them at camp, then I'm going to run some errands and do some packing, then I'll get them back here to clean up. Next, I'll take them for their haircuts, and afterward we'll come home and I'll make dinner."

"Don't forget to add *find replacement nanny* to that list, unless you think she's just going to magically blow in on the breeze."

Mabel laughed and punched my shoulder. "Maybe she will."

• • •

I followed my sister and the kids out the door, pulling it shut behind me. While they piled into her hatchback that was parked at the curb, I walked around to the driveway and jumped into a battered white pickup that said TWO BUCKLEYS HOME IMPROVEMENT on the side.

We did a little of everything—carpentry, painting, flooring, tile work, plaster repair, light remodels—and we did it well. Despite the fact that we could have made more money if my dad would just take on more employees, he'd always insisted that Two Buckleys would remain exactly that—a small family business.

Which was why it fell to me to hire on as the second Buckley after our uncle's death. Not only was I the oldest brother, but at that time, I was really the only one suited for the job. Xander had one year of school left and then planned on joining the Navy. Devlin had still been in driver's training and had *zero* interest in working with his hands. Dashiel was barely fourteen.

My dad had needed me, and I wanted to do right by him, like he'd done by us.

Waving to Arthur, our mail carrier, I made my way from our neighborhood down toward the harbor, usually only a five-minute drive. But even though it wasn't quite eight a.m., the traffic on Main Street was already slow, and the sidewalks were crowded with people looking for the perfect cup of coffee or handmade pastry. Many were already dressed for the beach or a day on the boat. With the truck windows down, I could smell the scent of fudge wafting through the air—I'd once read that Cherry Tree Harbor sold five tons of fudge every summer.

It was a small town with barely over a thousand year-round residents, but the population swelled each May to the point where it felt like every restaurant, inn, and shop was bursting at the seams, and stayed that way until September. It would pick up again for ski season, then quiet down in spring once more. Many of the seasonal visitors weren't just tourists, but families who'd owned homes here for generations.

The biggest ones were century-old Victorian "cottages" on Bayview Road, which curved along the shoreline, overlooking the crescent-shaped harbor that was nestled at the base of the bluff. I loved working on those old homes—restoring the exterior porches, gables, and trim, or the interior floors, moldings, and staircases. A few times, owners had asked me to restore original furnishings too, but what I enjoyed best was taking old materials like resawn beams, plank flooring, barn wood, or even whiskey barrels, and making them into something new.

I passed The Pier Inn, the popular hotel and restaurant at the harbor where Xander and Dash had bused tables every summer and Mabel had been the hostess. At the light, I waved to my Aunt Faye, who was crossing Bayview with her yellow lab, a cup of coffee in one hand. She was my Uncle Harry's widow and still kept the books for Two Buckleys.

Faye waved back, calling out, "Morning, Austin! Say hi to your dad!"

At the base of Lighthouse Point, a narrow strip of prime real estate jutting into the bay, I had to stop at the gatehouse and give my name. The attendant was an old friend of my father's, a mechanic who'd retired about five years ago and worked part-time at the gatehouse when he wasn't out fishing. He grinned as I pulled up and came out of the gatehouse to chat. "How's it going, Austin?"

I put the truck in park. "Pretty good, Gus. Catch anything

good lately?"

"You know it. I just told your dad he needs to give up this full-time stuff and get out on the water more often." He jerked his thumb up the road. "He was here a minute or so ago."

"I suppose he turned you down, huh?"

"As usual." Gus grunted. "I don't know why he wants to keep working so hard. I told him, I says, 'George, we're sixty-five, for cripes' sake. It's time to slow down.'"

"I agree with you." I adjusted the cap on my head. "But he doesn't listen to me either."

"I hear Xander's back in town. He could pass Two Buckleys on to you and Xander, easy."

"Nah, Xander's never had any interest. He's starting his own business." *Plus Xander and I would kill each other.*

"What kind of business? Private security stuff?" Then he laughed. "We don't have too many people that need bodyguarding around these parts."

I shook my head. "He's opening a bar. He just bought the old Tiki Tom's and he's working on renovations."

"Oh. Well, shoot. What about your brother Devlin? He still out east someplace?"

"Boston," I confirmed.

"Guess he's more of a suit and tie guy, huh?" Gus removed his bucket hat and scratched the top of his head with his thumb. "And I don't suppose your brother Dashiel has any interest."

"None at all." Dash had chased his dream of being a movie star out to L.A., where he was an actor on a popular show called Malibu Splash—something we gave him endless shit about, although we were proud of him.

"My granddaughters love that show he's on. They watch it all the time. Think maybe I could get them an autograph?"

"How old are they?"

"Ten and twelve."

I grinned. Dash was twenty-six, but he played a teenage lifeguard on the show, and his fan base was solidly prepubescent. "I bet we could arrange it."

"Thanks. They even have pillowcases with his face on them." He chortled, shaking his head. "Like Elvis or something."

"Right." Getting restless, I put the truck in drive again. If my dad was left alone on a job too long, he'd either do something dangerous like climb a ladder to check someone's gutters (for free), which made him dizzy, or waste time chatting away with the homeowner, adding on to the hours I'd have to spend finishing the work we'd been hired to do. "Well, I should get going, but next time I talk to Dash, I'll mention it."

"Thanks." Gus thumped the driver's side door of my truck. "Have a good one, Austin."

"You too."

Sure enough, when I arrived at the address and went around back, Dad was standing out on the homeowner's dock, holding a cup of coffee and nodding along as the homeowner chattered away gesturing toward his boat. Dad smiled and waved to me, but made no move toward the deck that needed refinishing, and I waved back before getting to work by myself.

In the back of my mind, I imagined what it would be like to spend a whole day working on my own projects, to be free to go after what I really wanted to do, the way my siblings were. Xander with his bar. Devlin with his pricey real estate deals. Dash with his movie career. Mabel with her treasure hunts.

But they were different from me. Their situations were different. They didn't have kids, and they didn't remember—maybe they'd just been too young to appreciate—how hard our dad had worked to raise us on his own after our mom was gone. They didn't understand how fully he'd supported me when I announced I was about to become a father of two, insisting we move in with him so he could help out.

I owed it to him to keep the family business alive and keep quiet about what I wanted for myself. And I owed it to my kids to be the kind of father they deserved. If that meant deferring my own dream, so be it.

That's what love was.

Chapter 3

VERONICA

*a*fter snatching my purse from the bride's room, I bolted out the chapel's front doors and down the steps. Plucking my veil from the back of my head, I tossed it in the air. It sailed up and caught the breeze, and I didn't even stop to look where it landed.

Pausing for a moment on the sidewalk, I looked right and left, intoxicated by the idea that not only could I go either way, but *I* could decide the direction.

Gleefully, I closed my eyes and spun in a few circles, and when I opened them, I was facing in the direction of Main Street.

I took off walking with a spring in my step, saying hello with a nod and a smile to every curious onlooker I passed. I realized I probably looked insane, traipsing down the street in a big poofy wedding dress, but at that moment, I didn't care.

Pulling my phone from my bag, I tried calling Morgan, but she didn't pick up. I left a cryptic message…"Hey, call me when you can. I have news."

When I reached Main Street, the smell of chocolate made my stomach growl. Neil had told me the town was famous for its fudge, but I'd been here for over twenty-four hours, and I hadn't even tasted it yet—something I planned to remedy immediately. But first, some real food.

For the first time in months, I actually had an appetite.

On the corner of Church and Main was an adorable fifties-style diner called Moe's, and the sign in the window said OPEN! COME IN FOR THE BEST BURGER IN TOWN! Ravenous for a thick, juicy cheeseburger, I opened the door and stepped inside.

I looked around, taking in the black-and-white checkered floor, the red vinyl booths, the signed movie star photos on the wall, and the jukebox in the corner. Above the din of clinking silverware and human voices, I heard the plaintive strains of Patsy Cline's "Crazy."

And then, slowly but surely...every conversation stopped. Forks, French fries, and milkshakes paused halfway to open mouths. Necks craned and heads tilted as people strove to get a better view of me. Only Patsy kept calm and carried on.

Gathering my voluminous dress in my hands, I squeezed past tables and chairs, excusing myself when I needed more room. All eyes followed me as I made my way to the old-fashioned counter, where there was one empty stool. I perched on it and smiled at the young guy behind the counter. He wore a white apron and paper cap, and his name tag said Steve.

"Hey, Steve," I said, trying to arrange my dress so it didn't take up too much room on either side of me.

"Hey." Steve looked behind me, possibly for the groom. "Just one?"

"Just one. Can I get a burger and a milkshake, please?"

"Uh. Sure." Steve and the other employee behind the counter, a young woman wearing a pink uniform and holding a coffee pot, exchanged a look. "What flavor milkshake?"

"Mmm, chocolate. And medium rare for the burger. Can I get fries too?"

"Yeah." Steve didn't move for another few seconds, then pulled a green pad from his pocket and wrote down my order. "It'll just be a few minutes."

"No rush. I don't have anywhere to be, contrary to what it looks like."

"So you're not, like, getting married or something?" The waitress—Ari, her name tag said—looked over my hair and face and gown.

"No. I mean, I was *supposed* to, but it didn't really go as planned."

Ari took a step closer, either forgetting about the coffee she'd been about to pour or not caring. "*Today?*"

Never one to shy away from a conversation, even with strangers, I nodded. "Right this minute, in fact."

"You don't say." The old guy in suspenders and a ball cap to my right, elbowed the old guy in suspenders and a ball cap to *his* right. "You hear that, Gus? She's supposed to be getting married right now."

"I heard it, Larry." Gus leaned forward to peer at me from Larry's other side.

"Were you jilted?" asked Larry.

"Oh, no." I poked a thumb on my chest twice. "I did the jilting."

"Really?" asked the woman to my left. She had silvery red ringlets escaping from a bun on the top of her head and wore long, dangly earrings. "Why?"

"Because he was cheating on me."

My audience gasped.

"And I just found out about it right before the ceremony started."

My audience gasped louder.

"How?" Ari's eyes were wide.

"He accidentally sent me a text message he meant to send to the other woman, referencing certain…" I glanced at the two old guys on my right. I didn't want to shock Gus and Larry's elderly sensibilities. "Salacious activities they were engaged in last night."

"Men," harrumphed Ari. She gave Steve the side eye as he set a milkshake down in front of me.

"It's not because he's a man, it's because he's used to doing whatever he wants and getting away with it," I explained. "He's rich and handsome. Born with a silver spoon and all that."

"Oh, honey. You can't fall for those guys." The lady with the dangly earrings patted the leg of a burly man with a bald head next to her. "You gotta stick with guys like my Bubba here. Good men, maybe a six or seven or even an eight out of ten, but definitely not a nine or above."

"Thanks, Willene," Bubba said, then paused. "I think."

"Those nines and tens don't have to work for anything," Willene went on. "You want the kind of guy who works hard for everything he's got. That way it means more when they treat you. And they *know* how to treat you." She leaned over and kissed Bubba's cheek.

"Believe me, I see my mistake now," I said after a long suck on the straw of my shake. "My god, this is delicious. I haven't enjoyed food in months."

"Why not?" Bubba looked horrified.

"I was afraid my dress wouldn't fit," I said. "I kept having this nightmare that it was my wedding day, and I'd go to get dressed, but my gown wouldn't fit. I just couldn't get it on, no matter what I did."

"It was a sign." Willene rapped the counter with her knuckles. "The universe is always sending signs."

"I should have seen this one sooner, I was just…" For a second, my mom's face popped into my mind. "I was confused."

"I dated a ten once," said the irascible Larry, as if he were still mad about it. "And that's how I felt all the time. Confused. All she had to do was smile at me, and I couldn't even think. I was bewitched, bothered, and bewildered, as the song goes."

I smiled at him sympathetically. "I hear you. I haven't done much good thinking over the last year myself. And now the problem is, everything I have, he gave me. My apartment, my car, my credit cards, my job. Even my phone. I don't have a thing to my name."

"Maybe he'll be generous," said Ari. "Since he was the one who cheated and all."

I took another long drink of my shake. "I doubt it, not since I dumped him at the altar with everyone watching."

"You went all the way to the altar?" Steve cocked his head. "Even after you knew?"

"I didn't want to, but Neil—that's his name—wasn't taking no for an answer. I told him ten times I wasn't going to marry him, but he just kept telling me I was being silly and insisting that I do as I was told."

"So how'd you finally convince him?" Gus asked.

"I kicked him in the face—but not until he insulted me in front of everyone."

"You kicked him in the *face*?" Ari was impressed. "How'd you get your leg up that high?"

"I used to be a Rockette," I said, sitting up a little taller.

"Wow, a Rockette." Gus was impressed. "I've seen the Christmas Spectacular three times. It's my favorite play. You girls are fantastic."

I laughed. "Thank you."

"So what will you do now?" asked Ari.

"I don't know," I admitted. "I guess I need to make a fresh start."

"Here in Cherry Tree Harbor?" Gus seemed kind of excited about that, like maybe more Rockettes would follow.

"If I could find a job." I glanced out the window. "It's not like I have anywhere else to go."

"Where's your family?" Willene asked.

"I don't have any."

"Could you get your old job back?" Gus wondered.

"I think so. But I missed auditions, so not this season."

"So you need more of a temporary gig," Ari said, one finger tapping her lips. "Hmm."

"Is there a dance studio around?" I wondered. "Maybe I could teach lessons."

"There used to be Miss Edna's, just outside town," said Gus, "but she closed up shop and moved to Florida. I once took salsa dancing there. I wasn't much good at it, or so the wife said."

"Hey, you know what?" Ari hurried over to a bulletin board by the entrance and pulled off a sheet of paper. Returning to the counter, she placed it in front of me. "My best friend Mabel was in here yesterday, and she put this up."

"What is it?" Larry asked, frowning as he pulled a pair of readers from his shirt pocket.

Willene leaned closer to me so she could read it too. "It's a flyer advertising a live-in nanny position."

"It's for Mabel's older brother, Austin," said Ari. "He's a single dad with seven-year-old twins."

"Boys or girls?"

"One of each."

"Are they nice?" I was thinking of The Sound of Music, where those kids terrorized poor Maria. Hadn't they put a frog in her bed?

"Yeah." Ari shrugged. "Austin is a little intense, but the kids are cool. They come in here sometimes, and they actually behave."

"What do you mean by *intense*?" I pictured stern, no-nonsense Captain von Trapp.

"He's just kind of…serious," she finished. "All work, no play."

"He didn't do all that much work in high school," said Willene drily. "Trust me, I was his social studies teacher three years in a row." Then she sighed. "But he sure grew up handsome. All those Buckley boys did."

"Those kids had it tough," Gus said. "Lost their mom so young and all."

"He put in a real nice split rail fence for us last year when I was laid-up because of my back," said Bubba. "Did good work. Nice wood."

"She doesn't care about his *wood*, Bubba." His wife smacked his shoulder. "She wants a job."

I might care about his wood, I thought, picturing a hot, shirtless guy chopping wood and then putting up a split rail fence, sweat glistening on his tanned pecs. Neil was slim and fit, but he hadn't been exciting in bed—at least, not when *I* was in it. And honestly, he'd been ignoring me sexually for months. I'd assumed he was just busy and distracted with work, but now I knew better.

"Mabel was supposed to be the nanny this summer," Ari explained, "but she just got this amazing offer to assist on some kind of archaeological dig in Virginia. She's really into that stuff."

"That's cool," I said studying the flyer more closely.

Wanted: Summer nanny for twins, age 7. Accommodations provided. Must have childcare experience, cooking skills, own transportation.

"Well, that's that," I said with a sigh. "I don't have any of those things."

"You could at least interview," Ari suggested. "Mabel said he's pretty desperate, and she feels terrible for abandoning them."

I looked at the address and phone number listed at the bottom and gasped. "Hey, they live on Sutton Street! Sutton is my last name."

"It's a sign," Willene said, knocking on the counter again.

I decided she was right and that I'd ignored enough of them. "I suppose there's no harm in applying. It's not like I have any better ideas."

Ari grinned. "I'll call her."

• • •

Twenty minutes later, I was sitting in a red vinyl booth at the back of Moe's when a petite, dark-haired woman rushed through the door and ran over to give Ari a hug. Ari pointed in my direction, and I sat up a little taller and waved.

Mabel waved back, had a brief conversation with Ari, and hurried over to where I sat, saying hello to at least three people on the way. She wore cut-off jean shorts and a T-shirt that said William & Mary.

"Hi," she said, sliding in across from me and holding out one hand over the table. "I'm Mabel."

"Veronica." I shook her hand. "Nice to meet you."

"You too. Sorry I'm a little out of breath. I was trying to do like ten things at once—pack my things, mind the kids, get dinner ready—but when Ari called and said there was someone interested in the nanny job, I dropped everything and raced up here."

"I appreciate it," I said.

"So." Her smile was warm and genuine. "Sounds like you've had quite the day."

I laughed. "You can say that again."

"Ari told me what happened." She shook her head, dark

ponytail wagging. "It's like a movie or something."

"Not the one I'd have chosen to star in."

"What kind of movie would you have picked?"

"A musical," I said right away.

Her eyes widened behind the lenses of her tortoiseshell glasses. "I *love* musicals. What's your favorite?"

I gasped. "Torture me, why don't you! But if I had to pick, I'd say *Hamilton*."

"Ob. Sessed." Mabel held up her hands. "That's my favorite too."

"For a couple months, I ushered at the theater where it played in New York," I told her. "I got to see it every night. And I was friends with some of the ensemble."

She moaned with envy. "That's amazing."

"I grew up dancing, and dance is such an important part of that show. It's not just like, 'oh, characters are happy, so now comes a happy dance,' it's like the choreography truly moves the story forward," I said rapturously. "It carries emotional weight, just like the music, just like the lyrics."

"Did you ever audition to be in it?"

"No." I laughed and shrugged. "Unfortunately, I am completely tone deaf. Precision? Technique? Musicality? I'm your girl. But you do *not* want to hear me sing."

Mabel laughed. "Ari said you were a Rockette."

I nodded. "For eight seasons. Then my mom got sick, and I moved back home to care for her. After she died, I got engaged and moved to Chicago—that's where my fiancé lives. Well, my ex-fiancé."

"And you don't want to go back there?"

"No." I shook my head. "And I wouldn't be welcome."

"Why stay here? Why not go back to New York?"

"I'll probably do that eventually," I said. "But I kind of like the idea of trying someplace new for a minute. Maybe somewhere slower-paced and quieter. A place where I can catch my breath."

"I totally get that." Mabel hesitated. "Are you sad about the guy?"

I looked out the window, where I watched a young family cross the street, a little girl on the dad's shoulders, a little boy holding his mom's hand. My heart ached fiercely. "I'm sad I wasted a year of my life on him. But I'm not sad it's over."

"Other fish in the sea, right?"

"I'm not worried about that right now. I think I'm better off alone for the time being."

"You sound like Austin—that's my brother. He's the one who needs a nanny this summer."

"Ari told me about the dig. That's awesome."

She smiled. "It is awesome—for me. But it leaves my brother with no help."

"And he's got twins, right?"

"Yep. Boy and a girl, age seven. They're high-energy, but they're funny and sweet and smart, and—" The alarm on Mabel's phone went off, and she pulled it from her purse. "Shoot. That's all the time I have. Okay, listen. I know we just met and all, but I feel like you'd be perfect for the job. Can you come up to the house later and meet my brother and the kids?"

"Sure." I wondered about the missing link—the twins' mom—but I didn't want to ask.

"Great," she said, sliding out from the booth. "The address is right there on the flyer."

• • •

About fifteen minutes later, I followed the directions Ari had written down for me on the back of the flyer and walked the three blocks to the Buckley house. Gus, Larry, Willene and Bubba, and even Steve offered to drive me, but I said I could walk.

Sutton Street was uphill from Main Street, and I was warm in my dress—the sun was just starting to sink, and the temperature still hovered in the low seventies. Probably I should have gone back to the inn to change my clothes, but I hadn't wanted to waste any time—showing up so soon would demonstrate how eager I was to get the job, right?

When I reached the address, I stood on the sidewalk for a moment and studied it. The two-story, white-painted house was charming and old-fashioned, almost storybook-like with its pretty front porch with the lattice skirt and gingerbread trim. It jogged a memory—my grandparents had lived in a house like this, but theirs was on a farm, and my mother had taken me there to visit once when I was little. We'd ridden on a bus overnight to get there, my mother tense and quiet, while I pretended I was on a grand adventure. The next thing I remembered was waiting in the living room and petting their dog while a terrible argument raged in the kitchen.

We were only there a short time, and we never went back.

Taking a deep breath for courage, I marched up the walk and climbed the porch steps. The wooden front door was open, so I knocked on the frame of the screen. A moment later, two kids came bounding down the stairs and stood in front of me.

"Hi, there," I said, giving them a smile and a wave.

One of them—a girl with gorgeous red-gold hair, looked me over head to foot. "Are you trick-or-treating?"

Laughing, I shook my head. "No."

"Then how come you're wearing that costume?" The little boy with the huge dark eyes and a fresh haircut pointed at my dress.

"Actually, this isn't a costume."

"Are you here to marry our dad?" the girl asked.

"I wasn't planning on it," I said, but just then, a wide-shouldered, dark-haired guy appeared behind them, and I thought maybe I'd spoken too soon.

Apart from the stern expression and furrowed brow, he didn't look anything like Captain von Trapp. He had close-cropped scruff, wore a ball cap, and his jeans were dirty. He was definitely their dad—he had the same brown eyes as his son, and the boyish ears that stuck out just slightly. The muscular arms and brawny chest weren't too far off my splitting-rails-man fantasy, although this guy was wearing a shirt. It said Two Buckleys Home Improvement on it. The armpits were dark with sweat.

"Can I help you?" His eyes traveled over my attire.

"Um, I'm Veronica Sutton. I'm here about the job."

"The job?" His expression was blank.

"Yes. The nanny job?" I showed him the flyer.

He pushed open the screen door and took the paper from me. As he read it, his face went from baffled to irritated. "I'm afraid there's been a mistake."

"You're not looking for a nanny?"

"No," he said firmly.

"Yes, we are, Daddy. Remember?" The little girl tugged on his shirt. "Aunt Mabel is leaving to go on a dig."

"A dig is like treasure hunting," the little boy told me with wide eyes. "And you get paid to do it."

Just then, Mabel came rushing up behind the man, holding a rubber spatula in her hand. "Veronica! You're here!"

I blanched at the surprise in her tone. "Aren't I supposed to be?"

"Yes, you're, ah, here just a little sooner than I expected. I thought maybe you'd want to go change your clothes or something. I haven't had a chance to tell Austin about you yet."

"Oh. I'm sorry, I—" Swallowing hard, I met Austin's unyielding eyes. "Should I come back later?"

"No, no." Mabel reached behind her brother and swung the door wider. "Come on in. This is my brother, Austin, and these are his kids, Adelaide and Owen."

The twins said hello while Austin gave his sister a scorching look and held up the flyer. "Mabel, what is this?"

"It's an ad for a new nanny," Mabel said, pointing the spatula at him like a weapon. "And she's the only applicant we have, so don't scare her off."

I glanced around—to my left was a living room, and to my right was a staircase. Shoes were lined up neatly on a rug by the door. Hats and light jackets hung just so on pegs at the bottom of the stairs. The wood floors were spotless, and I saw no clutter anywhere.

"Why don't we all take a seat in the living room?" Mabel suggested.

"Mabel, could I see you for a moment, please?" Without waiting for his sister to answer, Austin took her by the arm and pulled her up the stairs.

"We'll be right down," Mabel called as she disappeared. "Kids, why don't you introduce yourselves?"

I went into the living room and took a seat on the couch. The kids stood directly in front of me, staring curiously like I was a painting or an animal at the zoo.

"I'm Veronica," I said. "So you guys are twins, huh?"

"Yes, but I'm older," Owen told me.

"Only by four minutes!" Adelaide seemed a little miffed at their arrival schedule.

I smiled. "It must be fun being a twin. I don't have any brothers or sisters. But I always wanted them."

"Are you going to be our new nanny?" Owen asked.

"I don't know. I hope so. Got any tips for me?"

They each appeared to think deeply. "Daddy likes it when you make your bed," Adelaide said. "Tell him you always make your bed."

"And that you remember to turn off lights," Owen added. "Because we don't own the electric company."

"His favorite food is barbecue," Adelaide said. "Do you know how to make barbecue? Or cook on the grill?"

"No," I admitted. "I've never had a grill."

"Do you know how to make anything?"

I chewed my lip—I wasn't skilled in the kitchen at all. I overcooked chicken and undercooked pasta, and I never seemed to be able to time a meal right. "I know how to make fried bologna sandwiches. And I made a birthday cake once."

"What kind of birthday cake?" asked Adelaide.

"It was yellow," I said, neglecting to mention it was from a box. "With chocolate frosting and rainbow sprinkles."

"That sounds good," Owen said generously.

"If I get the job, I'll make you one," I promised.

"Can you make two?" Adelaide held up two fingers. "We always have to share a cake because we share a birthday."

"Absolutely," I said. "You'll each get a cake."

"Daddy is big on organization," Adelaide went on. "And charts. Do you have any charts?"

"Charts?"

"Yeah. Like chore charts," said Owen. "We each have one."

"They're on the fridge, right by the calendar." Adelaide pointed in the direction of the kitchen. "The calendar is very important too. If something isn't on the calendar, Daddy gets grumpy about it."

"Got it." I nodded. "So tell me about you two. What grade are you in?"

"We'll be in second grade this fall," said Adelaide. "We go to Paddington Elementary."

"It's named after a man, not the bear," Owen added with obvious disappointment.

"Yes, and the man's family still lives around here. I heard Daddy say they're a bunch of assholes." Adelaide grinned. "But I'm not supposed to repeat that word."

I mimed locking my lips and throwing away the key. "I won't tell."

"Your dress is pretty." Adelaide reached forward and played with the tulle skirt. "Are you getting married or something?"

"I *was*. But not anymore."

"How come?"

I hesitated. "The man I was supposed to marry wasn't being nice to me."

"Was he bullying you?" Owen asked.

I decided to go with that. "Yes."

"I hate bullies," the little boy said seriously. "But we're not supposed to fight back."

"Did *you* fight back?" wondered Adelaide.

I nodded defiantly. "I kicked my bully right in the face."

The twins exchanged a look of amazement.

"You did?" Owen blinked.

"Totally!" I jumped off the couch. "Here, I'll show you."

The twins backed up to give me some room, and I turned to face the fireplace.

"First, I had to get a little running start." Bunching up my dress in my hands, I drew back in dramatic fashion. "And then…" I took a few quick steps forward, added a twirl for flair, and executed a sharp hitch kick while shouting, "Hi-*yah*! Right in the kisser!"

That's when I heard a man's voice behind me. "*What* is going on here?"

Chapter 4

AUSTIN

I'd entered the living room just in time to see the crazy—and crazy beautiful—woman in a wedding gown jump off the couch and perform some sort of martial arts move in which her foot went flying toward the ceiling.

Honestly, it was fucking impressive. You had to be pretty damn flexible to get your leg to do that.

I shoved all thoughts of her looks and agility aside—this woman was clearly nuts, and there was *no way in hell* I was hiring her to live here and watch my children. Had Mabel lost her mind?

Actually, I already knew the answer to that, since she'd just spent several minutes upstairs trying to convince me to give this woman a chance.

"Mabel, you can't be serious," I'd argued. "That woman is not right in the head. She's wearing a wedding gown!"

"I know. Ari told me all about it," Mabel said. "She was

supposed to get married to some wealthy big shot today, and right before the ceremony she found out he was cheating on her. So she left him at the altar."

"And went for a burger at Moe's?" I shook my head, folding my arms across my chest. "This doesn't add up."

"Listen, you might be hungry too if you just defended your honor the way she did. This asshole controlled her life. Ari said it sounds like he was a real manipulative bastard who took away her old friends, made her delete all her social media accounts, and he paid for everything, so she was completely dependent on him."

"Why didn't she just leave?"

"Spoken like a true man." Indignant, Mabel's hands flew up. "I don't know! You know how those rich jerks are—so entitled, they treat everyone like dirt, bossing people around because they think everyone is beneath them. You're around that long enough, you start to believe it too."

I clenched my jaw. I knew exactly how those guys were, I'd worked on their summer homes all my life. But even if I understood how this girl had been manipulated, that didn't make her my responsibility. "Look, if that's true, I feel bad for her. But it's not my problem. And I don't appreciate you ambushing me like this."

"You're the one who told me to find a replacement nanny! Can't you just give her a chance? I felt an instant connection with her."

"Why, does she love Hamilton or something?"

Mabel's angry expression told me I'd hit the mark. "You would love it too, if you took the time to see it!"

"I'm busy, Mabel. I don't have time for shows, and I don't have time for this." I turned to go, and she whacked my shoulder with the spatula.

"You won't have time for anything if you don't hire a new nanny!"

I exhaled, feeling a painful stab between my shoulder blades. I must have pulled a muscle today. "Does she have any childcare experience?"

"Um. She might."

"You didn't ask her?"

My sister fidgeted. "We talked about other things."

I closed my eyes and pinched the bridge of my nose. "Mabel, this is ridiculous. This woman could be a serial killer."

"She's not." Mabel tugged my arm down and pointed her spatula at me. "Stop being so judgmental. She's here, she needs a job, and you need a nanny, so we might as well interview her. Maybe you'll like her."

"I doubt it."

"Then do it as a favor to me," she begged. "I can't go off to my dig feeling all guilty and ashamed. I won't do my best work, and then I'll blow my chances of getting into a good PhD program, and my life will have been one big waste. Do you really want that weight on your shoulders?"

I pinned her with my best older brother stare and held up one hand, fingers spread. "Five minutes. That's all I'm giving this. I've got shit to do tonight."

"Five minutes," she agreed. Then her eyes lit up with mischief. "She's pretty, don't you think?"

"I didn't notice," I lied.

"Well, she is. So try to be charming."

In the blink of an eye, I'd grabbed Mabel by the wrist and twisted her into a headlock—a classic big brother move I usually reserved for my male siblings since Mabel was almost ten years younger and much smaller, but I wasn't above employing it when she was really annoying me. "Twerp, I am *all* fucking charm."

"Ha!" She struggled to escape and couldn't. "You left charming behind a long time ago, along with easygoing, relaxed, and fun!"

"It's like you forgot you just asked me for a favor." I tightened my grip playfully and gave her skull a knuckle rub with my other hand.

Laughing, Mabel clawed at my forearm with one hand and slapped my legs with the spatula. "If you had a girlfriend, you wouldn't be so uptight. Now let me go! You smell like sweat!"

I loosened my grip, and she took off down the stairs, leaving me no choice but to follow her. On my way, I glanced at my shirt and noticed the pit stains. Shit. Should I change?

Fuck it, I decided, and kept moving. Maybe the girl was pretty, and okay, my pulse did pick up a little when I saw her standing there on my porch, and *fine*, I felt sorry for her if she'd been treated the way Mabel had described, but I didn't need to impress her. If she didn't like the way I smelled, she could leave. I didn't need a girlfriend, I needed a nanny.

What I appeared to have in my living room was a circus act.

"Wow," my sister said. "Can you teach *me* that move?"

The girl—Veronica—whirled around, her cheeks turning red. "Oh gosh! Sorry, I didn't see you there. I was just—uh—"

"She was showing us what she does to bullies," Adelaide said.

"Bullies?" I questioned.

"Yes. See, she was supposed to get married to this man who wasn't nice to her, so she kicked him in the face," my daughter explained.

"*Bam!*" Owen added, shooting his bare foot out and catching the leg of an end table. He grabbed his toes and hopped around in pain.

Veronica held up her palms. "But I promise you, that is not how I usually behave in a church. Or anywhere else. I don't believe in violence. I just sort of…snapped." As if she realized how that might sound, she quickly went on. "But I don't have a bad temper or anything. I'm actually very easygoing."

"She makes birthday cake with sprinkles," Owen said.

Adelaide nodded. "And she's going to make us each one for our birthday, so we don't have to share."

"Your birthdays aren't until February," I reminded them. "You two go up to your rooms please." I pointed toward the stairs and gave them a look that said I meant business.

They made eye contact with each other and had one of those twin conversations with their minds, during which they must have considered refusing to follow orders but decided it wouldn't be worth it. Defeated, they trudged toward the stairs.

Mabel cleared her throat. "So tell us about yourself, Veronica."

"Well, I grew up in New Jersey. I moved to New York as soon as I could save up the money, and I got my dream job as a Radio City Rockette. During the off-season, I waitressed or bartended."

"So you've got hospitality experience," said Mabel. "And a good work ethic."

"I learned it from my mom." Veronica's full lips curved into a proud smile. "She worked harder than anyone I've ever known."

"Do you have any childcare experience?" I asked, dismayed to find myself staring at her mouth. It was wide and lush and looked like a good time.

"Not really," she said reluctantly.

"Babysitting when you were younger?" Mabel prompted. "Maybe younger siblings or cousins?"

Veronica shook her head. "I was an only child and didn't grow up around any other family. It was just me and my mom. But I taught dance to kids." She lifted her bare shoulders. "Does that count?"

"Sure, it does!" Mabel sounded excited, but I wasn't in the market for a dance instructor.

"How about references?" I asked.

Veronica thought for a moment, then tugged up the strapless dress. "I don't really have any outside the dance world. I could try to track down some of the bar managers I worked for. They would tell you I'm honest, I'm a team player, and I always show up on time."

"Punctuality is so important," Mabel enthused.

"Do you have a valid driver's license?" I asked.

"Yes!" Veronica brightened up. "I definitely have a valid driver's license." Hurrying over to the couch, she pulled a wallet from her bag and handed her license to me as if I'd carded her.

I took it from her and studied it, starting with the photo. She was much prettier in person, but maybe that was because she looked sort of sad and serious in this picture. No smile, no light in her eyes, and her complexion was pale, almost gray. Her full name was Veronica Marie Sutton, and according to the birth date listed, she was twenty-nine years old. The issuing state was Illinois.

"I thought you lived in New York."

"I moved to Chicago to live with my fiancé."

"Did you have a job in Chicago?" I asked, handing her license back.

She hesitated, fidgeting with the card, flicking one edge with her fingernail. "Yes and no. My fiancé put me on the board of some charities his family supports, so I did some fundraising and special events."

"So you were in philanthropy." Mabel made it sound fancy.

"You could say that."

"And how did you end up in Cherry Tree Harbor?" I asked.

"My fiancé—ex-fiancé's—family owns a home here, and this is where they always have weddings."

"What's the family?"

"Vanderhoof."

I nodded. I'd heard of them. Rich family that liked to throw their name and their opinions around.

"But I'm afraid if you ask them for a reference, it will not present me in a very positive light," Veronica said quietly. "Needless to say, Neil and I did not end on good terms."

"So you have a driver's license," Mabel said, briskly moving on. "How about a car?"

"I had one." Veronica hesitated. "I might still have it. I'm just not sure."

"You're not sure?" Even Mabel's voice was wavering now.

"Well, technically it probably belongs to Neil. He bought it for me."

"How about cooking skills?" Mabel threw out the question, and I saw her crossing her fingers at her side. "Can you make any meals?"

"Besides fried bologna sandwiches?" Veronica laughed nervously. "Not too many."

"So you don't have any experience, you don't have a car, you can't cook, and you don't have any references," I said, mostly for Mabel's benefit.

"No," Veronica said. "I mean, yes. All that is true." Then she pressed her shoulders back and straightened her spine. "Other things I don't have include a college degree, a trust fund, a rich dad—or any dad at all—and currently, I am probably homeless. All in all, I realize I'm not an ideal candidate for any job right now. But." She lifted her chin. "I do have grit. And resilience. And self-respect—qualities that I think are important to teach kids. I'm creative and fun. I can turn anything into a game. Maybe I've never been a nanny before, but I like kids, I'm responsible, and I know how to memorize a routine. Bonus—I give really good hugs."

Her blue eyes pinned me with a stare, and I had to admit, her words were persuasive. Her delivery was confident. She truly believed she could do this job.

But I wasn't convinced. I couldn't trust my kids to a stranger—I just couldn't. And I didn't want to live with one.

Especially not this one, whose eyes and mouth and bare shoulders were doing things to my insides I wasn't comfortable with.

"I'm sorry," I said shortly. "But it's not going to work out."

And before either of them could argue with me, I strode through the kitchen and out the back door, and I didn't stop moving until I got inside my garage workshop, where I picked up a piece of sandpaper and started rubbing an old floor plank, just because it was the closest thing at hand.

It was fine, I told myself. It would be the usual kind of summer, and I loved those. I'd take the kids camping and hiking and swimming. We'd visit Mackinac Island and Sleeping Bear Dunes. We could go fishing and water-skiing and tubing off Xander's boat.

I paused, wiping sweat from my forehead with the back of my arm.

Maybe when the kids went out to stay with Sansa in July, I'd take a little road trip myself. I'd sold my bike after the twins were born, but maybe I could rent one. If I stayed in California, I could ride the Pacific Coast Highway. Or go somewhere new—the Badlands in South Dakota, or Independence Pass in Colorado. Maybe that's what I needed, open road and freedom. Solitude. Time off. Time out. Maybe this tension in my neck and back and shoulders would ease up.

Hell, maybe I'd meet a cute bartender in some roadside dive, somebody with long legs, blond hair, baby blue eyes, and a mouth that curved like the highway around the mountains. Maybe she'd take a ride with me and wrap her body around mine, the engine thrumming between our legs. Maybe later, she'd ride more than just my bike. Lost in the fantasy, I stopped sanding for a moment and relished the feeling of blood rushing to my crotch, my cock surging to life. I closed my eyes and imagined my hands on her skin, her breath in my ear, the taste of her tongue as she rocked her hips over mine.

But when I realized I was dream-fucking the potential nanny I'd just rejected, I tossed the sandpaper aside and went over to the small fridge at the back of the garage. Pulling it open, I grabbed a beer, pried the cap off, and tipped it up. The cold, crisp IPA went down fast, putting out the fire. I wandered out the open garage door and sat down in one of the four Adirondack chairs that circled a small fire pit on the stone patio behind the house.

The windows in the house were open, and through the screens I heard the usual dinner routine begin—Mabel shouting for the kids that it was ready, telling them to wash their hands. Adelaide yelling back "Okay!" and Owen protesting that he'd just washed them a little bit ago because he'd gone to the bathroom. The clatter of plates and forks. The clunk of pans on the stove. The argument over who got their milk in the giant plastic cup I'd won last year at the summer carnival. Owen claimed it was his night for the cup, but Adelaide insisted that Owen had traded it for her cookie at lunch today.

"You didn't even want that cookie!" Owen shouted.

"Well, I always want the cup," Adelaide said triumphantly. "So it was a good trade."

"Enough!" Mabel's tone was sharp. "I've got a million things to do and breaking up silly fights isn't one of them. Sit down and eat."

I was about to go in and rescue my sister when the back door opened, and she came out. "Hey," I said.

"Hey." She dropped into the chair next to mine. "Nice out here."

"At least until they start fighting again."

She laughed. "If you'd been talented enough to win a second

cup at that ring toss game, they wouldn't have a problem."

"I was going to offer you a beer, but now you can just fuck off."
I took another sip.

She smiled and crisscrossed her legs, rubbing her hands along
the chair arms. "What are you going to do without a nanny?"

"I'll manage."

"How?"

"I managed you guys, didn't I? And you were the worst of
them."

Her lips tipped up. "Yeah?"

"Smart-mouthed little know-it-all with too much sass."

"I needed sass with four older brothers. How else was I gonna
be heard?" She shrugged. "A girl's gotta do what a girl's gotta do."

I harrumphed and finished off my beer. "And now a girl's
gotta dig, huh?"

"A girl's gotta dig." She paused. "But speaking of sass…"

"No."

"Austin, you didn't even give her a chance."

"Yes, I did, and the answer is no." I got up and went into the
garage to get another beer, and Mabel followed me.

"The kids really liked her."

"They'd like anybody who promised them two birthday cakes."

"I really liked her."

I took out a beer and pointed the top at her. "You're leaving.
You don't get a say."

"Ari said everyone at Moe's adored her, even grumpy Larry."

"Larry likes a pretty face."

"And Willene Fleck."

"My old teacher? She hates me. She'd probably send me a bad
nanny on purpose." I uncapped the bottle and took a drink.

"Ari doesn't hate you."

"Ari is one degree of separation from being you. She can't

be trusted."

Mabel sighed and stuck her hands on her hips. "You're impossible. You did *not* give her a fair shake."

"I gave her as fair a shake as I'd give anybody," I argued.

"She's jobless and homeless now!"

I rolled my eyes. "A girl like that will be just fine."

"What's that supposed to mean?"

"It means any woman who's that attractive will have no trouble getting hired somewhere she's *qualified*," I said.

Mabel gave me a sly smile. "So you were attracted to her."

"I didn't say I was attracted to her, I said she was *attractive*. There's a difference." Although I was struggling to remember what it was at the moment.

"Of course." She crossed her arms over her chest. "Well, now it makes more sense."

Irritated, I rolled my neck and rubbed at my sore trapezius. "What makes more sense?"

"Your problem with her."

"Jesus Christ, Mabel, I don't have a problem with her!"

"Your problem," she went on in that infuriatingly calm tone, "is that you're afraid of her."

"Afraid of who?" Xander strolled into the garage with a saw he'd borrowed from me a few days ago. He was a slightly younger, slightly taller version of me, same dark hair and eyes, although his beard was thicker. His biceps were too, but I didn't like talking about that.

"This woman we interviewed today to replace me as the nanny this summer," Mabel said.

"Why's he afraid of her?" Xander set down the saw, went to the fridge, and helped himself to a beer.

"Because she's pretty."

"Ah." Xander nodded and he uncapped his beer. "That sounds

about right. Nothing sets Austin on edge like a beautiful woman."

"Will you two shut up?" I could feel my blood pressure rising. "I'm not afraid of beautiful women."

"Really? When's the last time you went on a date?" Xander pretended to think. "Was it high school?"

"Look, just because I'm not out every night with a different girl doesn't mean I'm afraid of them. It means I'm busy. And who said you could drink my beer?"

"Why don't you come over here and try to take it away from me?" he taunted, wagging the bottle at me like a red cape.

I thought about it for a second, but even though Xander was younger by one year, he was taller and stronger, and his time in Special Ops had taught him fighting tactics that gave him an unfair advantage. As much as I hated to admit it, we were no longer evenly matched in hand-to-hand combat. It didn't always stop me from messing with him, but right this second, I wasn't sure I had it in me.

Thankfully, I was saved by Adelaide, who ran into the garage out of breath. "She's back!"

"Who's back?" I asked.

"The bride lady. She's at the front door."

I looked at Mabel, who held up her hands, like it wasn't her fault.

"Bride lady?" Xander looked back and forth from Mabel to me.

"The pretty nanny he rejected," said Mabel. "She was supposed to get married today, but she found out he was cheating on her, so she left the jerk at the altar."

"But first she kicked him in the face!" Adelaide shouted, repeating Veronica's spin-and-kick move, but a lot less gracefully. "Hi-yah!"

"No shit." Xander looked impressed.

"I'll handle this." I strode out of the garage, but of course, Xander followed me. "I *said*, *I'll* handle this," I told him over my shoulder.

"But I want to see the pretty bride lady," Xander said, pausing only to scoop Adelaide under his arm and carry her, giggling, back to the house.

"I'm coming too," Mabel said, running ahead of me and reaching the back door first.

Right then, I envied Veronica being an only child.

Chapter 5

I did not want to go back to the Buckley house.

After Austin had said *thank you, next*—actually it was more like *fuck you, no*—I'd grabbed my purse and hightailed it out of their living room as quickly as I could. I could see that Mabel felt just as terrible as I did. The kids, who'd been sitting side by side on the same step, listening to everything, waved goodbye to me with sad faces.

"I wish you could be our nanny," Adelaide had said.

"Me too," echoed her brother.

For the first time, I thought about how much fun the job would have been and really regretted blowing it. I could have spent my summer in this charming, friendly little town, hanging out with those adorable kids on the beach, riding bikes, getting ice cream, eating fudge. We could have done crafts and colored. Baked birthday cakes and eaten batter from the bowl. Made up dances and put on shows in the backyard. I actually loved kids—I wanted my own someday.

Dammit, I could have been a good nanny! That uptight jerk hadn't even given me a chance. And did he even know how to smile?

As I plodded toward the inn, which, according to my nearly dead phone, was one mile across town, the adrenaline that had gotten me through the day was starting to fade. I swallowed hard several times, but the lump in my throat stubbornly refused to dissipate. Tears welled in my eyes. I took a few deep breaths and concentrated on picking out different scents in the air—fudge, the bay, the lilac bushes in someone's front yard. I nearly had my emotions under control when my phone buzzed in my bag.

It was Morgan.

"Well?" she squealed. "What's the news? Are you Mrs. Veronica Vanderhoof?"

"Actually, no. I'm not." God, it felt so good to say that.

Silence. And then, "Wait. What?"

"I didn't marry him."

More silence. "Are you being serious?"

"Yes."

"Halle-fucking-lujah! But are you okay?"

"I'm fine." I took a breath. "Or I will be. I think I'm still in shock."

"What happened?"

"About half an hour before the ceremony, he sent me a sext meant for someone else."

"Who's the someone else?" Morgan didn't sound surprised.

"Valerie. His assistant. He must have hit the letter V in his phone and not paid attention to whose name actually came up."

"That is because you were engaged to a complete fuckwit jackass who does not and never has deserved you," said Morgan, "but go on. I'll try to reserve additional judgment until the end."

"It seems like they might have been, um, *together* last night."

"Where?"

"I'm not sure. Maybe Valerie is staying at the family's vacation house. Or maybe he went to her hotel room. I stayed by myself at the inn you and I'd planned to stay at."

Morgan groaned. "God, Roni, I'm so sorry I'm not there. My baby had some nerve arriving so soon. I've never been early for anything in my life! He must get that from Jake."

I had to smile, remembering all the call times Morgan had nearly missed during our days as Rockettes together. "How's the baby doing?"

"Good." Morgan's voice warmed. "He's out of the NICU, breathing pretty well on his own and eating okay. The doctor is cautiously optimistic we can take him home within the week."

"That's awesome. I can't wait to meet him."

"Do it. Run away. Get on a plane back to New York right the fuck now."

"And do what? Live where?" I turned a corner and trudged further up the hill toward the Cherry Blossom Inn. "How would I even get on a plane? I have no money that's not his, and I refuse to spend one more Vanderhoof dime."

"He owes you, Roni. We can find you a job. You can live here."

"In your one-bedroom apartment with your husband and newborn?" Morgan had married a talented composer and music director, but even their combined incomes didn't stretch very far in terms of Manhattan rent, and their place was small. "No way. I am not intruding on you guys."

"Here's what you do." She continued like I hadn't spoken. "You go to the bank ASAP and drain every account you can— savings and checking. Then you—"

"Are you kidding? My name isn't actually on any bank

accounts, Morgan. I had a credit card that Neil paid off. He gave me an allowance in cash."

My best friend growled. "God, I hate him. And if I'd been a better friend through all this, I wouldn't have let you say yes to him and move away."

"It wasn't your fault. You were busy getting married and being pregnant and happy." My voice grew quieter. "And I'd made my mom a promise. I felt I owed it to her."

"You didn't owe her this." Morgan's voice was firm. "I know how much you loved your mom, Roni. I know how she got pregnant at eighteen. I know she was abandoned by the guy and disowned by her parents. I know how many jobs she worked to pay for your dance training. But you didn't owe her this."

"I don't know when she slept," I cut in, even though Morgan had heard all my stories early on in our friendship. "But she never once complained. She wanted my dream to come true."

"And it did," she said softly. "Don't you think your mom would have wanted you to keep dancing? She loved watching you!"

"But she loved seeing me with Neil too. She was so dazzled by him and his promise that he would always take care of me. She was in awe of his money."

"What about love? Don't you think she wanted you to find love?"

I bit my tongue. My mother's relationship with love was complicated. She'd fallen hard for someone who betrayed her, so she had made it very clear to me all my life that romantic love wasn't something you could trust.

Your heart could mislead you. Better to use your head.

Guard your heart like it's your home, she always said. *Be careful who you let in.*

"Because Neil was not capable of love," Morgan continued. "He saw something he liked on stage one night—the brightest, shiniest, most beautiful object he could imagine possessing—and when you turned him down the first few times, he was even more driven to prove he could have you, because he's used to getting what he wants. But that isn't love, Roni. It's just greed."

"I know. But I didn't love him either."

"I hope you told him that."

"I think it was implied when I refused to marry him."

"God, I wish I'd have been there." Morgan's tone lightened up. "So how did old Cornelius take the news? I can't imagine he was too happy to get dumped on his wedding day."

"He was not. Especially not the way I did it." I told her the full story, and she crowed with laughter.

"That's the best thing I've ever heard," she said. "He finally got what he deserved. So what will you do now?"

"Well, first I need to get out of this dress." Reaching the inn, I headed up the walk to the front entrance. "Then charge my phone. Then get a good night's sleep. After that, I'll be able to think straight."

"Wait, you're still wearing the dress?"

"Yes. I even interviewed for a nanny job in it."

"A *what* job?"

"A nanny job. But I didn't get it."

Morgan was laughing again. "You've had a hell of a day, Veronica Sutton. But if anyone can bounce back from this, you can."

"Thanks." I pulled open the door and entered the Cherry Blossom Inn's lobby. "I'll call you tomorrow."

"I love you, and everything is going to be okay."

"I love you too. And I hope you're right."

But she wasn't.

I was stopped on my way through the lobby by a nervous-looking employee named Randall who delivered a bombshell—

several of them, actually.

I'd been checked out. I had ten minutes to pack my bags and leave the premises. The credit card number that I'd given for incidentals was no longer valid.

"There must be some mistake," I started—and then it hit me.

Neil had done this. It was his way of showing me he was still in control. He still held my fate in his hands. I needed him. I was nothing without him.

Well, fuck that.

Just in case this Randall guy was being paid to report back to Neil, I refused to beg or fall apart. Chin held high, I went up to my room and—under Randall's watchful eye—threw all my things in a suitcase. "Can I have a minute alone to change my clothes please?" I asked.

He nodded and left the room. The second the door was closed, a sob tried to escape, but I choked it down. As quickly as I could, I ditched the wedding dress for a pair of denim shorts and a black T-shirt, knotting the tee at my waist the way I liked and Neil hated. In the bathroom, I scrubbed my face and yanked the pins from my chignon, leaving my hair loose around my shoulders. After putting my sneakers back on, I grabbed my bags and opened the door.

Randall looked beyond me into the room, his expression suspicious like I might be trying to walk out with a lamp or a pillow. "What about that?" He pointed at something.

I glanced behind me and saw my wedding dress in a sad, deflated heap of tulle and silk on the floor. "I don't want it. It's garbage."

"You're just going to leave it like that?"

"Oh—sorry." I went back into the room and balled up the dress as much as I could, then made a big show of attempting to stuff it in the tiny wastebasket. It overflowed like the foam on a beer poured too fast. "That better?"

Before he could answer, I walked out, dragging my suitcase filled with clothing for a luxury Hawaiian honeymoon behind me.

It was only when I reached the sidewalk outside the inn and realized I had absolutely nowhere to go and less than five dollars to my name that I gave in and shed a few tears, tugging my bag over the rough cement. But my mother had taught me there was no use crying over spilled milk, so I dug a tissue from my purse, mopped up my face, and made a plan.

Morgan could send me some money, right? All I needed was a train ticket back to Chicago so I could get some clothing and then plane fare to New York. And I'd pay them back plus interest as soon as I could get a job—I'd take anything.

I pulled out my phone to call her—the battery was dead.

"Okay, universe," I muttered to the twilight sky. "Now what?"

The universe was annoyingly silent.

"Fine," I mumbled. "Be that way." I decided to head for Main Street. Maybe Ari and Steve would let me charge my phone at Moe's.

But when I reached Moe's and looked through the window, Ari and Steve were nowhere to be seen, and unfamiliar servers were behind the counter. Too humiliated to walk in and explain the situation to a new crowd, I fought back tears and turned around again.

I only knew one other place to go.

Praying that Mabel would answer the door and I wouldn't have to face Austin Buckley again (now I knew what Ari had meant by *intense*), I knocked three times.

The twins came barreling toward the screen door like it was a race. Owen was there first and pulled it open. "Hi," he said.

"Hi, Owen. Hi, Adelaide."

"Veronica?" The young girl tilted her head. "You look different. I like your hair."

"Thank you." I tried to smile. "I was wondering if Mabel was here?"

"I'll get her!" Adelaide took off running, leaving Owen and me alone.

"You can come in," he said. "You're not a real stranger, so I don't think my dad would be mad."

"That's okay. I don't mind waiting out here on the porch."

Owen came outside, letting the screen door slap shut behind him. "What's that?" he asked, pointing at my suitcase. "Are you going on a trip?"

"I was supposed to, but it got canceled."

"Our trip to Sleeping Bear Dunes got canceled last year because Grandpa had a heart attack."

"Oh no!" I said. "I hope he's okay now."

"He is. We're going to California soon to visit our mom. We go every summer."

So she lived on the other side of the country. Interesting. "That will be fun."

"Not all kids live with their mom *and* dad," he went on. "Some kids live just with their dad, like me and Addie, and then some live with just their mom."

"Sure. I lived with just my mom."

"Did you visit your dad?"

"Uh, no. I didn't."

"Was it because your mom would miss you too much? Daddy says that's why we only go to California once a year. He misses us too much when we're gone."

"Something like that," I said, begrudgingly finding it sweet that Austin seemed to be such a devoted father. Too bad he was such a curmudgeon of a guy.

"Did you FaceTime your dad? We FaceTime our mom on Sunday nights."

Before I could answer, the screen door flew open and Mabel burst out onto the porch, followed closely by a scowling Austin and then a taller version of Austin but with a beard and a smile. Adelaide was the last one out the door.

"Veronica," Mabel said breathlessly. "Are you okay?"

"Yes and no," I said. "I'm sort of stranded at the moment, and my phone is dead. I'm so sorry to ask, but do you think I could charge it here? Maybe there's an outlet on the porch?"

"There isn't," Austin said, looking put out that I'd returned. Maybe I'd interrupted dinner or something.

"Hi," said bearded, smiling guy, offering a hand. "I'm Xander Buckley."

"Veronica Sutton. Nice to meet you."

"You're welcome to charge your phone at my house," Xander offered. "My dad and I live two minutes from here and we have plenty of outlets."

"That's ridiculous," said Mabel. "You can charge your phone here, Veronica. Let's just go inside."

Austin opened his mouth like he might argue, but Mabel silenced him with a look and a command: "Bring her suitcase in the house, Austin."

"Why?" the big jerk asked. "She's not staying here."

"I'll get it," Xander said with a grin. "Looks too heavy for Austin, anyway."

Chapter 6

AUSTIN

She was prettier than I remembered, which was annoying as fuck and immediately put me in an even worse mood.

She was even prettier than she had been in my motorcycle fantasy. Maybe it was that she'd let her hair down—it was wavy and pale blond and looked soft as cornsilk. Maybe it was that she'd changed into shorts, putting her legs on display—she definitely had the limbs of a dancer. Maybe it was that she'd washed the makeup off her face, and her blue eyes seemed even more vulnerable. I could tell she'd been crying, and it weakened my defenses.

She caught me staring as we took seats across from each other at the dining table, and I quickly looked away. Owen was to my right, Adelaide across from him, and they resumed eating their dinner. Xander sat at their end of the table, tipping the legs back on the chair I'd made, even though I'd told him a million fucking times not to do that.

"Veronica, can I get you something?" Mabel asked from the kitchen, as if this was a social visit. "A glass of wine maybe?"

"No, thank you. I just need to charge my phone for a few minutes, and then I'll be out of your way. I'm sure my friend in New York will send me train fare to get back to Chicago. I just need to call her."

"I plugged it in, so it's charging now," Mabel said, taking a bottle of white wine from the fridge and pouring herself a glass. "But since it's completely dead, I think you have time for one glass."

"She already said no, Mabel. Leave it." I glared at my sister, who stuck out her tongue at me.

Veronica spoke up. "Actually, a glass of wine sounds lovely. Thank you."

When I looked at her, she met my eyes directly. A little defiantly.

Mabel came to the table with two full glasses of wine, setting one down in front of Veronica. "Here you go. Austin, can I get you a beer? Take the edge off that mood?"

"What mood?" I knew I was being a dick, but I couldn't help it. Something about the woman sitting across from me had me tense as a tightrope. Maybe it was that mouth. Her lips looked puffy and inviting without the bright red color on them. Like a ripe peach.

"Maybe he's hangry," Xander suggested.

"Pasta is on the stove," Mabel said. "Anyone is welcome to eat."

"I'm not hungry," I snapped. What I wanted to taste were those lips.

"So Veronica, how long will you be in town?" Xander asked.

"I'm not exactly sure." She fit the tips of her thumbnails together and stared at them. "My circumstances are a little... uncertain at the moment."

"Where are you staying tonight?" Mabel asked.

"Um, that's sort of up in the air too." She took a sip of wine. "My ex-fiancé already cut me off. The inn where I was staying kicked me out. And my credit card has been frozen."

Mabel's jaw fell open. "Seriously? Your ex did all that *already*?"

"He's good at getting what he wants right when he wants it."

"Rich guys always are," I muttered.

"This guy was rich?" Xander asked.

"A Vanderhoof," I said.

"Oh." Xander nodded. "Yeah, I know that family. Bunch of douchebags. They used to come into the restaurant at The Pier every summer and complain about everything—their table, the service, the food. They were shitty tippers too."

"Veronica, do you have another credit card?" Mabel asked. "Or somewhere you can go tonight? What if you can't get ahold of your friend?"

"I'll figure it out," said Veronica, picking up her wine glass again. "I can always just sleep at the train station."

I knew what my sister was going to say before she said it.

"I think you should just stay here," said Mabel, right on cue.

"No," Veronica and I said at the same time.

Our eyes met once more. The air crackled with electricity.

Veronica looked away first, shifting her gaze to Mabel. "It's very nice of you to offer, but I really can't accept."

"Sure, you can. You can sleep in the room over the garage. I'll sleep in here on the couch."

"I couldn't take your room," Veronica protested.

"I insist," Mabel said, like the place was hers to rent out.

"You can always stay at Dad's house, Mabel," offered Xander. "Your old room is empty, and I'm sure Dad would love to have a little extra time with you before you leave for Virginia."

I gave him a scathing look.

"Good idea, Xander! That's what I'll do. I'm not quite done

packing yet," Mabel said to Veronica, "but it won't take me more than an hour. I'll put new sheets on the bed, and then the room would be all yours—if you're comfortable staying here, of course."

Veronica shook her head. "I really can't."

"But then where—"

"She said she's not comfortable with it, Mabel." I gave my sister a look that said *drop it.*

"I didn't say that."

"Huh?" I squinted at Veronica.

"I didn't say I wouldn't be comfortable with it," she clarified. "I just don't want to be a bother."

"You're not a bother at all," Mabel insisted. "In our family, we were taught to extend a welcome to everyone and offer a helping hand when it's needed. And after what you've been through, you could use a little generosity. Clearly, my brother can see that."

I clenched my jaw.

"You shouldn't leave Cherry Tree Harbor feeling like it's not a friendly place," Mabel went on. "Right, Xander?"

"Right." My dickhead brother nodded. "In this town, we open our hearts and homes to those in need."

"Then it's settled." Mabel's expression was triumphant. "She stays here for the night. Okay, Austin?"

I was caught in a trap. Unless I wanted my kids to see me act like a real asshole and toss this broke, stranded girl out on the street, I had to agree. "Fine. One night."

"That's really nice of you." Veronica smiled at me. "Thanks."

I swear I wasn't imagining the look in her eyes that said, *I won this round, didn't I?*

"Why don't you grab your bag and come out to the garage with me now?" Mabel suggested. "I'll show you the room and we can drink our wine while I finish packing. Then I'll head over to my dad's."

"Sounds good." Veronica pushed her chair back and stood up. Then she ran her fingertips over the smooth, glossy surface of the table, which I'd fashioned out of salvaged barn wood. "Wow. This table is *really* beautiful."

Okay, *fine*. She had good taste.

• • •

"Dude, I can't believe you turned her down for the job," Xander said to me after Veronica and Mabel had gone out to the garage, the kids in tow. We were in the kitchen, filling bowls with pasta from the pot on the stove.

"You'd believe it if you'd been here when she interviewed," I said, grabbing a beer from the fridge.

"Get me one too," Xander said as he headed for the table.

I hooked a second bottle with my fingers before bumping the fridge door shut with my hip. Taking my seat again, I sent one bottle sliding toward my brother.

He caught it easily. "So tell me why you didn't hire her."

First, I uncapped my beer and took a long pull. "She wasn't qualified."

"But she's hot."

"If you had kids, you'd know that being hot is the least important quality in a nanny."

"It doesn't hurt," Xander said. "Listen, I love those two kids like they *are* mine, and I'm just saying, I'd give that girl a chance. She seems cool. Honest. Trustworthy." He tapped his temple. "I have good instincts about that stuff."

"She has zero experience. No car. No references. And she can't cook," I said, digging into the pasta. "We'll starve."

"So you eat takeout."

"I'll go broke. And I'm not crazy about a stranger living here anyway."

Xander was quiet for a minute or two. "Don't go all grizzly bear on me for suggesting this, but what about a longer visit in California?"

"No." I shook my head. "Not an option."

"Austin, you have those kids fifty-one weeks a year."

"And the one they're gone is tough enough."

"But they're not babies anymore. Sansa can handle two seven-year-olds for a summer, can't she?"

"Not an option."

"But couldn't you—"

I leveled him with a look. "Not. An option."

"Okay, okay." Xander backed off. "Just trying to help. And it's never seemed fair to me that you're the only full-time parent."

"It's how things had to be," I said. "It was either full-time dad or nothing. She didn't want kids."

I hadn't either—not yet, anyway.

I could still remember the panic that gripped my heart when Sansa—an art student I'd met on vacation in Santa Cruz and spent several tequila-fueled, sex-filled days with at the beach—reached out to let me know she was pregnant. She was only twenty-one, still in college, up to her neck in student loans, scared out of her mind, not sure she even wanted children, and definitely not ready to be a parent at that point in her life. She was willing to have the baby, she said, but then planned to give it up for adoption.

My reaction was immediate. "I'll raise it," I told her, even though I was terrified. "Have the baby, and I'll raise it."

Of course, the phone call two weeks later came as even more of a shock—she was pregnant with twins.

"Do you still want them?" she asked.

"Yes," I said as the room spun around me. "I'll raise them both."

After we hung up, I passed out.

. . .

I helped Mabel load her bags into her car.

"Take care of yourself," I said gruffly, as we hugged goodbye in the driveway. I wasn't big on displays of affection. "Don't fall in any holes on the dig."

"I won't." She squeezed me tight—affection came easily to her. "Thank you for letting me go."

"No thanks necessary. Go show them all how smart you are."

"I will." Lowering her voice to a whisper, she pulled me down so she could put her lips at my ear. "Listen, if you change your mind about Veronica, she could always use my car this summer. I'll leave the keys at Dad's."

"I won't change my mind." I tried to release her, but she clung like a monkey.

"She could be good for you, Austin."

I shook her off me. "Get lost."

"Okay, okay. I love you."

"I love you too." My heart ached a little watching my sister leave. She was all up in my business when she was here, but I always missed her when she was gone.

She embraced the twins. "You be good for your dad, okay?" She pointed at each of them. "Send me pics of those weekly chore charts with all the boxes checked off."

"We will," they promised.

"I'm gonna miss you guys." She opened her arms for one last hug from them both at the same time. "Now go on up and brush your teeth for bed—two minutes, just like the dentist said!"

The kids went into the house, and Mabel turned to Veronica. "Well, good luck," she said, giving the taller woman a quick hug. "You have my number, right? Text me when you get to the East Coast. Maybe we can meet up sometime."

Veronica smiled. "I'd really like that. You've been so nice to me."

I wondered where on the East Coast she was headed. Back to New York? Home to New Jersey?

"I'll see you at the house," Mabel called to Xander before getting into her car and driving off.

"Guess I'll head home too," my brother said. Turning to Veronica, he extended a hand. "Nice meeting you. If you decide to stay in town, maybe I'll see you around."

"Actually, I think I'm going to head back to New York." She tucked her hands into her back pockets. "I just have to find my way to Chicago first and hope my ex lets me into the apartment to pack my clothes."

"Damn, that guy really did a number on you." Xander shook his head. "What a dick."

"I let him do it," Veronica said quickly. "I was stupid."

Wait a minute, she was taking the blame for the way he'd treated her? For some reason, that really bothered me. "It wasn't your fault," I said.

Both Veronica and Xander looked at me in surprise.

"Maybe not entirely," she hedged. "But I certainly didn't do myself any favors by becoming so dependent on him."

"If my bar was up and running, I'd hire you," Xander said. "But it will be a couple months yet."

She smiled. "I appreciate that. But I'll be okay."

Earlier today she'd told me she had grit and resilience, but I sensed how scared she was. I heard the tremble in her voice. My protective instincts were kicking in, and I had to sink my teeth into my tongue to prevent myself from doing something ridiculous, like hiring her.

"If you change your mind, let me know." Xander pulled a card from his wallet and handed it to her. "My place should be open in a couple months."

"Xander Buckley, Cole Security," she read. "Virginia Beach."

"I'm not in private security or Virginia Beach anymore, but the phone number's still good." He gave her a flirtatious grin that bugged me.

"Private security, like a bodyguard?" Veronica sounded impressed.

"Yeah." My brother shrugged, as if he was humble. "Just for a couple years, after I left the Navy."

At least he hadn't mentioned being a SEAL, which surprised me, since it was usually the first thing out of his mouth when a cute girl was around.

"I was a SEAL," he added, puffing out his chest.

Annnnd there it was.

"I should go in," I said. Maybe these two wanted a moment alone.

"Me too, actually." Veronica flicked the edge of Xander's card with her fingernail. She had long, graceful fingers, and when I thought about the way she'd caressed the wooden table earlier, my body warmed. "Thank you again for letting me stay the night."

I folded my arms over my chest. "No problem."

She looked at Xander, then me, her eyes lingering on mine. "Well…goodnight."

"Night," Xander said.

We watched her disappear up the driveway and around the back of the house.

Then my brother turned to me and stuck his index finger in my face. "You're a fucking idiot."

• • •

I'd always been a light sleeper—any noise in the house will wake me, and with the windows open, any noise in the yard will too. So when I heard the door of the garage apartment open and close, then footsteps on the exterior stairs, I got out of bed.

Peeking around the shade, I saw Veronica, looking like a ghost in a white T-shirt that barely covered her ass, reach the bottom of the steps and move on bare feet across the lawn to the patio. Perching on the edge of one of the Adirondack chairs, she took out her phone. She appeared to send a text, then she put her phone down on the edge of the fire pit and buried her face in her hands. A moment later, her shoulders began to shudder, and I heard soft, pitiful sobs.

"Fuuuuuck meeeee," I moaned quietly. Frowning, I rubbed my sore shoulder and listed all the reasons I didn't need to go down there.

She wasn't my problem. I couldn't solve hers. She was a total stranger. I was good with crying kids, not crying grownups. She would be embarrassed if she knew I'd seen her. *I'd* be embarrassed.

But even as the list grew, I found myself tugging a shirt over my head and pulling on a pair of gray sweatpants. I glanced at my hair in the mirror over my dresser and saw it sticking up on one side pretty badly, so I grabbed a cap and tugged it on as I left my room.

On my way out to the yard, I yanked a handful of tissues from a box on the kitchen counter. When I pushed open the back door, she looked up, startled.

"Oh!" she said, frantically wiping away her tears. "I'm so sorry. Did I wake you?"

"I'm a light sleeper, and the windows are open." I dropped into the chair next to her. "We should be quiet, though, so we don't wake the kids."

"Of course," she whispered. "Sorry."

I held out the tissues. "Here."

"Oh. Thank you." She sounded surprised. Our fingers touched

as she took them from my hand, and I immediately pulled mine back, conscious of the heat that traveled up my arm.

She dried her tears and blew her nose while I tried not to stare at those long, bare legs in the moonlight. Crickets chirped, and a warm breeze whispered through the leaves of the red oak on the back lawn.

"You okay?" I asked.

"Yes. But also no."

"You had a rough day."

"Yeah."

"Look, I'm sorry about the interview. I didn't mean to come off as rude. I just don't like surprises, and Mabel sort of sprung you on me. To be honest, I'm not sure I'd hire any stranger to live here and take care of my kids, whether they were qualified or not."

"It's not that."

I looked at her. "Is it the guy?"

"No." She hugged her knees to her chest, her bare feet on the edge of her chair. "I lost my mom last summer, and I feel like it's hitting me all over again. I just feel really alone."

I rubbed the back of my neck, but my chest felt tight too. "I'm sorry."

"Thanks. We were close—it was just the two of us when I was growing up. She worked so hard to give me a good life. She cleaned houses during the day and waitressed at night. Probably half her pay went to a sitter for me, until I was old enough to stay on my own. Then all her money went to my dance training. She also cleaned the studio and sewed costumes so I'd get a break on tuition."

"You didn't have any other family around?"

She shook her head. "I wish. My mom got pregnant with me when she was eighteen and the guy took off when she told him. She asked her parents for help, but they were very religious and told her she had sinned and shamed herself and her family."

"So you've never met your father?" It was unfathomable to me—abandoning your own child.

"Never. And I don't want to." She paused. "I did meet my grandparents once."

"Your mother's parents?"

She nodded. "My mom took me to their farm once when I was four. I think she was hoping enough time had gone by that they'd be more forgiving. Or maybe she was hoping they'd see me and feel some kind of instinctual love, but…it didn't happen."

I tried to imagine it—being rejected by your own grandparents, right there, face to face. "That's…that's tough."

"I remember sitting in the living room with their dog listening to them fight with my mom in the kitchen. I remember being scared and hearing a lot of words I didn't understand. They seemed so mad at her."

"I'm sorry." It was hard not to contrast her experience with mine. When I told my dad about the twins, and how I was going to raise them on my own, he was proud of me. No questioning my decision, no judgment of me or Sansa. He was actually excited to be a grandpa.

"Eventually my mom came to the living room and got me," Veronica went on. "She grabbed me by the hand and we walked out. I never saw them again. No birthday cards, no Christmas gifts, nothing."

"Sounds like you were better off without them."

"After that we went and got ice cream. I had vanilla with rainbow sprinkles."

I looked over at her, and she suddenly looked so *young*, her chin resting on her knees, her eyes luminous in the dark. "You actually remember what flavor you had that day?"

"It was always my favorite. It still is."

I nodded slowly, sort of wishing I could buy her a vanilla ice cream with rainbow sprinkles right this second.

She sighed. "I bet there's a great ice cream parlor in this town."

"Several," I confirmed. "Cherry Tree Harbor is great for anyone with a sailboat or a sweet tooth."

"I never even got to see the harbor. Or eat any fudge."

"You should get some before you leave."

"Are there free samples? Currently I have about five bucks to my name."

Sympathy tugged on my heart. "Did you ever talk to your friend? Is she able to help you out?"

"She wants to." Veronica stretched out her legs, and the shirt rode dangerously high on her thighs. "But I don't really have access to a bank account right now, so even transferring money to me is difficult. We need to find a Western Union or something."

"Right." My body was reacting to her bare skin, and my dick was perking up like it wanted a better look. Forcing my eyes away from her legs, I thought for a minute. "I think there's one in Petoskey. That's about twenty minutes from here."

"Twenty minutes walking?" she asked hopefully.

I shook my head. "Driving."

"Right." She pointed and flexed her feet. "How many miles do you think it is?"

"Maybe ten or so." I kneaded my aching shoulder.

"That's not so bad. I can walk it."

"I'll drive you."

She shook her head. "No. You've done enough."

"I *said*, I'll drive you." God, this fucking muscle was tight as the crotch of my pants.

"You're too busy."

"I'll find the time."

"I don't want to be a bother, Austin."

"Too late, *Veronica*." Our eyes met, and her lips parted, like I'd offended her. I thought maybe she'd continue to fight me, but then she smiled.

"Okay," she said. "Thank you."

Giving up on my neck, I sat back. "Do you always argue so much?"

"Are you always so bossy?"

I gave her the side eye. "Yes."

Her lips tipped up. "Mabel said you're the oldest of five siblings."

"Mabel talks too much."

"People say that about me too."

"I believe it."

"Mabel said you were an awesome big brother," she went on. "A little overprotective, but always there for her."

"I was protective of her." I shifted in the chair. "Our mom died when I was twelve, and Mabel was only three, so I sort of helped raise her."

"Oh, I'm sorry," she said softly. "That must have been really hard."

"We managed."

She hugged her knees again, going quiet for a moment. "I always wished I had siblings."

"Take one of mine. Preferably Xander."

She smiled. "You two don't get along?"

"Eh, we get along fine. He just knows how to push my buttons."

"I have a feeling it's mutual," she said.

"Xander doesn't have too many buttons. Not much bothers him."

"But a lot bothers you?"

"I just like things the way I like them," I said tersely, rubbing my shoulder again.

"What's going on here?" She gestured toward the hand gripping my sore muscles. "Did you pull something?"

"Probably."

She rose to her feet. "Let me help. Stand up."

"You don't have to—"

"I *said*, stand up." She mimicked my tone from before.

Slowly, I pushed myself out of the chair. We stood close, nearly chest to chest. "Now who's bossy?"

Her smile was as tempting as her bare legs. "Turn around."

I rolled my eyes. "Veronica."

She drew circles in the air with one finger. "Come on. About face."

Reluctantly, I made a half-turn, presenting her with my back.

Placing her hands on my right shoulder, she began kneading the muscle so hard I winced. "Too much?"

"No." I closed my eyes and tried not to moan.

"We had an awesome trainer for the Rockettes," she said. "She was a wizard at getting the kinks out of sore muscles." One of her hands slipped beneath my T-shirt. "Is this okay?"

"It's fine," I said as she worked her thumb beneath my shoulder blade. How long had it been since I'd felt a woman's hands on my back? My mind drifted into dangerous waters—my hips between her thighs, my body rocking above her.

"But as tall as I am, I do wish I was just a little bit—hang on." She jumped up on the chair and rotated me so I faced away from her. "This is better. Now I can use my elbow."

I groaned as she dug her elbow into my flesh. "Fuck. This is brutal. Is this because I didn't hire you?"

She laughed. "Yes. It's a revenge massage."

"It's very—*Christ, that hurts*—effective." As she tortured me, I tried to keep myself from making too many noises—they all sounded sexual—and from thinking about her hands anywhere else on my body.

Or my hands on hers.

Those mile-long limbs were so pretty. And she was so flexible. What kinds of positions could she get herself into? I imagined them flung over my shoulders, or maybe pressed together and straight up, my hands locked around her ankles as I slid into her tight, wet—

"I think that's good." I took a step away from her.

"Did I get it?"

"Yeah." I turned around to help her off the chair at the exact moment she hopped down, and our chests collided. She stumbled back, and I caught her by the elbows.

Laughing, she quickly regained her footing. "Sorry! I thought you were walking away, and I…" She lifted her chin, her voice growing soft. "Jumped."

Our lips were close. I hadn't kissed anyone in so long, and it seemed really fucking unfair that I couldn't kiss this girl right here, right now, in the dark.

No one was looking. Could I?

I dipped my head slightly. Heard her quick inhale.

But it would be wrong. She was so vulnerable—what kind of jerk would take advantage of a woman who'd been through what she had today? After she'd sat here crying about how lonely she felt? After she'd been so honest with me?

As badly as I wanted to taste that mouth, I couldn't bring myself to do it. I wasn't that guy.

I took my hands off her and stepped back.

That's when she threw her arms around my neck and crushed her lips to mine.

Chapter 7

AUSTIN

For a few seconds, I was so shocked, I couldn't even kiss her back. I just stood there like I was made of stone—I didn't even close my eyes.

Then she opened hers and pulled back, covering her mouth with her hands. "Oh my god." Her words were muffled. "Oh my god, I'm so sorry."

I couldn't seem to find my voice. All I could hear was Xander in my head.

You're a fucking idiot.

Veronica uncovered her mouth and flapped her hands at the wrist. "I don't know what just came over me. I must have lost my mind. Please accept my apology."

"It's fine." My voice cracked, and I cleared my throat. "It just surprised me. You were right about giving good hugs."

Flustered, she began to ramble. "It's been such a weird day, and I was feeling so overwhelmed, like I don't have a handle on any of these things that a functioning adult should have a handle on, my own money or a job or a place to live. Everything is out of my control."

I wanted to tell her it was okay and also ascertain if I could have another shot at getting my tongue in her mouth, but she kept talking and *would not shut up.*

"And then grief hit me all over again and I was out here crying and you were finally being nice to me after being such a meanie, and then I probably shouldn't have put my hands on you but you have a really nice body and it sort of did things to me that I wasn't expecting and haven't felt for a *really, really* long time, and I thought you were going to kiss me and then you didn't, so I took control of the situation and kissed you—but then it was obvious you didn't want that, and—"

"Fuck it." Without waiting for her to finish, I grabbed the back of her head and forced her to stop talking by covering her mouth with mine.

This time it was her turn to go still with shock, and I took advantage of her immobility by opening her lips with mine and stroking between them with my tongue. Recovering her senses, she moved her hands up my chest and clutched the front of my shirt while I devoured her mouth like a starving animal. When her tongue met mine, just as hungry and desperate, I slipped one arm around her lower back, pulling her body against me, lifting her onto her toes. Sliding one rough hand into her soft blond hair, I moved my mouth down her throat, catching the scent of her perfume, tasting it on her warm skin. She moaned, and the hum of it against my lips sent a lightning bolt straight to my cock.

I took my hand from her hair and slid it up her side, beneath her shirt, spreading my fingers over her ribcage. My thumb brushed the bottom curve of her breast, and when she looped her arms around my neck, I took it as permission to keep going, letting my thumb skim over the taut peak of her nipple. Goddamn, I wanted my mouth on it. My mind was wild with the thought of tearing our clothes off and getting inside her right here under the moon. Or we could go up to the garage apartment. Or I could invite her up to my bedroom.

My bedroom...with my kids right across the hall.

Fuck.

I released her from my arms and stepped back. "Jesus. Sorry."

"It's okay." She stared at me, wide-eyed. Her pebbled nipples were visible through the thin white material of her T-shirt, and I cracked my knuckles, just to give my hands something to do.

"Well, I should go back inside. Check on the kids. If it's too hot over the garage, you can turn on the window unit," I said, because I was burning up. "It cools the place off pretty fast."

"Okay." She hesitated. "Thank you again for letting me stay. Honestly, I don't know what I would have done if you hadn't."

"No problem. Goodnight." Anxious to get inside before I lost control and kissed her again, I headed for the back door, carefully skirting around her so I wouldn't be tempted to touch.

"Night," she called softly.

Upstairs, I checked on the kids—sound asleep—then slipped into my bedroom and closed the door. After yanking my shirt off, I couldn't resist moving closer to the window and peering around the shade again.

The light was on in the garage apartment, and the shade on the window facing the house was up. She came over to the window and looked out.

I knew she couldn't see me, but I still held my breath. For a second, the teenager in me hoped she might take off her shirt. Those tantalizing nipples poking through white cotton lingered in my mind. I could practically feel them between my fingertips, beneath my tongue.

But after a moment, she pulled down the shade, and the light went off.

I got into bed and lay on my back, overcome with the urge to slide my hand into my pants and work off the pent-up tension with a quick orgasm. My dick was so hard, and it would feel so good. I untied the drawstring and eased the waist below my hips, closing my fist around my cock.

Closing my eyes, I thought of her. I pictured her long, lithe body. I tasted her on my tongue. I inhaled the scent of her skin. I heard the soft, sweet moan escape her lips. I felt her hands on my back.

I imagined what it might have been like if our circumstances were different. If I'd had the house to myself tonight. If she were in bed with me right now. Naked. Panting. Greedy for my cock. Maybe she'd talk dirty to me, or like it when I said filthy things to her. Maybe she'd love the way I used my tongue on her clit, the way I made her come with my fingers. Maybe she'd get on her knees for me, let me fuck that gorgeous mouth. Maybe she'd beg me to fuck her. I could practically hear my name on her lips, smell the sex in the room, feel her pussy tighten around me as she whispered—*yes, yes, yes…*

Swallowing the groan that threatened to escape, I tightened my fist and jerked myself harder and faster, coming in quick, hot pulses that left a sticky mess on my stomach.

Jesus.

After my heartbeat quieted and my breathing returned to normal, I made my way into the bathroom to clean up. Two minutes later, I was back in bed, hands behind my head, staring up at the ceiling.

Was she asleep? Was she thinking about me? I wondered if I'd made the right decision not to hire her, or if I'd dismissed the idea too quickly. Would it be so bad to have her around this summer?

Xander's voice was still in my head.

You're a fucking idiot.

• • •

The following morning, the first thing I did was reach for my phone and Google her. She didn't appear to have social media accounts, which surprised me until I recalled Mabel telling me Veronica's ex had made her delete them. I saw a couple articles related to being a Rockette—she'd been interviewed on different blogs or news media—but the item that caught my eye was a wedding announcement from a Chicago newspaper.

I clicked on it and held my breath as the photo popped up. She looked beautiful, sitting there in a chair in front of her fiancé, who stood with his hand on her shoulder, as if to keep her down. But she also looked kind of miserable. No smile, no light in her eyes, no sign of love or chemistry between them. She looked like a caged bird.

Setting my phone aside, I threw on some clothes and went downstairs, feeling torn about what to do.

I hadn't slept great, so I was a little groggy as I sipped my first cup of coffee, looking out the kitchen window at the backyard. For a second, I thought my eyes were deceiving me—was Veronica lying on the lawn?

Squinting, I chugged more caffeine as she pressed her hands into the ground and peeled her upper body off the grass, her face lifting to the bright blue sky.

Fuck, she was doing yoga.

She wore a black sports bra and little black shorts that showed off her legs. Her blond hair sat in a nest on top of her head, and her feet were bare. I moved a little closer to the window.

She held that pose for a moment and then shifted into a new

one, moving through a plank to an inverted V shape, her legs perfectly straight, her heels on the ground, her arms stretched out, and her head tucked between her biceps. I was mesmerized by the perfect lines her body created—especially her spine, which formed a gentle concave curve from her tailbone all the way to the back of her neck.

I was even more impressed when she extended one leg to the sky in a slow, dramatic arc. She held it there for a moment, toes pointed, legs split in a perfect straight line—a work of art. Then she brought her foot back to the ground and repeated the process with the other leg. I was so enthralled I didn't even hear Adelaide come down the stairs.

"Dad?"

I spun around so fast my coffee sloshed over the side of the cup and went *splat* as it hit the floor.

Adelaide stood there in her pajamas looking at me strangely. "What are you doing?"

"Morning, June bug. Nothing." I grabbed a paper towel and wiped up the spill. My heart was beating erratically, as if I'd been caught with my hand in the cookie jar.

"You were looking out the window at something." She went over to the back door and peered out the glass. "It's Veronica!"

"Addie, don't—"

But it was too late, she'd already yanked open the back door and run outside. "Hi! What are you doing?"

Veronica came out of her pose and popped to her feet. I wondered what it would be like to have bones and muscles that moved so easily in the morning. I always felt stiff as a board for a couple hours. Although, I had to admit, my neck and shoulder seemed a little less tight than they had yesterday. Maybe the revenge massage had worked. Standing at the screen door, I glanced over at the fire pit, where we'd kissed last night. A hot spark zipped up my spine.

"I'm doing yoga," Veronica said with a smile. "Want to join me?"

"I don't know how to do yoga." Adelaide folded her arms behind her back. "Can you teach me?"

"Of course! Come on. We'll start with an easy one." Veronica stood up tall. "This is called Mountain Pose. Stand like this with your big toes touching but not your heels."

Adelaide turned her legs completely inward so she was pigeon-toed. "Like this?"

"Not quite so much space between your heels." Veronica bent down and adjusted Adelaide's feet. "There. Now stand nice and tall, feel the ground with all your toes, the balls of your feet, and your heels. Stretch your legs and pull your belly button in toward your spine." She placed a hand on Adelaide's stomach and tailbone. "Good, that's really good."

Adelaide beamed. "What should I do with my arms?"

"Like this." Veronica stood opposite Adelaide, as if she was a mirror. "Palms forward toward me, and spread your fingers out. Good! Now you're going to lengthen your neck. Roll those shoulders back—we want a nice broad chest for deep breaths. Imagine you're wearing long, dangling earrings and you want to show them off."

Adelaide's neck did suddenly look longer.

"Perfect! You're so good at this. Now imagine one straight line from the top of your head all the way down your spine."

"I'm picturing a skeleton," said Adelaide.

Veronica laughed. "That's a good way to do it. I once had a dance teacher who had a plastic skeleton in the studio so she could show us what she wanted our bones to look like."

"Am I doing it right?" Adelaide asked.

"Yes. Doesn't it feel nice to stand so straight and tall?"

It did feel nice—I realized I'd unconsciously followed the last few instructions about rolling my shoulders back, broadening my chest, and lengthening my neck. Even my palms were facing the screen door.

"What are you doing, Dad?"

Caught off guard again, I turned around to find Owen standing there in his pajamas, hair matted on one side, expression curious.

"Nothing. Just watching your sister learn some yoga poses." I went to the fridge and took out the almond milk, pouring a little in my second cup of coffee. "Are you hungry? I could make you a—"

But Owen was already racing out the back door.

"Good morning, Owen," I heard her say cheerfully.

"Can I learn yoga too?" he asked.

"Of course. We're just about to do cat-cow. First, you get down on the ground like this."

Watching out the kitchen window, I groaned inwardly as Veronica got down on all fours. Her ass looked spectacular in those shorts.

"Okay, so for the cat, you want to make a rainbow with your back. Like this. Think about your belly button being sucked up toward the sky—the very top of the rainbow." Her gorgeous spine went convex, and I could practically feel my hand gliding over each vertebra as I lined my hips up behind hers.

"Like this?" The kids imitated her pose, and I felt like a total pervert for fantasizing about having sex with her while she was giving my children a yoga lesson.

"You are a terrible person," I muttered to myself. But I kept watching.

"Yes, but don't forget about your head," Veronica said patiently. "Let it be the pot of gold at the end of the rainbow. Drop it down."

They followed her directions, and she nodded. "Perfect. Now

the cow."

This time I caught myself moaning out loud. But I couldn't help it—now she was arching her back, which drew attention to her sumptuous apple-cheeked butt and curvy hips. I thought about kissing her in the dark last night, my hands in her hair, her fingers clawing my shirt like they'd claw at my sheets if I—

Don't think about it.

She picked up her head. "Now think about your belly button lowering back down to the ground. Your back is making a sort of bowl shape. Good cows, you guys!"

"Moooooo," said Owen.

"Daddy, come out here!" Adelaide called. "Come look at our cows!"

Shit. I wasn't prepared to face her yet. I tried to think of a reason why I couldn't go out there and couldn't come up with anything except the fact that I felt an erection coming on. "Just a second!"

I took a couple deep breaths, forcing myself to think about mundane, unsexy things. When I was sure I could be seen without embarrassing myself, I ran a hand over my hair and went outside.

Veronica scrambled to her feet. "Morning."

"Morning." I was careful to keep my eyes where they belonged. "What's going on out here?"

She glanced at the kids, who were still on their hands and knees. "I was just teaching them a few yoga poses."

"This one is the cow," said Owen.

"And this is the cat." Adelaide rounded her back the way Veronica had shown her. "Try it, Daddy. It feels good."

"Maybe another time. Are you guys ready for breakfast?"

"Can we go out for breakfast?" Owen asked.

"I guess we could. Where do you want to go?"

"Moe's!" the twins shouted. That was their first choice for

breakfast, lunch, or dinner, because they loved to play songs on the jukebox. I'd probably given them a hundred bucks' worth of quarters for that thing over the years. But the food was good, the prices were reasonable, and Moe and his wife Judy were good people. After my mom died, Judy had stocked our freezer with enough casseroles to feed an army. Their daughter Ari was Mabel's best friend.

"Okay," I said. "Go get dressed."

"Can you come too, Veronica?" Adelaide asked as she got to her feet.

Veronica smiled at my daughter. "Thanks, but I can't."

"Would you like to come to breakfast?" I asked her, knowing that she was probably hungry but had very little money. "Our treat."

"Are you sure?" Her eyebrows rose.

"Consider it payment for the yoga lesson."

She smiled, and the memory of kissing her hit me all over again. "Okay. I'll come."

"Yay!" Adelaide clapped her hands and jumped up and down. Even Owen looked excited as they raced each other into the house.

"Make your beds!" I yelled after them, which caused Veronica to giggle.

"What's funny?" I asked.

"Yesterday, when you and Mabel were upstairs, and I was alone with the kids, they were giving me tips on how to get the nanny job, and one of them was to tell you I always make my bed."

I shook my head. "And do you?"

"Pretty much never."

"What else did they tell you?"

She shifted her weight to one hip and ticked things off on her fingers. "Let's see. Don't ever leave lights on, because you don't own the electric company. Your favorite food is barbecue. And it would be good if I had some chore charts to show you, because you're big on responsibility and organization."

"Jesus," I grumbled. "They didn't make me sound like much fun, did they?"

A smile teased her lips. "Actually, you gave me that impression all on your own."

I took another sip of coffee, glaring at her over the edge of the cup.

"But you redeemed yourself later," she added.

Our eyes locked, and my body warmed instantly.

"And who knows?" Her pretty shoulders rose. "Maybe if I'd had a chart or two, I'd have gotten the job."

"Veronica, I—"

"It's okay," she said, laughing again as she put a hand on my arm. "I'm just messing with you. You were right, Austin. I'm unqualified. I'm not saying I wouldn't have done a good job, but I understand. I'm not what you're looking for."

Actually, right now I was afraid she was exactly what I was looking for.

"Could I have fifteen minutes to get ready for breakfast?" she asked. "I just want to rinse off really quick and change clothes."

"Of course." *Don't think about her in the shower. Don't think about her in the shower.* "Just knock on the back door when you're ready."

"Thanks." She gave me one last smile before turning toward the garage.

I watched her walk away from me, imagining what my life would be like if I asked her to stay.

Chapter 8

VERONICA

*F*ifteen minutes later, I stood at the back door with my bags packed. Adelaide answered my knock.

"Hi," she said, opening the door. Her eyes widened as she looked at my outfit—a cropped halter top and maxi skirt with a thigh-high split in a tropical print, which I wore with sandals that laced up my calves. "Wow, you look fancy."

"Thanks." Leaving my suitcase outside, I stepped into their kitchen. "The clothes I packed were for a Hawaiian vacation," I explained, although truth be told, there were more casual outfits in my suitcase. I'd worn this for Austin's benefit.

What I'd said before was true—I didn't blame him for not hiring me. I thought he should have given me the opportunity to prove myself, but I understood that his kids were his world, and he wasn't the kind of guy to take chances with them. Plus, he liked things to go according to his plans. Did I really need to spend my summer being bossed around by a man who thought he could do everything so much better than me? Hadn't I just gotten out of that kind of situation?

Still, I'd lain awake for hours last night thinking about that kiss. I couldn't even remember the last time someone had kissed me that way, like he couldn't hold back. Like he was suffocating, and I was oxygen. I'd felt that kiss from my head to my toes.

I felt it now when he walked into the kitchen and stopped in his tracks at the sight of me.

Make grumpy single dad's brown eyes pop? Check, I thought with satisfaction. *Put that on my chore chart, you big hot lug.*

He looked delicious again this morning in jeans and a fitted navy T-shirt. I remembered my hands on his back muscles last night and felt a little tingle between my legs.

His eyes traveled down my body and back up again. "You've been to Moe's, right? It's not really a dressy place."

I shrugged. "I know."

"But doesn't she look pretty, Dad?" Adelaide pressed.

"Did you mark your chore chart, June bug?" he asked her, going over to the fridge to look at it.

Behind her dad's back, Adelaide rolled her eyes. "Yes. For making my bed *and* watering the living room plants."

"Good job. Where's your brother?"

"Still getting dressed."

"Can you go tell him to hurry up, please?"

Adelaide sighed and left the room.

"We can head to Western Union right after breakfast," he said, placing his coffee mug in the dishwasher.

"That sounds great, thanks. I'm all packed up." I glanced around the kitchen—not a dirty dish left anywhere. Not a crumb on the floor. Not a stray set of keys or stack of junk mail or crumpled dish towel on the gleaming counters. Again I thought maybe I'd dodged a bullet being rejected for the job. I wasn't a slob, but I wasn't obsessive about neatness either.

He turned around and leaned back against the sink, folding his arms over his chest. "You're a good teacher."

"I'm sorry?"

"I heard you giving the kids the yoga lesson out there. You're a good teacher. Very patient."

"Oh!" I laughed and played with the ends of my hair. "Thanks. I taught dance for years. And I like kids. Yours are great—very polite and funny. I can tell they're smart too."

"Thanks." He glanced the way Adelaide had just gone. "They're good kids."

I hesitated, but decided to ask. "Owen mentioned their mom lives in California."

"Yeah. She—we—" Austin exhaled, shaking his head. "It's not a typical situation. They were sort of...unplanned."

"A surprise gift?"

He nodded. "Their mom and I met while I was out in California on vacation. I was shocked when she called and told me she was pregnant."

"She didn't want kids?"

"No. I didn't, either, not at that point. I was just twenty-five. After spending a lot of my childhood helping to raise my siblings and going to work for my dad right after graduation, I was enjoying my independence. In fact, I almost—" He shook his head. "Never mind. Anyway, that week in California, I clearly enjoyed myself a little too irresponsibly."

"But you chose to raise them on your own." My heart beat a little faster, learning this about him. It made him even sexier. "That's responsible. That's amazing, in fact. A lot of guys would have run the other way."

"Sometimes, I have no idea what I'm doing."

It surprised me—the admission of insecurity. He seemed so sure of himself. "It looks like you're doing a great job, Austin."

"I've had a lot of help," he said. "From my dad and sister especially. We lived with them up until two years ago. I don't think I'd have survived that first year without them."

"Mabel said you work for your dad's company?"

"Yes. And he was so understanding about my schedule when they were small—he always said being a dad came first, letting me arrive late and leave early, paying me more than he was taking." He shook his head. "He saved me."

My admiration for—and envy of—his tight-knit family grew. "That's what family is for, right? And accepting help from others when you need it is okay. The problem is when accepting help turns into letting someone else call all the shots in your life." I took a breath. "I'm never doing that again."

A few seconds ticked by. "Veronica, it's none of my business, but…"

"You can ask."

"It's just that you seem very independent too. How did he gain that kind of control over you?"

"I've asked myself the same thing many times," I said with a sigh. "And the truth is, it was little by little. Almost like I didn't notice it was happening until it was too late. Neil had this way of making it all seem like 'taking care of me.'" I made air quotes with my fingers. "And I'd promised my mother I'd try to let him."

"Your mom liked him?"

I shrugged. "She didn't know him, not the way I did. Honestly, I didn't know the real him back then either. We dated long-distance—I was in New York, and he was in Chicago. But he was in Manhattan a lot for business. And in all his big talk and promises, she saw a life for me that looked like a fairy tale."

"And you wanted that life?"

"I thought I did," I said honestly. "But—"

"Okay, we're ready!" Adelaide burst into the kitchen, Owen right behind her. "Can we go now?"

"Yes." Austin grabbed his keys from a hook next to the back door. "I'll load your bags in the car, Veronica."

"Thanks," I said, watching him leave. A hollow pit had formed in my stomach, and I realized it was because I hadn't gotten to finish what I was saying—that while I *thought* I'd wanted that life, it was no fairy tale. It hadn't dulled the pain of missing my mom, of not having her unconditional love in my life, the only one I'd ever known.

My father had abandoned me before I was born. My grandparents didn't want me. And no man I'd ever dated had inspired the kind of trust necessary for a healthy relationship. When I lost my mom, I'd been completely untethered, adrift in cold, lonely waters. Neil had at least been a buoy in the storm. But he hadn't loved me. His family hadn't accepted me. I hadn't belonged.

Then again, I thought as I followed the kids out the door, pulling it shut behind me, maybe it was better I hadn't spilled my guts like that.

Austin didn't like a mess.

Chapter 9

*W*hen we walked into Moe's, Veronica was greeted like a celebrity.

Gus, my dad's old friend, and grumpy Larry, who owned the barber shop, were on their way out, and we crossed paths just inside the door.

"Veronica!" Gus exclaimed with a grin on his face. "You're back!"

"I'm back. Hi, Gus." Then she smiled at the usually cantankerous barber. "Hi, Larry."

The old curmudgeon actually blushed. "Hi, Veronica."

"Hey!" Ari, who'd been pouring coffee for someone at the counter, set down her pot and came running over to envelop her in a hug, like they were long-lost friends. "You're still here!"

"I'm still here," Veronica said with a laugh. "For the moment."

"I'm so glad it worked out with the job." Ari smiled from me to the kids to Veronica again.

"Oh." Veronica's cheeks went pink. "Actually, I'm not staying in town."

"We just came in for breakfast," I said, feeling like an asshole again for not hiring her.

"But what about the job?" Gus persisted.

Veronica glanced at me. "It didn't work out."

"You didn't hire her?" Larry turned to me, his face arranged in its usual get-off-my-lawn expression. "What's wrong with you?"

"Nothing." I looked past him to Ari. "Can we get a table please?"

"Sure thing, Austin. Right this way."

We followed her to the back of the diner and slid into opposite sides of an empty booth. Owen got in next to Veronica, and Adelaide pouted. "I want to sit by Veronica!"

Her brother shrugged. "I got here first."

"Because you pushed me out of the way. Dad, Owen pushed me."

"Enough." I looked at my daughter. "Now sit down."

"Fine." Looking mad about it, Adelaide flopped into the booth and crossed her arms, like sitting next to me was a punishment.

"Maybe you could take turns," Veronica suggested. "Owen can sit on this side while we wait, and then you can switch when the food comes? Like musical chairs."

The twins looked at each other and nodded. "Okay," Owen said. "Dad, can we have some money for the jukebox?"

"What was the point of the argument about where you're sitting if you're just getting up to leave?" I griped, but I reached into my jeans pocket and pulled out a handful of quarters. "And what do you want to eat?"

"Chocolate chip pancakes," said Owen, sliding out of the booth.

"French toast." Adelaide took the quarters from me and followed her brother to the corner of the diner where the jukebox sat.

"Now they'll argue about which songs to play," I said moodily. "And who gets to choose the first one."

Veronica laughed. "I hope you gave them an even number of quarters."

Ari approached with menus and a coffee pot. "Coffee, you two?"

"Yes, please." Veronica turned over the plain white mug on the placemat in front of her.

"Can I have almond milk please?" I asked.

"Sure thing. Give me one sec." Ari poured two cups of coffee and left the menus, but since I knew everything on it by heart—not much changed from year to year in Cherry Tree Harbor, and the menu at Moe's was no exception—I covertly studied Veronica instead. She licked her bottom lip as she read the menu.

She was so fucking pretty. Would it be so bad having her across the table from me all summer? The kids liked her. My brother and sister liked her. Even the town grump liked her.

And she was so down on her luck—I understood that. She needed a break. I could give her one, and she'd be helping me out too.

It would only be for eight weeks, since I'd taken the last two weeks of August off for vacation. I could resist temptation for eight weeks and do a good thing, couldn't I?

Ari returned with the almond milk and took our orders, and when we were alone again, I leaned forward, elbows on the table. "Veronica, I've been thinking. Maybe—"

"Oh, no." She was looking at her phone.

"What is it?"

"My phone. I think it's been shut off." She handed it to me, and sure enough, it was completely dead.

"You charged it last night?"

"Yes. Mabel left me an extra charger and it was plugged in all night. When we left your house, it was at one hundred percent. It's Neil—he must have cut service to my number."

"Seriously? He controlled your phone?"

She nodded tearfully. "He's punishing me."

I wanted to show up on this guy's doorstep and fucking punch his rich-ass lights out. "Okay, that's it. You're hired."

"Huh?"

"You're not going back to Chicago or anywhere near that apartment he owns. You're staying here."

"I can't do that."

"Yes, you can. You are." My jaw ticked. "It's final."

"I don't need to be rescued, Austin." She shook her head. "And I'm not trading one bully for another one."

"Sorry." I took the edge off my tone and eased up on the commands. "I didn't mean to order you around. I just don't like the idea of sending you alone back to Chicago to face him."

"I'm not afraid of him." Her blue eyes were bright and clear, her chin lifted.

"I believe you. But I'd still like you to stay."

"What about clothes?"

I thought for a moment. "Can you get along with what you have for a few weeks? Once the kids are out in California, I could take you to Chicago to get what you want."

Her eyes widened. "You'd do that?"

"Yeah. I'm making a table for a couple in Saugatuck that will be ready by then. I'll deliver it on the way."

"You make furniture?"

I shrugged. "Here and there. So what do you say? The job includes room and board, and I'll pay you weekly on top of that.

You'd have to commit through the middle of August. You'd have time off when the kids visit their mom next month."

She appeared to think about it, knotting her hands together on the tabletop. "Okay."

"So you'll take the position?"

"I'll take it."

"Good." Our eyes met, and my body hummed—a warning. "But I think we should probably..." I glanced over at the kids. "Set some boundaries."

She sat up taller. "Definitely."

I lowered my voice. "What happened last night can't happen again."

"I agree completely."

"It was just..." I grappled for what it was. The full moon? A moment of weakness? A fear deep in my gut that my brother was right and I was indeed a fucking idiot?

"I don't think it was any *one thing*," Veronica said.

"Whatever it was, it stays between us."

She mimed zipping her lips, then smiled at me, her eyes twinkling.

Great, now we had a secret. I couldn't remember the last time I'd had a secret with someone. It made me feel closer to her, which was precisely the opposite of how I wanted to feel.

Maybe that's why I said what I said next.

"It never should have happened in the first place."

She looked a little taken aback. "Probably not, but—"

"It was my fault," I interrupted. "Completely."

"I don't think we need to assign blame, Austin."

"You were lonely and vulnerable and confused. It affected me."

"Okay, wait just one minute." She held up one hand. "Maybe I was lonely, but I wasn't vulnerable and confused. I knew what I wanted." Those eyes pinned me with an icy stare. "And you did too."

"Not really." I picked up my coffee cup and took a sip without tasting it.

"You're saying you didn't want to kiss me?"

"I'm saying it was late, it was dark—"

"*Dark?*" Her eyebrows shot up. "What does that have to do with anything?"

"Lower your voice, please." I set the mug down, frantically trying to think of a way to extricate myself from the mess I'd just made. What the fuck was my problem? "All I'm saying is that I got carried away. I felt sorry for you, and I acted totally out of character."

"You felt *sorry* for me?" She leaned forward. Her gaze traveled downward—toward my lap. "Is that what that was against my stomach?"

My face burned. "Look, I don't even know what we're arguing about. Bottom line, while you're working for me, we'll have to keep our distance."

"It won't be a problem, because I have no intention of working for you." With that, she dropped her dead phone back in her purse and left the booth.

When I heard the bell over the door jingle, I closed my eyes.

You're better off, said the rational voice in my head. *Having her around would have been a disaster. You heard her—she doesn't need to be rescued. You're too attracted to her, and she gets under your skin too easily. You'd be on edge all the fucking time.*

But where the hell was she going to go?

"Dad, can we have some more quarters?"

I opened my eyes to see the twins standing at the side of the booth. "No. That's all I brought."

"Where's Veronica?" Adelaide asked, looking at the empty

side of the booth.

"She left."

Owen glanced behind me, toward the door. "Where'd she go?"

"I don't know," I said irritably.

"What about her suitcase? It's in our car," Adelaide reminded me.

"Fuck." I pinched the bridge of my nose.

The twins looked at each other and gasped.

"Yes, I said a bad word," I barked. "Get over it."

"Why are you so mad?" Owen asked as Ari arrived with the food.

"I don't know, I just am! Now sit down." I pointed at the seat Veronica had vacated. "Both of you over there."

Adelaide looked concerned, glancing toward the door. "But what if Veronica comes back?"

I was more worried about her *not* coming back. "Let's just eat."

But I wasn't hungry.

While the kids gobbled up their breakfasts, I drank coffee and brooded over Veronica's abrupt departure. Every time I heard the bell over the door ring, I turned around and hoped to see her walking toward our booth.

The twins kept badgering me. Where had she gone? Why had she left without saying goodbye? What were we going to do with her suitcase? Would we ever see her again?

"Stop with the questions already." I put my empty mug down. My hand was shaking, I'd had so much caffeine. "We'll find her."

"But why would she run away like that?" Adelaide persisted.

"She ran away because I hurt her feelings," I finally said, signaling to Ari to bring the bill.

"What did you say?"

"It doesn't matter. But listen, you two." I leaned my elbows on the table. "What do you think of having her as your nanny this summer?"

"Yes!" Owen said, stuffing a forkful of pancake in his mouth. "I like her. She's fun."

"You guys might have to learn to cook," I said.

"I know how to make some things already," Adelaide boasted. "I can make nachos, fruit kebabs, and Pop Tarts."

Ari brought the check and glanced at Veronica's untouched Belgian waffle. "Did she…have to go?"

"Yeah, because Dad hurt her feelings," said Owen.

"I'm going to apologize," I said, giving Owen a dirty look. "As soon as we find her."

"She's going to be our new nanny," announced Adelaide.

Ari smiled. "She seems like she'll be a really fun nanny."

"Did you know that's our uncle's picture on the wall over there?" Adelaide pointed to Dash's black and white headshot, which was signed, *To everybody back home at Moe's, Dash Buckley.* "He's a TV star."

The smile slid off her face as Ari glanced at the wall behind her. "Yeah. I know your uncle."

"Don't you like him?"

"Everybody likes Dashiel Buckley. He told me that himself." Ari grabbed the check and my credit card. "I'll take that up for you."

I nodded, wondering if something had gone on between Mabel's best friend and Dash at some point. "Thanks."

$$\cdots$$

"So where should we look?" Owen asked when we were standing on the sidewalk outside Moe's.

Shielding my eyes from the sun, I looked down the block to the right and left. Downtown was always busy on Sundays, and

Main Street was crowded with people ducking in and out of shops and restaurants or strolling down toward the harbor with cups of coffee.

I remembered how Veronica had remarked yesterday that she hadn't seen it yet—and how she wanted to at least taste some fudge before she left town. "Come with me," I told the kids. "I have an idea."

They followed me into the nearest fudge shop, where I let them each choose a small piece—chocolate peanut butter for Owen and chocolate mint for Adelaide. For Veronica, I purchased plain vanilla, wishing there was some way to add sprinkles to it.

As the kids munched on their unexpected treat—I didn't normally let them have dessert at ten a.m.—we walked to the corner and turned onto Spring Street, which sloped down toward the harbor.

After crossing Bayview Road, we stood at the foot of Waterfront Park, which was packed with picnicking families, dog walkers, joggers, and couples stretched out on blankets beneath the shade of a huge maple tree. Behind the lenses of my aviator sunglasses, my eyes scanned the crowd. Was she here?

"I see her!" Owen shouted, pointing toward the seawall.

"Where?"

"Over there—sitting on the rocks."

I followed the direction of his finger and spotted the pale blond hair blowing in the breeze. My pulse picked up. "Okay. I don't want you two near the water. Can you stay here please? Under this tree?"

"I think we should talk to her too," Adelaide said. "What if you hurt her feelings again?"

"Then she won't be our nanny and we'll be stuck with *you* all the time," Owen added.

"I'm not going to hurt her feelings again," I said impatiently.

"Now stay here."

They groaned, but I held up one hand. "Listen, I just bought you guys fudge after breakfast. Give me a break."

They exchanged a look that served as an agreement and plopped down beside the tree. "Fine," Adelaide said, "but don't mess this up."

"Thanks for the vote of confidence." Turning around, I took a deep breath and approached the seawall.

Veronica was sitting on one of the bigger boulders, staring out at the bay, her arms wrapped around her knees. Carefully, I made my way over to her and dropped down on the large, flat rock beside her.

It was windy by the water, so she might not have heard me approach, but when she didn't even look over at me after I sat down, I knew I was being ignored.

"Hey," I said.

She didn't answer. Just pushed her sunglasses up her nose. They were round and oversized, like a movie star might have worn several decades ago. In fact, she could have been a movie poster sitting there by the water in her fancy outfit, the sun glinting off the gold in her hair. My heart began to beat faster.

"You okay?" I asked.

"Fine."

I adjusted my hat and looked out at the sailboats and cabin cruisers in the harbor. The Pier Inn Marina was to our right, and out on the restaurant's deck, people sat enjoying brunch under huge striped umbrellas. To our left was the unimpeded view of the water offered to the giant homes along Bayview Road. Lighthouse Point curved out into the bay just beyond the marina, each house boasting its own dock lined with water toys—boats, jet skis, giant inner tubes, dinghies. At the tip of the peninsula stood the lighthouse itself, looking pretty much the same as it had since it was built in 1884—white-painted bricks, windows on all four sides, the keeper's two-story brick dwelling beside it.

Things were slow to change in Cherry Tree Harbor. And we had a historical preservation committee that liked to keep every stone, tree, and brick just as it always had been for the last one hundred and fifty years. People liked to complain about that whenever they wanted to modernize their home or business, but I sort of understood it. I was resistant to change too.

And I had a feeling the woman next to me could change everything.

I pushed that fear aside and focused on the task at hand. "You missed breakfast."

"I wasn't hungry anymore."

"So you probably don't want this fudge I got for you."

She looked down at the bag I held out. "What kind is it?"

"Vanilla. They didn't have any sprinkles—I asked."

She didn't laugh. "No, thank you."

"Come on, Veronica. I'm trying to apologize."

"You are?"

"Yes."

"Because usually an apology sounds like 'I'm sorry' and not just 'I got you some fudge.'"

"I'm sorry."

Now she pushed her glasses to the top of her head and looked me in the eye. "For what?"

"For making you feel bad about last night. The truth is, I *do* feel guilty about taking advantage of you in a vulnerable moment, but that's not why I kissed you."

Apparently finding me sincere, she replaced her glasses on the bridge of her nose. "Thank you. I accept your apology." She held out one hand. "And your fudge."

Relieved, I gave her the bag.

She reached inside, took out the slice, and bit off a piece. "Mmm. Want some?"

I started to say no, but she held it up for me to take a bite right from her fingers. As it melted in my mouth, I thought, *This is what she would taste like right now if I kissed her—creamy, buttery, sweet.* My insides twisted like a corkscrew. "Thanks."

"So what's *your* favorite fudge flavor?" she asked.

"I don't eat many sweets."

"But you must indulge sometimes."

"Not often. I'm pretty disciplined."

She took another bite of fudge. "What do you do for fun?"

"I make furniture."

"But that's still work," she pointed out. "I meant in your spare time."

"I spend all my spare time with my kids."

"You don't do *anything* just for you? Like, to let off steam?"

"I run, if I have the time. I used to have a motorcycle, but I sold it when the twins were born."

"Jeez. You *are* all work, no play."

"Who said that about me?" I asked testily. "Mabel?"

"Actually, it was Ari."

I rolled my eyes. "Same difference. She's like the second little sister I never asked for."

"You're lucky. I wish I had *one* little sister." Veronica sighed and focused her attention out over the bay again before tilting her face to the sun. "It's so beautiful here."

I admired the curve of her throat. "Then stay for the summer."

"I'm not sure I should, Austin."

"Why not? Did you get a better offer since I last saw you?"

"No," she admitted. "But I don't want to be where I'm not wanted."

"You're wanted here. Jesus, everyone you've met adores you—

my kids, my siblings, even crusty old Larry."

She paused, looking at me sideways. "What about you? Do you like me?"

"Yes. As a friend."

Her brows peeked over the tops of her sunglasses. "A friend, huh?"

"Yes, Veronica. If you stay, we'll be friends."

"My friends call me Roni."

"Roni." I took a deep breath and counted to five. This woman could test the patience of a monk. "Will you take the job?"

"I'm considering it. But maybe I should ask you some questions first."

I ran a hand over my jaw and glanced back at the kids—they were right where I'd left them, licking their fingers. "Like what?"

"Do you have a criminal record?"

"No."

"Are you going to make me use a chore chart?"

"Maybe."

"Will you fire me if I serve fried bologna sandwiches every night?"

"Definitely."

"Good to know." She nodded succinctly. "I accept your offer. Of employment and friendship."

"Thank you," I said, although I wasn't sure why I should thank her when it was me doing something for her. "We can go over your duties, the schedule, and payment when we get back to the house."

"Deal."

I stood up, then offered her a hand, which she accepted, although she was remarkably sure-footed as she made her way over the rocks.

"Mabel offered you the use of her car for the summer," I said when I reached the grass where she waited for me.

"Oh, that's so sweet." We began walking toward the tree where the kids were scrambling to their feet.

"And we should get you a new phone number right away. I need to be able to contact you. And set up a bank account."

"Okay." Veronica waved at the kids, who came running over.

"I found you first!" Owen yelled happily. He had chocolate all over his mouth.

"I'm so glad you did." She ruffled his hair, then pulled a package of wipes from her bag and gave him one. "Here. You've got a fudge beard and mustache going."

"Do I look like my dad?"

She laughed. "Exactly like him."

"Are you going to be the new nanny?" Adelaide asked.

"Yes." She stood tall and saluted. "Roni Sutton, nanny, reporting for duty."

"Dad, can we show Roni the lighthouse?" Owen asked as he wiped his mouth and chin.

"Okay, but not the inside tour." I checked my watch. "I promised your Uncle Xander I'd help him out with something this afternoon."

"But the inside tour is the best," Adelaide whined. "You get to see where the keeper lived, the bedrooms and kitchen and everything. And you get to climb the stairs and look out from the top!"

"I know, but we have to get Veronica a new phone, and it's already—"

"Come on, Daddy, don't be a stick in the mud." My daughter turned to Veronica and said, "That's what Aunt Mabel calls him when he doesn't want to do something fun."

"Or a party pooper." Owen giggled at saying one of his favorite words. "We call him that a lot too."

"He can't be that bad," said Veronica, winking at me. "I bet he's fun when he wants to be."

They took her by the hands and pulled her in the direction of the lighthouse, leaving me standing there wondering if I'd just made the best decision ever or the biggest mistake of my life.

Chapter 10

Veronica

"I'm so confused," Morgan said. "I thought you didn't get the nanny job."

"I didn't. Not at first." I'd called her from my new phone number while I was unpacking my bags at my cozy new apartment. It was small—just over four hundred square feet, Austin said—and it didn't even have a kitchen, just a sink and a refrigerator tucked beneath a square of counter space, but it was perfect for me. I'd spent the last year living in a gorgeous penthouse apartment with a view of Lake Michigan, the Magnificent Mile at my feet, and I'd been miserable. "The guy, Austin, changed his mind."

"Why?"

"I'm not entirely sure," I said, shoving some underwear in a drawer.

"Did you blow him or something?" She laughed at her joke.

"It didn't get that far."

She gasped. "I was kidding! You messed around with the guy?"

"Calm down, it was just a kiss." I sat on the side of the bed and looked out the window that faced the house. My eyes lingered on the chairs by the fire pit.

"You *kissed* him?"

"Just once. Well, twice. But the second time, he kissed me."

"Holy shit! So there's something going on between you guys?"

"No, no—it was just a moment of insanity last night. We both agreed that boundaries need to be in place now that I work for him."

"But you're attracted to him."

"I mean, I *guess.*" I picked at a loose thread in the comforter, remembering the warmth of the skin on his strong, muscular back. "He does have this sort of anti-Neil, blue collar, sweaty handyman thing happening that I find *very* appealing."

"Well, I think you've earned a sweaty summer fling with a hot handyman," Morgan said. "Go for it. Get hammered. Get nailed."

"I'm not here for a fling," I said, laughing. "I just want to earn some of my own money. I never want to be dependent on a man again."

"So you'll stay there for the summer?"

"Yes. And since I'll live for free, eat my meals with the kids, and have the use of his sister's car—he's even going to cover gas money—I can bank just about every dollar he pays me and come back to New York in the fall."

"That would be incredible! Just like old times!" She sighed. "Except I'm old and tired now."

"You have a *baby,*" I reminded her. "And that's wonderful."

"It is. Sleep deprivation just gets to me sometimes. But listen—are you *sure* you don't need me to wire you any money to get you through?"

"I'm positive. Austin gave me a little advance already, and he let me use his credit card to set up my new phone number."

"Are you sure this is the same guy you called a big grumpy jerk yesterday?"

"Yes."

"You must be a *really* good kisser."

Through the window, I saw Austin come out into the yard, and I stood up, moving closer to the glass. It looked like he was walking toward the garage. "Listen, I have to run, but I'll keep you posted. Give that baby a kiss for me. Love you."

On my way from the bedroom area to the living room, I ran my fingers through my hair. I heard him knock, and just before I opened the door, I took a breath.

It whooshed from my lungs when I saw him waiting on the landing.

"We're heading over to my dad's now," he said. "He's going to spend some time with the twins while I help Xander tear out the old floor at the bar he just bought. I thought maybe you could come along and get Mabel's car."

"Of course. What else can I do to help?"

He looked confused. "With what?"

"Anything. With the kids, or maybe doing some grocery shopping or cooking so dinner is made when you all get back?" Frantically, I wondered what I'd make if he took me up on the offer.

He shook his head. "Kids are all set. They're going to order pizza and eat at my dad's. You can have the night off, get settled in."

"Then what about helping you and Xander out?"

"Doing what?" he asked, his eyes wandering over my tropical two-piece outfit and strappy sandals. "The bar isn't open yet. It doesn't need a hostess."

"I know that. But I could be useful."

His expression was dubious. "I can't imagine how. But if you want to come along, maybe I can talk through the weekly schedule and routines. You can take notes."

"Fine," I said, aggravated by his dismissive attitude. It reminded me of the way Neil had treated me like window dressing. His little teacup. "Let me just change my clothes."

"Okay, but hurry up. I'm already running late today because I didn't plan on the lighthouse tour or the cellular phone place."

I arched a brow. "Listen, pal, I managed a seventy-eight second head-to-toe costume change in four shows a day for eight years, including hat, gloves, earrings, and heels. I can be downstairs in shorts and a T-shirt in less than a minute." I snapped my fingers, shut the door in his face, and already had my top off by the time I entered the bedroom again.

I hoped he was standing there thinking about it.

• • •

"Okay. Monday through Friday, up by seven, supervise them getting their own breakfasts, make their lunches," I said, looking over the notes I'd typed into my phone. I was seated on a stool at the lone high-top table that had been left in the former tiki bar Xander was renovating. "Send them up to make their beds and brush their teeth by seven-thirty. Pack their bags for camp—must have bathing suits, clean towels, sunscreen, goggles, flip flops, lunches. Check their progress by seven-forty. Leave by quarter to eight."

"Make sure they've turned off the lights." Austin ripped up another section of rotting floorboards. "Owen will leave the cap off the toothpaste and forget to brush his hair, so he needs a little extra attention in the morning. Addie usually does everything on her own, but she sometimes likes help with her hair too. Do you know how to do braids?"

I nodded. "I was in show business. Hair and makeup will not be a problem for me."

"No makeup," Austin said sternly.

"Don't worry," I chided. "Once I get the false eyelashes on her, she won't need more than some brow gel, rouge, and a nice red lip."

He glowered at me. "No red lips."

"Party pooper."

Xander chuckled as he pried faux bamboo off the front of the bar. "So Veronica, what made you decide to stay in town?"

"Austin made me an offer I couldn't refuse." I slipped off the stool and took a bottle of water from the case on top of the bar. I'd run out to grab them a little bit ago, along with more trash bags—more than one of which I'd helped to fill and carry out back to the dumpster. "Water anyone?"

"Yeah, thanks." Xander uncapped the bottle I offered and drank the entire thing all at once. "Hot in here."

"Yes." It was hot—I glanced over at Austin, who was sweating through his blue T-shirt. He straightened up and twisted his torso right and left before rubbing his right shoulder. Then he looked over and caught me staring, and I quickly looked at Xander again. "So when did you buy this place?"

"Just a few weeks ago." He looked around. "It's a little off the beaten path, but I think it will do well. There aren't any sports bars on Main Street. But all this tiki shit has to go."

"What will it look like when you're done?" I asked, glancing around at the faux bamboo on the walls, the thatched roof over the bar, the framed posters of fancy tropical drinks with flowers and paper umbrellas in them.

"I'm going for rugged and masculine but high-end," Xander said. "I want it to look like an up-north Michigan bar—casual and relaxed—but have great beer and craft cocktails, comfort food that's not all greasy and fried, big screens to watch games, and a kick-ass sound system."

"Wow. That's a tall order."

"An expensive order," added Austin. "Where the hell are you going to get the money for that sound system?"

"I'll figure it out."

"Will you replace the wood floor?" I looked at the cement that had appeared where the wood used to be.

"Nah. I'm going to leave the cement, and behind all this fake bamboo on the walls, there's brick. So once I yank that down, the bones will look a lot more like I want them to. Then I'll focus on the furniture."

"What about the bar?" I ran my hand over the scarred and stained surface, its varnish peeling.

"Actually, I want my big brother over there to make me a bar top out of reclaimed wood," said Xander. "But he keeps refusing."

Austin scowled in his brother's direction. "I didn't refuse, I just said I wasn't sure when I'd have the time. That's a big project."

"So the furniture you make, it's out of reclaimed wood?" I asked Austin.

"You know that table in his dining room?" Xander pointed at his brother. "He made that."

My jaw dropped. "Oh my god, that table is so beautiful!" I looked at the bar again, imagining a long length of gorgeous, gleaming dark wood. "Something like that would be perfect in here, give it just the right character."

"Exactly," said Xander. "This jackass is so fucking talented. So ask him why he's still working for my dad every day instead of working for himself."

"Why?"

Austin busted up some floorboards. "It's complicated."

"No, it isn't." Xander tossed his empty plastic water bottle into a recycle bin. "Want my theory? Austin won't quit working for our dad because he'd have nothing to complain about if he did."

Austin shook his head and pointed the handle of a hammer at his brother. "You're a dick."

"So then what is it?" Xander asked, leaning back against the bar, arms folded.

"You know what it is." Austin tossed the hammer aside and picked up a garbage bag. "I'm not going to abandon Dad."

"He wouldn't want you to keep working for him if he knew what you really wanted to do," pushed Xander. "He could hire someone else to take over for you. Hell, he should sell the business. He needs to retire anyway."

"Drop it."

"But I want my reclaimed wood bar."

"Then hire someone else to rip out your floor." Austin attempted to shove rotted boards into the bag, but it wouldn't stay open. I hopped off the bar and went over to help.

"Are you scared your business wouldn't succeed?" Xander refused to give up.

"Fuck you."

"Because it would. I know it would. *You* know it would."

"Would it?" I couldn't resist asking.

"Probably." Austin kept filling the bag I held open. "But I can't quit on my dad. He never quit on me."

I nodded, recalling what he'd told me this morning about his father being so supportive when he'd announced he was bringing newborn twins home. And what he'd said last night about losing his mom when the kids were all still young. I knew how hard it had been for my mom to raise me alone—I couldn't imagine raising *five* kids after losing your partner, especially when you were also dealing with grief.

I'd met their dad at the house before we'd come to the bar, and it was immediately apparent where Mabel had inherited her wide smile and her welcoming nature. George Buckley had greeted me like I was already one of the family, inviting me to stay for dinner, insisting I sit down with an iced tea and tell him about myself, showing me a photo album from the time he and his wife had visited New York City.

Mabel had already told him about me last night, but he'd also gotten an earful from his friends Gus and Larry, who'd stopped by after their usual Sunday breakfast at Moe's—George would have been at the diner too, he said, but he'd had to take Mabel to the airport. But what did I think of Moe's? How did I like Cherry Tree Harbor so far? Had I tasted the fudge? Seen the lighthouse? Had dinner at The Pier Inn? Taken a ride on the old ferry?

If Austin hadn't been standing there tapping his toes and checking his watch, I could have sat there sipping iced tea and chatting with the sweet old man all evening. After a year of being in the company of people who had no interest in me outside of grooming me to become the future Mrs. Neil Vanderhoof, it had been lovely to sit across from someone genuinely curious about my life. He was like the father or grandfather I wished I'd had.

"I understand," I said quietly. "Your dad is wonderful."

When Austin looked up and met my eyes, goosebumps swept down my arms. He grabbed the bag from me. "Thanks. Should we keep going with the schedule?"

"Sure." I went back to the table and perched on the stool again, listening with one ear while he went through the rest of the daily routine—quiet time with a book and a non-sugary snack after camp. Outside playtime was fine, but no wandering more than three houses in any direction. Library visits on Tuesday. Water the plants on Wednesdays (Owen) and Sundays (Adelaide). Kids have to bring down their dirty clothes and sort it all into baskets in the laundry room on Fridays. Laundry should be done on Saturday, including sheets and towels. Kids could help fold—Owen was good at towels and pillowcases, Adelaide liked matching everyone's socks—and should put everything away immediately.

"You can do your laundry with theirs or separately," he said. "Washer and dryer is in the basement."

"Got it."

"Please make sure they check off chores on their charts. It's how they earn their allowance."

"Will do."

"Grocery shopping can be done any day, but there's a list of things to keep stocked that I can text you. As for dinners, we usually eat around six o'clock in the summer. If I'm working late, eat without me."

"Okay. And what should I make?"

Exhaling, he straightened up and rubbed his shoulder. "An effort."

I laughed. "Deal."

7

Chapter 11

*T*wo weeks later, I had to admit Veronica was a better nanny than I thought she'd be.

The kids were on time for camp every day. Chores were checked off the charts. Library books were returned on time, plants did not die, and no one suffered any life-threatening injuries. She was, as advertised, *not* a good cook, but nobody starved—although the hockey pucks she called hamburgers and the soggy, salty casserole did have me momentarily considering a hunger strike.

But the kids didn't seem to care one bit. When I came in to grab dinner before heading out to the workshop each evening, they were full of stories about the fun things they'd done that day— yoga at the beach, dance routines in the backyard, chalk art on the driveway, karaoke contests on the front porch. I'd gotten two calls from parents in the neighborhood wanting to know where I'd found the awesome new babysitter their kids had raved about.

"Through my sister," was all I said. The entire town was buzzing about the bride who'd jilted a Vanderhoof at the altar and taken off running, and as much as I liked the story, I wasn't sure I wanted it going around that I'd hired her.

The Fourth of July came around, and I took the day off work so we could all go out on Xander's boat. The weather was gorgeous, and we had a fantastic time, water-skiing and tubing and cruising around on the lake. I did my best to keep my eyes off her body in the little black bikini she wore, but I'm positive she caught me staring more than once—and adjusting myself in my swim trunks afterward.

On her second Saturday with us, it rained, and even though it was technically her day off, she took the kids to a movie. Later that afternoon, the twins came running from the house into the garage, shouting, "Look at our tattoos, Dad!" I glanced up from the table I was working on to see both of my kids with full sleeves.

"They're temporary! They're temporary!" Veronica yelled, running in behind them. She was barefoot, wearing that flowery skirt and top again, the one that tied behind her neck and back and showed some of her stomach if she moved in just the right way. Her hair was up, but damp pieces fell in soft curls around her face.

"I hope so," I said, setting my saw aside to examine Owen's skinny right arm. "You've got more ink than Uncle Xander."

"Look, this one is like yours, Daddy." Adelaide shoved her elbow in my face and pointed at her deltoid. "It's a bear."

"I see that," I said, although the smiling animal on her arm looked more like Winnie the Pooh than the grizzly on my shoulder.

"Do I look like a rock star?" Owen asked, playing air guitar along to the music on my speakers.

"Totally." I looked up at Veronica, who seemed relieved I wasn't mad. "Got any tattoos?"

Her cheeks turned a little pink. "Uh, none that are visible."

Great, now I could add that to the list of things about her body I fantasized about. I'd managed to respect the physical boundaries we'd set without any problem so far, but my mind? That was another matter entirely.

If I had to add up all the minutes I'd spent thinking about her over the past fourteen days, the sum total would be embarrassing. But I couldn't help it. There was something about her that got to me. It was her looks, sure, but it was also the easy rapport she had with the kids and my dad, the kindness she showed to everyone around her, the way she remembered everyone's names and something about them, how quick she was to offer a hand with anything. She'd signed herself and the kids up to walk a 5K benefiting a nearby animal rescue, and said yes to a request that she teach a free dance class for senior citizens at the weekly 65-plus mixer at the library.

With every passing day, I was more impressed by her generosity, her work ethic, and her ability to find silver linings. Sometimes I'd overhear the kids ask about her childhood or life in New York City or what it was like to perform on stage every night, and she answered all their questions with patience and excitement, like she was glad to be asked. One night I overheard her telling them how an occasional shoe would fly off into the audience during routines with lots of kicks—the sound of the kids' laughter made me smile.

There were things I wanted to know about her too, but I tried hard to maintain a professional distance between us.

Especially after dark.

After saying goodnight to the kids, I'd usually go back out to the garage and work on something. I would see her walk from the back door of the house to the stairs leading up to her apartment, and she always lifted a hand and called goodnight, but she never stopped to talk.

I'd hear her feet moving around above me, and I'd turn off my music so it wouldn't keep her awake. Sometimes I heard the TV, sometimes I'd hear her talking with a friend, and I'd go perfectly still, trying to hear what she was saying about her life here or catch my name, but I couldn't ever make anything out.

Then the shower would come on, and I'd imagine her taking off her clothes, getting beneath the water, and moving her hands all over her body. After a few minutes, the water would shut off and I'd picture her stepping out, dripping wet, reaching for her towel. After rubbing it all over her skin, she'd hang it up and walk into her bedroom naked, where she'd pull that white T-shirt over her head before crawling into bed. (In my fantasy, she never wore underwear.) Then she'd lie there and think about me in the garage beneath her and hope I'd come up and knock on her door.

I'd be hot and sweaty after a day's work, covered in sawdust and grime, but she wouldn't care. She'd act surprised to see me, maybe she'd even pretend she didn't want this. She might say things like *we can't, we shouldn't, we better not*…but all the while she'd be backing up toward the bedroom.

She wanted this. Of course she did.

And I would—

"Austin?"

Jolted out of my daydream, I realized I was standing there in front of her and my kids. Immediately I went and stood behind the table I was working on, since my dick was clearly trying to get her attention. "Sorry, what?"

"Is it okay if we order pizza for dinner?" She sighed. "I think the kitchen and I need a little space in our new relationship."

I laughed. "It's fine with me. Xander is supposed to stop by, so get enough for him too."

"Okay. What about your dad? Should we invite him as well?"

I shook my head, touched that she'd suggest it. "It's poker night. His crew gets together at Gus's house every other Saturday and they go a little wild. They split a six-pack and eat high-sodium snacks."

She giggled. "Good for them. Okay kids, let's leave your dad alone so he can get his work done."

"Thanks," I said.

"You're welcome." She smiled at me over one shoulder, and honest to god, my heart nearly jumped from my chest onto the table in front of me.

• • •

After a dinner break, during which I struggled to keep my eyes off her, I came back out to the garage to work while Veronica and the kids settled in the living room to watch a movie. She wanted to show them some old movie musical that had been her favorite as a kid, and they were totally into it. If I had suggested a movie from *my* childhood, they'd have pitched a fit, but somehow every idea Veronica had was automatically fun. Seeing them snuggle up with blankets and pillows and popcorn on the floor in the living room sort of made me want to blow off work and join them.

Xander followed me out to the garage, hurrying through the rain, which had started up again. After helping himself to a beer from my fridge, he jumped up on my tool bench and watched me lay out the boards for a Parsons table I was making from some red and white oak.

"So how's it going with Veronica?" he asked.

"Fine." I grabbed my tape measure and extended the metal strip. "Although she wasn't lying about not being able to cook."

He laughed. "You *are* looking a little skinny. Want to arm wrestle?"

"I'd still kick your ass."

"Okay, big brother." Xander's tone let me know he was giving me this one for free. "Now tell me how it's going between you and the nanny."

"She's a good employee." I scribbled some measurements on a scrap of paper. "Does what I ask her to."

"Have you asked her for a blow job?"

I gave him the finger without looking in his direction. "If you're going to be an asshole, you can leave. She *works* for me. She takes care of my *kids*."

"I'm just saying, I don't think she'd complain. She looks at you."

I lined up the tape measure on the next board without even looking at the number. "Fuck off."

"I'm serious. She does it when you're not paying attention. And when you're looking at her, she's focused on the kids. You guys look at each other. Trust me."

A sweat broke out on my back. "We're not looking at each other like *that*."

"It's like that," he said confidently. "Not that I blame you. She's gorgeous."

"So you ask her out." I said it, but at the thought of his actually doing it, a jolt of hot, electric rage shocked my system. I immediately regretted my words.

"Nah," he said, thank fuck. "She's not interested in me. Plus, I'm looking for a wife, and I feel like she's probably not looking to get serious with someone so soon after her bad experience."

Finally, I turned around and stared at him. "A *wife*? Are you joking?"

"No. I feel like it's time I settle down. I'm thirty-one, you know? I've sown my oats. Once I get my business going and move out of Dad's house, I'll be like two-thirds of the way to respectable adulthood. I just need a wife and a couple of kids to complete the picture. But not like you did it," he said, taking a swig from his beer. "Not two at once. That's too much work."

"Dude, the longest relationship you've ever had was like four weeks."

"I was married to the U.S. Navy," he said defensively. "I was serving my country—and I was good at it, until I got injured. I think I'll be a fucking *great* husband."

"You do?"

He grinned and spread his arms. "I'm great at everything else, aren't I?"

Ignoring him, I turned around and got back to work.

"You know what? I'm so confident you and the nanny are going to bang that I'll place a bet on it."

Xander was always looking for a way to win, especially if it meant I lost. "What kind of bet?"

"The bar I want you to make. If you keep your hands to yourselves for two more weeks, I'll quit bugging you about it. If you can't, you owe me some reclaimed wood."

"Deal," I said. All it would take to win this bet and get Xander off my ass was mental fortitude. That, I had.

I hoped.

• • •

I put up with Xander for another couple hours, then kicked him out and went into the house to put the kids to bed. Veronica had already seen to it that the leftovers were put away and their chore charts marked off, and she said goodnight to the twins and promised to teach them some tap dance steps tomorrow.

"Tap dance, huh?" I said.

"Yes. Roni said we can make our own tap shoes!" Adelaide said excitedly.

I looked at Veronica. "You can?"

"Sure." She grinned and tucked one of those curls behind her ear. "We just need some sneakers, packing tape, and spare change."

"I think we can manage that," I said, impressed by her ingenuity.

"I thought it might be a fun project since it's supposed to rain all day again tomorrow." She laughed and struck a pose with jazz hands. "Then we can put on a show for you tomorrow night!"

"Yay!" The twins clapped their hands and jumped up and down.

"Sounds like fun. Okay, you guys, head upstairs." I nudged them both out of the kitchen, and they went dancing toward the front of the house. Then I turned toward Veronica. "You do know you have tomorrow off, right?"

She loaded a dinner plate in the dishwasher. "I know."

"And that you had tonight off as well? You don't need to clean up the kitchen."

"I don't mind." She shut the dishwasher door and turned around, leaning back against the sink with her palms draped over the edge. "And it's not like I have anything better to do tonight. Just laundry."

"As long as you know I don't expect you to work on your days off."

"I know." Her blue eyes stayed on mine for a moment, then drifted over my T-shirt, which was coated in sawdust and damp with rain and sweat. She sucked her bottom lip between her teeth as her eyes traveled lower, to the crotch of my jeans. I thought about what Xander said—*she looks at you*—and the back of my neck grew warm.

I glanced at the fridge and thought about a dirty chore chart for her and everything I'd put on it. *Give me a handjob. Sit on my face. Suck my dick.*

My cock twitched.

I was a bad person.

"Well, goodnight," I said, desperate to exit the room and her line of sight.

"Night," she said softly as I left the room.

Halfway up the steps, I paused and closed my eyes, my hand gripping the banister, my pulse beating a little too fast.

What was the bet I'd made with Xander? Two weeks?

I had a sinking feeling I might lose.

• • •

After putting the kids to bed, I went out to the garage to put away the tools I'd left out—I never left it messy at night. The rain had stopped again, but it was hot and humid, and I was anxious to get everything in order and grab a cold shower.

I needed one. A cold beer sounded good too.

The lights in the apartment above the garage were off, and I assumed Veronica had already gone to bed, so it surprised me when I heard the back door to the house close. I looked up and saw her walking toward the garage, carrying a laundry basket on one hip. She gave me a wave.

I lifted a hand, and before I could stop myself, I held up the beer I'd just opened. "Want one?"

She hesitated, glancing back at the house.

"It's okay. They're fine. I actually still have the baby monitor in here for nights when I want to work late."

"Oh. Okay, then." She entered the garage and I glanced at her bare feet.

"You should probably put shoes on though. I haven't swept in a few days, and I don't want you to get a splinter or step on a nail or anything."

"My shoes are upstairs." She looked at the laundry basket. "I was just going up to fold my laundry."

"You can fold down here if you want." I gestured toward a work table. "I can put a clean drop cloth on this."

"Oh. Okay." She set her laundry basket on the floor. "Then I'll be right back."

I watched her leave the garage on her tiptoes, being careful where she stepped, and heard her going up the stairs. After she was gone, I threw a clean cloth over the work table, then placed her laundry basket on top of it. I couldn't resist peering into the jumble of clothing—on top were her whites and I saw bits of lace and satin that made my blood rush faster.

When I heard her feet on the stairs again, I backed away so I wouldn't be caught looking at her panties like a creeper. I went over to the fridge and grabbed her a beer.

She appeared in a pair of flip flops. "Safe to enter?"

"Safe to enter." I handed her the bottle. "Here you go."

She clinked hers to mine. "Cheers."

I watched her bring the bottle to her lips and saw her throat work as she swallowed. Damn, it was hot in here.

"Thank you," she said, noticing the cloth over the table where I'd placed her laundry basket. She took another sip, set her beer down, and began to pull items out and fold them. "So did you get a lot done today?"

"Yeah." I leaned back against my workbench and tried not to notice what each piece was as she folded—bras, panties, little tank tops, the white T-shirt she'd worn the night we kissed. "Thanks again for working the extra hours. I'll pay you for them."

She smiled. "You're welcome."

"So how did your first two weeks go as a nanny?"

"Great. The kids are so fun. And this town is delightful." She scrunched up her face. "Sorry about the food. I'll work on it."

"It's okay."

"I've worked in a bunch of bars and restaurants, but I just never learned to cook. And my mom never taught me."

"No?"

She shook her head. "I think it was also a rebellion against her mother, who pretty much lived in the kitchen. Very traditional beliefs about where a woman belonged and all that. They never got along."

I tipped up my beer. It was easy to remain silent around her—the woman was a *talker*.

"They were just so different, you know? My grandmother was totally subservient and submissive to my grandfather. My mother was independent and feisty. Always bucking the rules." She folded a pair of shorts in half. "And I was her daughter through and through. Which is why I cannot believe I let Neil do what he did."

I took another couple of cold swallows.

"God, I miss her." She was quiet a moment, staring at the clothing in the basket. "What was *your* mom like?"

"She was tough. She had to be, with four rowdy sons. She was so determined to teach us good manners and we were like a pack of wild animals, always wanting to tear each other apart." I laughed. "Sometimes she used to just give up, set a timer, and let Xander and I fight in the backyard for three minutes."

Veronica smiled. "Like a boxing round?"

"Exactly."

"So who'd win?"

I gave her a dirty look. "Me, of course."

Her grin widened. "Of course."

"Then she'd have to listen to us howl in pain while she cleaned us up, and she'd tell us it was our own damn faults and we'd never learn."

She folded a pair of shorts. "I feel like she was on to something there."

"But she was funny and outgoing and always saw the good in everyone."

"What did she look like?"

"A lot like Mabel. Dark hair. Blue eyes. A loud laugh, a big smile." The rain started up again, drumming on the garage roof.

Veronica smiled and picked up her beer. "Did she and your dad get along?"

I nodded. "They always claimed it was love at first sight. On their first date, he told her he was going to marry her. And he did. Six months later."

"Really?" Her eyes widened. "That's incredible."

"Or crazy."

"And he never dated again? I mean, after she was gone?"

"Nope." I could hear his voice in my head. "He always said, 'It only happens once.'"

Nodding slowly, Veronica placed her folded clothing into neat piles inside the basket, then hitched herself up on the edge of the table so she sat right across from me. "What about you? Have you ever been in love?"

"Nah." I scraped at the label of the bottle with my thumbnail. "I had a few girlfriends before the twins were born. But never anything serious."

"Are you one of those guys who doesn't do feelings?"

I frowned at her. "You sound like my sister. It's not that I 'don't do feelings.' I have plenty of them. I just think certain emotions are kind of pointless. What a person *does* is more important than how they *feel*."

She held her ankles together and stared at her feet. "Actually, I've never been in love either."

"Not even with your ex?"

"No." Cheeks coloring, she shook her head. "And he wasn't in love with me. We had no business getting married."

"Good thing you didn't."

She sipped her beer. "Did you think about marrying the twins' mom?"

I shook my head. "The first thing she said to me after 'I'm

pregnant' was 'I'll have the baby, but I'm not going to keep it.' So there was no reason to consider it."

"And since then you've been single?"

"Since then, I've been single. I like my independence."

"You don't get lonely?"

"Never," I lied.

She nodded. "I like my independence too, but I do think it's nice to share things with someone. One of the reasons I loved being a Rockette was because we were like a family. I never should have let Neil talk me into quitting."

"Why did he want you to quit?"

"He didn't think it was a *suitable job* for a Vanderhoof wife." She made air quotes and wrinkled her nose. "It was probably something his mother said."

I grunted. "Every time I hear something about that guy, I despise him a little more."

She grinned. "It's too bad you weren't at the wedding. You'd have enjoyed the show."

"I can picture it pretty vividly. I've heard the story enough times."

"From the kids?"

I shrugged. "It's a small town."

Her jaw fell open. "You mean people are talking about me?"

"Of course they are." Amused, I folded my arms across my chest. "I'm surprised the Harbor Gazette hasn't called you for an interview yet."

"Oh no!" She slapped a hand to her forehead. "That is so embarrassing."

"Why? You put an asshole in his place. He can't just go around treating people like shit and expect no one to mind."

"I know, but…" Her cheeks grew even more pink. "I just don't want that to be people's first impression of me. I'm a friendly person. I have nice manners. I'm a good girl."

"Are you?" The question slipped out.

Her hand slowly fell to her lap.

I don't know what made me do what I did next—maybe it was all the talk about her ex that got me worked up. Maybe it was the way she was blushing.

Hell, maybe it was the crop top.

I pushed off the workbench in no hurry, crossing the three feet of space between us until I stood in front of where she sat on the edge of the table. She opened her knees, and I took a step closer. Her thighs now straddled mine. I touched her lips with my thumb, tugging the lower one down slightly. I felt the barest caress of her tongue as her eyes held mine captive.

Her skirt had a slit that exposed one knee, and I took my hand from her mouth and placed it on the top of her thigh. Slowly, I slid it up her leg until my thumb and fingers bracketed her hip. I squeezed gently.

She inhaled sharply.

With my other hand, I touched one of those curls that fell around her face. It felt like silk between my callused fingers. She turned her cheek into my palm and rubbed the heel of my hand with her chin. I closed my eyes, my entire body tense with restraint.

"It's okay," she whispered.

"It's not," I said between my teeth.

And when I still couldn't bring myself to move, she kissed my palm, then the inside of my wrist, then my jaw. When I opened my eyes, I saw her lean back on her elbows, her top riding up to expose a strip of skin on her belly.

Unable to resist, I lowered my mouth to her abdomen. Her muscles trembled. Slowly, I kissed a path across the ribbon of soft, warm skin. Then I rested my forehead on her stomach, breathing in her scent, wanting her, aching to untie the top, put a hand up her skirt, claim her mouth with mine. My desire for her had the strength of a nuclear bomb.

"Daddy?" I bolted upright and looked at the open garage door, expecting to see Owen standing there with a confused look on his face. But no one was there.

"It's the monitor." Veronica was still breathing hard, her chest rising and falling quickly.

Heart pounding, I hurried out of the garage into the rain.

I was surprised it didn't sizzle on my skin.

Chapter 12

VERONICA

*a*lone in the garage, splayed on his table like a centerpiece, I felt the weight of embarrassment settle over me like a wet blanket.

But I shouldn't be embarrassed. The guy came at me. *Again.*

He asked the flirty question, *he* came and stood between my legs, *he* put his hands on me first. It was obvious he wanted me like I wanted him. We were just having fun. So what was his problem?

I propped myself up on my hands and took a minute to catch my breath and wrangle my thoughts.

Was it the kids? Was it the boss/employee thing? Was he still worried about taking advantage of me in a vulnerable state? He was definitely a guy with a strong moral code—he'd flat out said he thought a person's actions were more important than their feelings. If he believed a thing was wrong, he wouldn't do it.

As my pulse decelerated, I had to admit there were plenty of reasons to put the brakes on before we did something we might regret.

You need this job, I reminded myself, pushing off the table and picking up my laundry basket. *So maybe it's good that one of you isn't thinking with your hormones right now. The last thing you need is to mess this up.*

As I hurried up the stairs in the drizzle, I grew even more thankful that nothing had happened. *Okay, maybe not one hundred percent thankful,* I admitted, thinking about his lips on my stomach, his hand on my thigh, that bulge in his jeans. But at least ninety percent. Possibly eighty-five. Eighty if I was being *super* honest.

Kicking the door shut with my foot, I headed into the bedroom area and set the laundry basket down. But rather than put it away, I went over to the window and looked out at the house. The windows in Austin's bedroom were dark, and I couldn't tell if the shade was up or down. The kids' bathroom light appeared to be on, although the shade was lowered.

I hoped everything was okay.

Moving backward, I flopped across the foot of the bed and stared at the ceiling, my arms above my head. Closing my eyes, I fantasized about Austin stretching out above me, his weight pressing me into the mattress. I wondered if he'd be rough, like he was the night he kissed me by the fire pit, all greedy tongue and grabby hands, or tender, like he'd been downstairs just now, all soft lips and gentle fingers. I wouldn't mind a little of both, I thought, bringing my hands to my breasts and wishing they were his. I just wanted to *feel* him.

I kicked off my flip flops and brought my heels onto the bed, knees apart. Bringing one hand to my leg, I let it glide up my inner thigh just like he'd done. But where he'd stopped, I didn't—I placed my hand over my panties and rubbed slowly and firmly, allowing the hum to build in my lower body. Then I slipped my fingers inside the edge of the lace—

A knock on the door made me bolt upright, heart pounding like I'd been caught touching myself. Jumping to my feet, I glanced out the window and saw that the house was completely dark. But Jesus Christ, I'd left the shade up!

If it hadn't been raining, I'd have taken a moment to make sure my face wasn't too flushed, but I didn't want to leave him out there getting wet. Fanning my face, I quickly went to the door and pulled it open.

The sight of him, all dark and rugged and wet with rain, did nothing to cool me down. "Hey," I said, my voice cracking.

"Hey." He shoved his hands in his pockets.

"Want to come in?"

He shook his head. "That's a bad idea."

"Austin, you're getting wet. Just come in. I won't bite."

Tentatively, he stepped across the threshold. "Okay, but leave the door open."

I rolled my eyes, but I backed up and put some space between us. The rain thrummed on the roof above our heads. "Everything okay at the house?"

"Yes. Owen had a bad dream. Then he wanted a glass of water. But he's fine, already back to sleep."

"That's good."

"Anyway, I just came up to apologize." His eyes lingered on my stomach.

"You don't have to."

He held up his hands, raising his gaze to mine. "I want to. *I* made the big deal about setting boundaries when I hired you, and tonight, I pushed them."

"I wasn't putting up a fight, in case you didn't notice."

Dropping his arms, he exhaled. "Maybe you should have."

"Why? It doesn't seem wrong to me."

"It doesn't?" He looked angry. "All I can think of when I see you in that outfit is untying your top—with my teeth."

I gasped. "Really?"

"Really. And it's fucking wrong. You work for me."

"Okay, maybe it's a *little* bit wrong, but you know what?" I tossed my hands up. "I don't care. I spent the last year doing exactly what I was told, so I guess you're getting me in a rebellious phase. I'm sorry."

"It's not your fault. I'll do a better job of keeping my distance."

I didn't want him to keep his distance. I wanted him to untie my top with his teeth. "Okay. I will too."

He nodded. "So…goodnight."

"Night."

Then he was gone, pulling the door closed behind him.

Back in the bedroom, I went over to the window and looked out to see him hustle across the driveway and enter the house. A minute later his bedroom light came on, and I thought he'd notice the shade was still up and come over to lower it. But he must have been distracted or something because he disappeared into the bathroom for a moment—turning on the shower?—then came back out, grabbing his shirt at the back of his neck. Walking toward the window, he yanked it over his head and tossed it aside.

That's when he saw me.

My breath caught. Framed in the window, he stood there for a moment, gorgeous and bare-chested. He reached up to pull down the shade.

I reached behind my neck and untied my top.

He paused with one arm raised.

Leaving the halter ties dangling over my shoulders, I turned around and unraveled the knot at my back. Then I let the top fall to the floor. With one last look over my shoulder—he was still there watching—I walked away from the window and switched off the light.

I walked into the bathroom with a little smile on my face.

• • •

Austin stuck to his word.

I wasn't sure if he was just following through on his promise or punishing me for the mini-strip tease routine, but the following week, he did an excellent job keeping his distance.

On Sunday, he took the kids to Moe's for breakfast, and even though the twins invited me to come along, Austin said nothing. I insisted they go without me and took advantage of the break in the rain with a jog down to the harbor and back. Later, when the drizzle started up again, the kids and I made tap shoes by taping pennies and nickels in the shape of taps to the bottoms of old sneakers. Then I taught them some basic steps on the tiled basement floor, and that evening, they invited their dad down to see their new skills.

He gamely applauded and praised their talent, examining the bottoms of their shoes and offering to get them a big piece of plywood if they wanted a better practice surface.

But he barely even looked in my direction.

The week began smoothly enough—I had the morning routine down pat, and running errands was quicker now that I knew my way around town. I was good at remembering names and faces, so it was nice to be able to call out a personal greeting when I passed someone on the street or grabbed coffee on Main Street or checked out at a shop downtown.

On Wednesday evening, I taught a social dance class for seniors at the library, and the librarian—Noreen, whose sister Faye had been married to Austin's Uncle Harry—said it was the most crowded the mixer had ever been. She asked if I'd come back every week during the summer, and I said yes.

Thursday night was my biggest culinary triumph yet—I managed to serve a meal that Austin finished. And then he had seconds! Granted, it's hard to screw up tacos, but whatever. It felt like a victory.

Afterward, however, he disappeared into the garage like he had every other night, while the kids and I ate popsicles on the front porch. Then they played outside with the other neighborhood kids until it got dark, when I corralled them into the house for showers and one last snack.

At some point during the bedtime routine each night, Austin would come in and say, "Thanks, I'll take over," and we'd change places without directly meeting each other's eyes. I'd say goodnight to the kids and head back to my place above the garage, and he'd get the kids tucked in. Sometimes I heard him come back out to the garage and work a little more, but he never invited me to have a beer with him again, and he certainly didn't come knock on my door.

By the weekend, I was feeling kind of lonely and isolated. Owen and Addie were great, and the seniors in dance class had been adorable, but I was sort of craving interaction with someone my age. Friendship. Camaraderie. It has been missing from my life ever since I'd been engaged to Neil. I'd never made girlfriends of my own in Chicago—just his sisters or the wives and girlfriends of his work or golf buddies. And I'd had *nothing* in common with those women.

I couldn't call Morgan every night—she was busy with a newborn baby. Mabel had texted me a couple times over the last couple weeks asking how things were going, but I didn't want to burden her either. I especially didn't want to admit that part of my problem was a strong attraction to her brother.

But all physical urges aside, I really did like it when Austin and I had *talked*... Neil had not been a good listener. He'd pretend to listen, he'd say things like "right" and "uh huh," but his eyes would glaze over, and he always found a way to bring the conversation around to a topic he could mansplain to me. We just never understood each other.

But somehow, I felt like Austin *got* me. Maybe it was because he'd lost his mom too. Maybe it was because I was a lot more myself around Austin than I had been around Neil. Maybe it was simply because Austin wasn't a rich selfish prick.

Whatever the reason, I felt the loss of his friendship even though it had barely begun. I started to think about maybe trying to go see Morgan while the kids were gone, if I could scrape the money together to get there. Then while I was in the city, maybe I could see about a job and a living situation for the fall.

On Friday morning, after I'd dropped the kids at camp, I called her.

"Speak of the devil!" she said when she picked up. "I was just talking about you."

The familiarity of her voice made me smile. "You were?"

"Yes. I might have solved your employment issues! Jake went to a meeting yesterday about a new show that's opening this fall. Scott Blackstone is the choreographer, and apparently, he's looking for a new assistant."

I gasped. I'd taken Scott's musical theater dance class for years when I lived in the city, and I loved both his choreography and his teaching style. He'd asked me to assist him in the past during my off-season whenever he'd do college workshops or festivals, and we worked really well together. But I hadn't been in touch with him since I left New York. "Oh my god, that would be perfect!"

"I know! I told Jake to float your name. Okay to give Scott your new number? He adored you. I bet you'd get the gig."

"Of course! Thank you—I'm so anxious to get back to New York."

"The job isn't going well?"

"No, it is, I just…" I didn't feel like explaining the whole Austin situation to her. "I guess it just doesn't feel like home here yet. I was thinking maybe I'd come visit you while the kids go to visit their mom in California."

"Yes!" she shrieked. "Do it!"

I laughed at her excitement. "I'll check ticket prices. I don't want to blow all my earnings. I'm going to need them this fall."

"Let me know," she said. "I cannot wait to see you!"

We hung up, and I felt a little better.

Then I got a message from Austin.

> The kids leave tomorrow for California.

> I know. It's on the calendar.

> I'll help them pack when I get home tonight. Could you make sure all their laundry is done?

> Yes.

Then I took a deep breath and asked my question.

> Are you still planning to take me to Chicago while they are gone to get my things?

> I said I would.

I frowned.

> It's okay if you don't have time. I know how busy you are.

> I said I would, and I will. We'll go Sunday.

Annoyed, I tossed my phone aside and stomped upstairs to get the kids' laundry.

. . .

On Friday evening, Xander showed up with burgers and hot dogs, and he and Austin grilled while I stuck frozen French fries in the oven and tossed a salad together. Austin sat across the table from me, but never seemed to look up from his plate, much as he'd done all week.

After dinner, the kids begged their dad to take them into town for ice cream.

"Not tonight," he said firmly. "We need to get you guys packed."

"All their laundry is done," I said before he could ask. Then I got up and began clearing the table. "I just have to bring up the last load from the basement. The rest is already folded and put away."

Austin didn't look at me, but I could sense Xander's eyes moving back and forth between me and his brother.

"Tell you what." Xander spoke up. "I'll take the kids for ice cream right now, and you guys can get their bags packed without interruption."

"Yay! Can we, Daddy?" Adelaide asked.

"I guess." Austin didn't sound too happy about the plan, and I wondered if it was because it meant being alone in the house with me.

"Let's go." Xander stood up and shook his keys. "Last one to the car is a rotten egg."

As soon as they were gone, Austin brought his dishes to the sink. "I'll clean up in here. Can you bring those last loads of laundry up to their rooms? Then you can be done for the night. I can pack their bags myself."

"Fine." Wiping my hands on the towel, I glanced sideways at him. "Everything okay?"

"Why do you ask?"

"I don't know. You haven't been talking to me much this week."

He was silent for a moment. "I'm just doing what I said I'd do."

"Right. Okay." I left him standing there and went down to the basement, where I emptied the clothing from the dryer into the basket, then carried it all the way up to the second floor.

On the landing, I glanced into Austin's bedroom. The bed was made, although the comforter was wrinkled on one side, like maybe he'd sat there to put on his socks and shoes. I wondered if he'd ever had a woman in that bed, or if he'd slept alone every single night for the last seven years. He said he never got lonely. But how could that be? Wasn't he human?

I went into Adelaide's room and dumped the clothes out onto the bed, separating them into piles of his and hers, then folding them neatly. I was placing things into Addie's dresser drawers when I heard Austin's voice behind me.

"Thanks," he said. "I'll take over."

I closed the drawer and turned around, leaning back against the dresser. "You don't want help?"

"No, thanks." He went over to the bed, knelt down, and pulled a small purple suitcase from under it. Rising to his feet, he opened it on the bed.

"Are you just going to ignore me like this for the rest of the summer, Austin? Because I'm not sure I can stand it."

"I'm not ignoring you." He went to the closet and took out a couple pairs of shoes. "I'm treating you like I'm supposed to. Like an employee."

"I thought we were going to be friends."

He placed the shoes at the bottom of the suitcase. "I thought we could, but I don't think that's possible anymore."

"Why not?"

"You know why not." He went to the closet again and took a couple sundresses off their hangers.

"Because we like each other?"

"It's more than that." Laying the dresses on the bed, he came over to the dresser where I was standing. "Excuse me. I have to open this drawer."

I wouldn't budge. "Answer the question, Austin. Why can't we be friends?"

His eyes were focused on the dresser top.

"Is this about the thing in the window the other night? I'm sorry, okay? I was trying to get under your skin the way you'd gotten under mine. I won't do that again."

He swallowed. His jaw twitched.

I pivoted so I could see his expression in the mirror over the dresser. It was hard and unrelenting. "So that's it? We can't be friends because we're attracted to each other?"

Lifting his head, his eyes found mine in the glass. "We can't be friends because I spend every minute of the day thinking about fucking you."

I sucked in my breath. "That's—that's not what I thought you'd say."

"It's the truth."

My core muscles clenched. "Maybe we could—"

"No." He opened the drawer and took out the items he wanted. "It's out of the question."

"Even if I told you I think about it too?"

"Don't tell me that." He went back to the bed and began placing socks and underwear inside the suitcase.

"But we're two consenting adults."

"It's more complicated than that. You work for me. I pay you."

"What if I quit?"

But I couldn't quit, and he knew it.

Downstairs, the front door opened, and we heard the kids' voices. A moment later, they came running up the steps and appeared in Adelaide's bedroom doorway holding the drippy remains of their ice cream.

"Uncle Xander let us get double scoops!" Owen shouted.

I plastered a smile on my face. "Looks delicious, but let's go outside with those cones. You can each tell me what flavors you had."

They followed me down the stairs and out to the front porch, where I sat and listened to them chatter on about their desserts and who they saw in town and how excited they were about their trip on an airplane by themselves.

"Last year was the first time Daddy let us fly alone, and the pilot let us go in the cockpit and see all the buttons and steering things," Adelaide said. "We got to get on the plane first, and we got snacks and drinks before anyone else."

"Wow." I smiled. "It's like you guys travel like movie stars."

But my mind was stuck on a loop.

I spend every minute of the day thinking about fucking you.

Chapter 13

I was furious with myself.

And with Veronica.

If she hadn't pushed me, I never would have said those words out loud. And furthermore, if she didn't look so beautiful all the time, maybe I could get a moment's peace! Why did she have to wear those crop tops? And that red lipstick? Or have such gorgeous legs?

And would it kill her not to smell so good? Every time we crossed paths—although believe me, I'd tried to avoid it all week—I caught the scent of her perfume or shampoo or whatever it was, and it nearly brought me to my knees. She smelled like a goddamn cupcake.

Not to mention that little show she'd put on in the window. How dare she take off her top like that! I couldn't even breathe watching her untie those strings. The memory of her bare back haunted me, along with the feel of her tongue on my thumb, the apex of her hip along my hand, the softness of her stomach beneath my lips.

I was going to lose that fucking bet.

I frowned as my dick began to get hard, shifting uncomfortably in the driver's seat of the truck. I'd just left the airport after seeing the kids off, and I was in a shit mood. I knew they were safe—I'd watched the gate attendant walk them right onto the plane, the flight was nonstop, and they'd be escorted off as "unaccompanied minors" and delivered right to Sansa in San Diego, who'd be waiting at the gate.

And they were so excited. They'd barely slept last night after getting off FaceTime with their mom, and they'd chirped endlessly on the ride to the airport about all the fun things she'd promised them they could do—surfing and pottery and swimming in the ocean. When they hugged and kissed me goodbye, they hadn't shed a tear.

You should be glad about that, I told myself. *You're raising brave, curious, outgoing kids who aren't afraid of an adventure. And it's good for them to know their mom.*

But a week without them was tough.

It wasn't that I didn't trust Sansa to take care of them—for all her ambivalence about being a mom, she adored them and was actually really good with them, like a cool aunt.

But already I missed their little voices in the back seat, laughing or asking questions or even arguing. Veronica had offered to make the drive with me, but I'd told her I didn't need company. Being alone with her didn't seem like a good idea.

I was dreading that trip to Chicago. Just the two of us in close quarters, a six-hour drive, the prospect of running into her ex and having to keep my temper in check. I'd even asked Xander to come with us, but he said he couldn't spare that much time away from the bar—he was hoping to open before MLB playoffs began.

Frankly, I thought he was bullshitting me, because he kept dropping hints all the fucking time about me and Veronica hooking up. He was at the house when I got home, walking out of the garage with my circular saw again.

"Dude. You could at least ask," I said, meeting him halfway down the driveway. I wondered if Veronica was home, and refused to let myself look up at her apartment.

"I was going to." Xander shrugged. "You weren't here. Kids get off okay?"

"Yeah."

"When do they come back?"

"Week from tomorrow."

"You alright?"

I shrugged.

"You should come out tonight. There's a great band at The Broken Spoke."

"I don't feel like it."

"Come on, it's Saturday night! Don't be such an old man. We'll drink a few beers, hear some good music, talk shit about people we don't like, get in a bar fight."

I grunted. "Don't tempt me."

"I'll pick you up at eight, Grandpa," he said, continuing down the driveway with my saw. "Be ready."

• • •

I should have known he'd invite her too.

She was already sitting in the front seat of his SUV when I walked out to it, and even though I felt like turning around and going back inside the house, I couldn't see a way to do it without looking like an asshole.

As soon as I got in the car and slammed the door, they

both looked back at me—Xander with a *gotcha* grin, Veronica's expression apologetic.

"I'm sorry," she said, pressing her tempting scarlet lips together. "I didn't know you were coming, or I'd have gotten in the back seat."

"It's fine." I gave Xander a dirty look.

"Are you sure you have enough room?" she asked. "I can trade with you. Or move my seat up."

"I'm sure."

"Have you heard from the kids?" she asked. "Did they make it out there okay?"

"Yes. They called me about an hour ago. They're fine."

"Oh, good." She looked relieved. "I've been thinking about them all day."

She really needed to stop doing and saying sweet things. I wasn't sure I could handle wanting her any more than I already did. I turned my attention out the window and set about the task of ignoring her for the rest of the night.

But it was impossible.

Sitting across from her at a table at the back of The Broken Spoke, my leg was twitching beneath the red-checkered tablecloth, and it wasn't in time to the music. The bar was housed in a repurposed barn on an old dairy farm a little ways outside of town, more popular with locals than tourists. It was packed tonight, and everyone else was enjoying the music, dancing to current favorites and old classics, drinking beers, shooting pool, talking and laughing and flirting while the place pulsed with the sweltering beat of a small-town Saturday night.

Since Xander had driven, I had allowed myself a couple more beers than usual, hoping the alcohol would numb what I was feeling.

It wasn't working.

Moody and tense, I sat there scowling while everyone else had a good time. Familiar faces stopped by our table, slapped Xander on the back and asked about the progress on his bar, introduced themselves to Veronica, and nodded at me. Several people tried to engage me in conversation, but I remained broody and uncommunicative.

A couple times, friends asked if I was okay, and I snapped, "I'm fine." Then I'd go back to drinking my beer and pretending not to see the woman across from me, my body on fire for her. She'd turned her chair to face the band, not that I blamed her. I wouldn't want to look at my glowering mug either.

In contrast, her skin seemed to glow under the strings of party lights that formed a canopy above our heads. She wore a little red skirt with flowers on it that twirled out every time she danced, showing off the tiny black yoga shorts underneath. And she danced a lot—every time someone asked her. And she was the best dancer out there, spinning and stepping effortlessly, making even the clumsy, arthritic old guys look like Fred Astaire. With every song, she grew more flushed and beautiful, while I got more mad and sullen, slumping lower in my chair.

A song came on and she jumped to her feet. "Oh, I love this one! Anyone want to dance with me?" She looked hopefully around our table.

"I'm a little tired," said Xander, lying through his teeth. "Austin, why don't you go dance?"

"No." I grabbed my beer and took a drink.

"Please, Austin?" Veronica looked at me hopefully, and my chest tightened.

"Go on." Xander elbowed me. "She can even make *you* look good."

"I don't feel like it," I snapped.

Her face fell, and she was about to sit down when a guy I didn't recognize came over to the table and smiled at her. He was good-looking, maybe in his twenties, tall with blond hair and a wiry frame. I wanted to kick his ass immediately.

"Hi. Would you like to dance?" he asked her politely.

Veronica began to shake her head, thank god, but then suddenly she glanced at me and then beamed up at him with ruby-lipped delight. "Thanks, I'd love to!"

He offered his arm, and she slipped her hand through it, and they headed for the dance floor.

My spine snapped straight in my chair, and I gripped my beer so hard my knuckles turned white.

"Something wrong, brother?" Xander drawled.

Watching the blond guy take Veronica in his arms felt like someone had just injected my veins with molten glass. I couldn't even answer the question, seething with fury as she laughed at something he said, her head tipping back.

"Dude, you look insane," Xander said. "Why didn't you just fucking say yes when she asked *you*?"

The guy's hand on Veronica's back was moving treacherously low. I might have growled.

"You're being ridiculous. When this song ends, go ask her to dance."

"I don't like dancing."

"Well, she does, so unless you want to sit here and watch her dance with other guys while you grunt like a jealous caveman all night, you better go cut in."

"I'm not jealous," I said hotly.

"Oh no?" Xander laughed. "So if he asks her to hang out after this, you'd be fine with that? Maybe take her back to his place? Bring her home late?"

"Fine by me," I lied, the urge to flip the table building in my chest and radiating through my arms. "It's her night off. She's free to do as she pleases."

"Jesus Christ. I can't watch this. I'm going to get another beer, you want one?"

"No." All my focus was on that dance floor. I didn't want anything except her. I wanted her so badly that when the song ended and everyone paused to applaud, I got up from the table and headed their way.

"Excuse me." I tapped her on the shoulder. "Can I have the next one?"

"Sorry." Her expression was cool. "I've already promised the next one to Daniel here."

I gave Daniel a look of barely contained rage. "Would you mind?"

He swallowed. Looked at the width of my shoulders and the way my hands were curled into fists. "No, it's fine. Maybe I'll see you later, Roni."

I fumed as he walked away. He was already calling her Roni?

When he'd gone, she faced me, her expression livid. "Really? *Now* you want to dance?"

"Yeah."

The band started up again, a slow blues this time, but I couldn't bring myself to put my arms around her and sway like the couples around us—I was too worked up.

She cocked her head to one side. "What's the matter? Scared to touch me?"

"No." But I was. If I touched her, it was all over.

"So you don't really want to dance with me, you just don't want me to dance with anyone else." She rolled her eyes. "Figures."

She walked off the dance floor, but instead of going back to the table, she headed toward the bathrooms. I followed her, even though I felt like every eye in the place was watching us. But instead of entering the ladies' room, she blew right by it. Bursting out the back door, she stomped off around one side of the building, in the opposite direction of the parking lot.

"Hey!" I called, hurrying to catch up with her. "Where are you going?"

"Leave me alone. I want some air."

"It's dark out here!"

"Then you better keep your distance—you know what happens with us in the dark. You might start to *feel sorry* for me again!"

"Will you stop?" I got close enough to grab her by the elbow and spun her to face me. "I want to talk to you."

"Let go!" She shook off my grip and faced me, her eyes shining with anger in the moonlight.

"I'm sorry." I held up my hands. "I didn't mean to manhandle you. I just wanted to—"

"To what?" She crossed her arms over her chest, her eyes going wide. "Punish me for dancing with someone else? It's obvious you didn't like it."

"I didn't," I admitted. "I wanted to fucking lay him out."

"That's ridiculous. We were just dancing."

"He had his arms around you," I seethed.

"And you were jealous?"

"Yes!"

"So put your fucking arms around me, Austin! No one is stopping you!"

Pushed to the limit, I did exactly what she said—threw my arms around her and crushed my mouth to hers. My tongue swept between her lips, insistent, hot, demanding. I poured all my anger and jealousy and frustration into that kiss, desperate to smother my fired-up feelings.

But her arms wound around my neck, and she jumped up, wrapping her legs around me, which only stoked the flames. My hands moved beneath her ass, and I put her back against the old barn wall, which throbbed with the pounding drums inside. I ground my cock between her legs, rubbing my hard length against her pussy through those little black shorts.

She moaned against my lips, and I wondered if we'd get caught if I fucked her right here in the dark against the side of The Broken Spoke—although frankly, I wasn't even sure I'd last long enough to get caught. I was about to come in my pants.

The song came to an end, and I heard whistles and applause from inside the bar. Returning to my senses, I set her down and took a step back. Both of us were breathing hard.

"God," she panted, wiping her mouth. "You can be *such* an asshole, but you sure know how to kiss."

I grimaced, even as my chest filled with pride.

Adjusting her skirt, she leaned back against the wall. "So what happens now? You going to apologize again? Promise to stay away from me?"

"I should."

She glared at me, her eyes catching the moonlight. "Don't bother."

"What is this, Veronica?" I blurted. "What are we doing?"

"Hell if I know! I know what we *would* be doing if you'd just relax and have some fun. What are you so afraid of?"

I opened my mouth, but I couldn't put it into words.

"The kids are gone for a week, Austin. The tension between us is driving us both crazy. If you weren't such a chicken, we could get it out of our systems!"

"I'm not a chicken!" I told her. "It's not just about the kids."

"Then what? Are you worried about me? Are you afraid I might think you're my boyfriend if I let you get to third base? Please." She held up one hand. "The last thing I'm looking for is another relationship."

Her words were tempting me to kiss her again. To take her home and run for third base—fuck that, I wanted to score. But something was holding me back.

"It's not right," I said stubbornly.

She tilted her head. Then she moved close enough to stand chest to chest with me, placing her hand over the bulge in my jeans. "That feel wrong to you?"

I couldn't lie, so I said nothing. Always my default.

Her lips tipped up, and she shook her head. "Next time you kiss me, Austin, do it because you want to, not because you don't want me kissing somebody else." She dropped her hand. "Or don't do it at all."

Then she turned on her heel and walked away.

• • •

When we left the bar, she rode home in the back seat, stiff and silent. I didn't say anything either, and Xander gave up trying to make conversation and turned up the radio.

At home, Veronica jumped out of the car quickly. "Thanks for taking me, I had fun," she said without any emotion whatsoever. Then she slammed the door and marched up the driveway toward the garage.

"What the hell happened with you guys tonight?" Xander asked as we watched her go up the stairs to her apartment, illuminated by Xander's headlights.

I exhaled and rubbed the back of my neck. "I fucked up."

"Before or after you borrowed her lipstick?" Xander reached over and swiped at my neck.

I knocked his hand away and rubbed at the spot. "This stuff is like industrial marine varnish. It doesn't come off."

"You know what your problem is? You've got no finesse."

"My *problem* is that she *works* for me, asshole," I snapped. "What kind of dad screws the babysitter?"

"Don't make it into that," Xander shot back. "It's not like she's a teenage innocent and you're a pervy old man. The kids aren't even around."

"What happens if things go badly?"

Xander laughed. "You mean what if you're a two-pump chump?"

"Fuck off! I'm being serious, Xander." I rubbed the back of my neck. "I mean, what happens if I sleep with her and then it's awkward, and we're stuck having to practically live together for the rest of the summer? Or what if things go wrong and she leaves?"

He shrugged. "I don't know."

"And not only is messing around with her a risk in terms of the job, but she's just getting out of a terrible relationship. That guy was a real dick to her."

"That's why she needs you. Show her that not all guys are like that."

"What if she's not thinking straight? What if she's just lonely and vulnerable and I'm the jerk that took advantage of her?"

Xander sighed. "Look, I don't know her that well, but she doesn't strike me as fragile."

"She hides it well," I said, remembering things she'd told me about her past.

My brother was quiet for a minute, staring out at the garage. "I don't know, dude. Maybe I'm not reading the signals right. But from where I'm sitting, she's into you, you're into her, and you both seem like you could use a good time with someone you trust. That's all."

Xander had hit on something—Veronica trusted me. Maybe that was the problem. I didn't want to ruin it.

Leaning across me, he opened the glove box and pulled out a condom. "But for god's sake, be careful this time."

"I'm not going to sleep with her, Xander."

But I took that condom with me.

Chapter 14

VERONICA

I let myself into my apartment and slammed the door behind me. Then I flopped facedown on the couch and screamed into a pillow.

What was the matter with him? Did he want me or not? Maybe it was just the forbidden aspect—he was hot for the nanny.

Or maybe I was the problem. What was the matter with *me* that I wanted *him* so badly? Was I trying to prove that I was still desirable because Neil had cheated on me? Was I just desperate for physical affection since Neil had been so stingy with it? Maybe I just needed to give up. Was sleeping with my boss really going to make my life better? Or would it just make me feel worse about myself?

Dragging myself into the bathroom, I stripped off my sweaty clothes and took a shower. I thought about tomorrow, when we'd be stuck in the car together for six hours—and that was just one way. What the hell were we going to talk about? Knowing Austin, he could be silent for the entire ride, but I'd lose my mind.

After I got out of the shower, I towel-dried my hair, brushed my teeth and put on the big white T-shirt I always slept in. It had been Neil's at one point, and I sort of hated that I still liked sleeping in it, but it was comfortable, and I'd had it for so long that I never thought of it as his anyway. Plus, the only other pajamas I'd packed was a slinky lace nightie Neil had gifted me to wear on our honeymoon. I'd already thrown it out.

I checked my phone for messages—nothing—plugged it in, and turned off the light.

Stay away from that window, I told myself. *The shade is already down, so you have no reason to go over there.*

I went over there.

Timidly, I peeked around the side of the shade. Austin's bedroom light was already off. Was he in bed already? Maybe he—

Three sharp knocks on the apartment door made me jump. With one last glance across the yard at his window, I slowly made my way to the door. *Don't get your hopes up,* I admonished myself. *He's probably here to list all the reasons why he shouldn't be here.*

After a deep breath, I pulled the door open.

Damn, he was hot.

He'd showered too—his hair was damp and messy, and he wore the sweatpants he'd had on the night we'd kissed by the fire pit. His feet were bare.

So was his chest.

Deep in my body, things went loose, and then tight. My nipples tingled, and I folded my arms across my chest to hide their pointed tips. "Yes?"

"I want to leave early tomorrow. Can you be ready by eight?"

I tilted my head. "You came over here with no shirt on to ask me if I could be ready by eight?"

"Yeah." He looked mad about it.

"You could have texted," I pointed out.

"I wasn't sure if you'd already gone to bed," he said defensively. "You might not have seen it."

"So you were going to wake me up?"

His scowl was back. "Look, just be ready."

"I will."

"Fine."

"*Fine!*" I slammed the door in his face. "Jerk!"

Pouting, I stood there for a moment, fisting my hands in my hair, listening to the furious rapid firing of my pulse.

Then suddenly the door swung wide and he charged in, taking me in his arms without a word. Our mouths slammed together as he kicked the door shut, his scruff rough against my jaw, his hands sliding beneath my shirt. I slanted my head as his tongue plunged between my lips and ran my hands up his chest, chiseled with muscles and covered with hair. He backed me deeper into the apartment, never breaking the kiss.

He came back! He came back!

But part of me needed to know why.

"Wait," I said breathlessly, gripping the back of his neck as his mouth worked its way down my throat. "Wait a minute. Why are you here?"

"Isn't it obvious?" One hand moved down the back of my panties, his fingers grabbing my ass, kneading hard.

"I want to hear it."

"Fine. I'm here to fuck you. Want me to narrate it too?"

I laughed, because it felt so good to be touched this way, to hear him talk this way, to know he wanted me like I wanted him. The scent of him—clean and masculine—filled my head. "Yes."

Suddenly he swept me off my feet and carried me to the back of the apartment. "I'm taking you into the bedroom now." He tossed me onto the bed, whipped the shirt over my head. "I'm tearing the clothes from your body." He yanked my underwear down my legs, his eyes roving all over my skin. "I'm looking at you naked and wondering how the hell I thought I could stay away from you."

"Willpower?" I suggested as he grabbed me behind the knees and yanked me toward the edge of the bed.

"No one has that much willpower." He leaned over me, bracing his hands on the mattress by my shoulders, and covered my mouth with his. His kiss was deep and demanding, his tongue moving against mine in a way that made my entire body shiver with anticipation. I grabbed handfuls of his damp hair as he kissed his way down my neck and chest, closing his lips around one hard nipple. He sucked greedily, sending bursts of desire swirling through me. Then he switched his attention to the other breast, tracing a circle around its taut peak with his tongue, biting it gently. Then his mouth moved from my belly button straight south, the velvet softness of his lips a delicious contrast to the texture of his scruffy jaw. He pushed my legs apart and rubbed his nose against my clit, inhaling deeply and teasing me with one long, languorous stroke of his tongue.

"Oh god," I whimpered.

He straightened up again. "Okay, so here's where I'm going to preview the coming attractions—see what I did there?—because my mouth is going to be busy from now on."

"Okay." My insides quivered with nerves and excitement.

He ran his hands up the insides of my thighs. "I'm going to put my hands all over your body. I'm going to lick every last inch of your skin. I'm going to fuck you with my fingers and my tongue, and after you come just like that, I'm going to fuck you with my cock, deep and hard. And I'm not going to stop until I feel you come again. How does that sound?"

"That—that sounds good," I panted, my toes curling over the

edge of the mattress.

It was better than good—it was *spectacular.*

And he took his time about it too—especially when he knelt on the floor beside the bed and buried his head between my legs, lavishing my clit with more attention, skill, and patience than any man had ever offered. His tongue was a marvel, a tool of incredible dexterity and versatility, an instrument that could play any melody you requested, while his fingers accompanied it in perfect harmony.

And believe me, I danced to the tune.

I writhed and arched and undulated beneath him, my fingers twisting in the sheets, in his hair. He growled and moaned, every sound from the back of his throat taking me higher. I hooked one leg over his shoulder, lifting my hips in sync with the rhythm of his fingers inside me. He sealed his mouth over my swollen clit, teasing it with quick flicks of his tongue, sucking it with ravenous abandon until I was feverish with need, my lower body humming with rapture, my cries growing louder and more frequent and higher pitched until fireworks exploded in the blackness behind my eyes and my body convulsed with pure, primal pleasure. My god, it felt good to surrender to desire this completely, to have it course through me in waves that released all the tension from my muscles.

And it wasn't over yet.

With one final, rasping growl, Austin tore his mouth from my body and rose to his feet. Breathing hard, I propped myself up on my elbows and watched him shed his clothing until he stood naked in front of me. Light spilled in from behind him, illuminating the outline of his body—the wide shoulders, the heaving chest, the narrowing torso, the solid arms. I watched one of those arms begin to move as he took his cock in his hand and worked his fist up and down its length.

"I wish I could see you better," I whispered.

"You like to watch?" His voice seemed even deeper.

"Maybe next time." I reached for him, pulling him over me. "Intermission is over, and I'm very eager to experience the second half of this show."

A low, sexy laugh erupted from his chest as he stretched out above me, positioning his hips between my thighs. Then he stopped. "Fuck. Hang on."

"What's wrong?"

He hunted around for his sweatpants and pulled a condom from one pocket. "Nothing is wrong. I'm just careful. Always."

I was on birth control shots, but I understood his fear.

"Just so you know, I haven't been with anyone in years," he said quickly.

"Years?" I repeated, stunned by the admission.

"I don't mess around—this town is too small."

"So you just walk around with condoms in your pocket at all times?"

"Xander gave it to me earlier." He knelt between my legs again. "Even though I swore up and down nothing was going to happen."

I reached between us to wrap my fingers around his heavy, hard cock, rubbing the tip of it up and down my slick center. "I'll keep your secret if you keep your promise about making me come again."

His erection thickened in my palm. "I am a man of my word, Veronica Sutton."

"I know you are," I said, easing his smooth, wide crown inside me. Then I let him take over, running my hands over his rippling abs and up his chest, squeezing his biceps as he notched deeper.

"God, you're beautiful," he said as he slowly worked his way into my body with slow, measured thrusts, giving me a little more each time. "You're so beautiful, and so tight, and so wet—fuck." His eyes closed, and his cock throbbed once.

I giggled—I couldn't help it. "It *has* been a while, hasn't it?"

He growled at me. "Be good, little girl. Or I won't give you what you want."

"I'm sorry, I'm sorry." I pulled him closer and buried my face in his neck, kissing his throat, his jaw, his collarbone. Rubbing my lips against his scruff. "I'll be good."

He pushed in deeper, so deep I gasped. Then I closed my eyes against the sharp twinge, my breath caught in my lungs.

"Breathe, baby," he said in that low, sexy voice I wanted to drown in. He began to move inside me with long, unhurried strokes, and my body trembled and tightened, the need building in me all over again.

"Yes," I whispered, running my hands all over his arms and back and neck. "I want this. I want you. Since the moment I saw you."

My words seemed to ignite something within him, and his thrusts grew faster, harder, deeper. I clung to him like he might drive me right off the edge of the mattress. Our breathing grew ragged, our bodies slick with sweat.

I moved my hands down either side of his spine to his ass, thrilling at the muscles working beneath his heated skin. Curling my fingers into his flesh, I pulled him into me, meeting every punch of his hips with a lift of my own, delirious with the effortless way our bodies moved together.

"Fuck—close," he rasped, slowing his pace a little.

"Don't stop," I begged, opening wider for him, lifting higher, taking him deeper—so deep that he touched a magical spot inside me that made my entire body involuntarily contract around him almost painfully tight. "Oh, god—right there… I can't—I'm going to—" But I lost the ability to form words as the tension snapped and the second orgasm crashed through me, relief rippling throughout my entire body, from my core to my limbs to my fingers and toes.

As if he'd been waiting for me, Austin's climax hit as mine waned, so I could feel every pulse of him inside me. Beyond the fading thunder of my heart, I heard his guttural moan. Beneath my hands, I felt his muscles twitch and shudder and still.

I couldn't help the smile that crept onto my lips as he collapsed on me. *A stellar performance*, I thought. *Technique? Ten. Choreography? Ten. Artistry? Ten. I loved every single moment from the entrance to the exit, and I want an encore.*

Austin picked up his head. "Are you laughing?"

"Was I?"

"Yes. And as much as I like the way you laugh, that was not supposed to be funny."

"It wasn't! I swear, it wasn't funny. It was very serious. I had two *very serious* orgasms."

"That's more like it." He nodded with cocky satisfaction.

"I was just thinking about something that made me smile."

"Oh yeah? What?"

"You standing there on my doorstep with no shirt on, a condom in your pocket, pretending like you'd come over to give me tomorrow's departure time. Did you really think you'd fool me?"

"I wasn't thinking much at all. I just wanted to see you." He brushed the hair back from my face.

"You didn't need to pretend otherwise."

"You know how I am."

"I do." I locked my ankles behind his thighs and my hands behind his neck. "And I appreciate that you want to be respectful of me. But I'm a big girl."

"You are. But there's something about you that makes me feel protective. I can't help it. Sorry if that's toxic male patriarchy or something."

I smiled and pulled his head down so I could kiss his lips. "You are not the toxic male patriarchy. You're just a little bossy sometimes. And a lot stubborn. And sort of dictatorial about the way things have to go. But as someone who hasn't ever had a man be protective of her, I have to say it feels pretty good."

"So does that mean I can fight your ex-fiancé if I see him tomorrow?"

"No! I'm going to handle him myself." I laughed. "It would not be much of a fight anyway, trust me."

"I still want to do it."

I smiled again at the ferocity in his voice. "I appreciate that. But actually, I think you should thank him. If he hadn't been such a jerk, I wouldn't have been stranded here in need of a job."

"That's true. And I don't know what I'd have done without you this summer."

My entire body tingled with pleasure at his words. "You're not just saying that because it was fun to fuck the nanny?"

He groaned as he tipped to one side. "Don't say that."

"Why not? It was a riot to fuck the boss." Laughing, I slipped from the bed. "I'll be right back."

In the bathroom, I cleaned up and washed my hands. In the mirror, I saw flushed cheeks, puffy lips, wild hair. But the girl who looked back at me was happy.

As I dried my hands, I wondered if Austin would still be lying there in bed when I went out. Was this like an overnight kind of thing? Would I get my encore? What if he was all *This can't happen again, Veronica* when I walked out? Pulling on his sweatpants? Racing for the door?

But when I opened the bathroom door, I saw him lying on the bed, right where I'd left him. My insides tightened once more. Quickly, I switched off the living room light and hurried back to him.

"You're still here," I said, lying on my side with my hands tucked under my cheek.

"Is that okay?" He propped his head onto his hand.

"Yes. You can stay as long as you want." I chuckled sheepishly. "I've been a little lonely up here all by myself."

"Have you?" He ran his hand down my arm, shoulder to elbow.

"Yeah. I'm an extrovert, and I think I've just been starved for meaningful social interaction over the last couple years. I was pretty isolated caring for my mom. And I went right from her house to orbiting Neil, who kept me close while also keeping me sequestered. But I suppose it's been good to have time to think."

"What did you think about?"

The outline of his broad shoulder was tempting me, and I put my hand on his chest, brushed my fingers through the soft, dark hair. "Well, I'd like to say I've been up here contemplating the meaning of life, world peace, self-actualization. But the truth is, I've mostly been up here fantasizing about your naked body."

He laughed. "Then we're even. That's all I've been doing over there. Or sometimes just one floor below you."

"And how was the reality compared to the fantasy?"

"So much better. No comparison." His hand skimmed the dip at my waist and over my hip.

My heart fluttered. "Good."

"But now I have a problem." In one easy move, he'd turned me onto my back beneath him, shackling my wrists with his hands, pinning them to the mattress above my head.

"I'm going to want it all the time." He buried his face in my neck and inhaled deeply. "God, you smell good. Every single time you walk by me, I want to fucking eat you with a spoon."

"I don't see a problem with that. Not for the next week, anyway. After that, you'll have to behave again." It was good that we had an agreed-on end date. No potential for hurt feelings or misunderstanding.

"Then I better not waste any time." He kissed his way back up to my mouth and claimed it with his own.

We got very little sleep that night. But as I drifted off wrapped in Austin's arms, I felt happier than I had in years.

Chapter 15

AUSTIN

I woke up to the sound of Xander pounding on the back door to the house.

"Bro!" he was yelling. "You made me get up early on a Sunday to help you, and you're not even awake? Get your ass out of bed!"

"Shit," I mumbled, tossing the covers back and going over to the window. When I peeked behind the shade, I saw him standing at the back of the house shouting up at my bedroom window. I'd left my phone at the house last night, so I couldn't text him, and I didn't want to wake up Veronica by yelling back.

"I'm giving you five minutes!" Xander shouted, then plunked himself down in one of the Adirondack chairs by the fire pit.

I noticed he had a cardboard cup of coffee in his hand, so I figured he'd be fine for a few. Going back to the bed, I slipped in beside Veronica again, curling up behind her.

The bedroom window faced the east, so the light filtering

through the shade was soft and pink. It made her skin glow angelically, and her gossamer hair was like a halo around her head. She had the sheet pulled up to her hip, but it was low enough that I noticed the tiny pattern of stars just above her right butt cheek. They were connected, like a constellation. I wished I knew enough about astronomy to recognize it.

She inhaled, her ribs expanding, and I heard a contented little sigh as she exhaled. I leaned over and pressed my lips to her ink.

"Good morning," she said sleepily.

"Morning. I found your tattoo."

"I noticed."

"What is it?"

"It's the constellation for Virgo. That's my sign."

"Ah."

She rolled onto her back and gave me a smile. "What's yours?"

"Aries. Are we compatible?"

"No. Actually, those two signs are terrible together."

"Hm. That's too bad." I lowered my mouth to her chest, taking one perfect pink nipple in my mouth, teasing the pebbled tip with my tongue. Her fingers moved into my hair, and she arched her back, moaning softly. My cock stirred to life, and I wished I'd woken up fifteen minutes earlier.

Outside, my brother yelled, "You're down to three minutes, asshole!"

Veronica laughed. "Is that Xander out there?"

"Yeah. He's here to help me get the table into the truck. I forgot I told him to come at seven. Actually, I didn't forget, I just had no idea what time it was and didn't really care." Reluctantly, I picked up my head. "And I really don't want to stop what I'm doing, but I don't think Xander would appreciate the wait or the sound effects."

"I agree. But you know what he will appreciate?" She giggled.

"You walking out of my apartment with no shirt on."

"I wish there was a way to sneak back to the house. He's going to give me *so* much shit about this." I groaned. "Fuck! I owe him a bar now."

"A what?"

"The bar top he wants out of reclaimed wood. He bet me I wouldn't be able to keep my hands off you, and he was right."

She laughed. "Serves you right for taking that bet."

"I guess you're right." After planting one last kiss on her breast, I dragged myself from the bed and looked around for my clothing. "And you know what?"

"What?" On her side, she watched me get dressed, her cheek propped in one hand.

I tugged up my pants. "It's worth it."

Her smile validated that sentiment.

I dropped a kiss on her forehead. "Eight o'clock," I reminded her as I headed through the living room.

"I'll be ready, Dad!" she shouted.

Frowning, I yanked the door open. "Jesus, don't call me that!"

I heard her laughing as I let myself out. Moving down the stairs slowly, I tried to play it cool.

When Xander heard my feet on the steps, he looked over. Probably expecting Veronica, he pushed his sunglasses to the top of his head and squinted at me. When it registered that I was exiting her apartment wearing nothing but sweatpants, he started to laugh.

"Dude," he said, replacing his sunglasses. "I knew it."

Ignoring him, I went straight for the house and opened the back door.

"The door was open?" Xander followed me into the kitchen. "Didn't you check?"

"No. I knocked, and you didn't answer, so I just assumed it

was locked and you were still in bed." He grinned, leaning back against the counter, taking a sip of his coffee. "And I was only wrong about one of those things."

I looked at my phone, glad to see I hadn't missed any calls from the kids or texts from Sansa.

"I want details."

"Too bad." I switched on the Keurig and stuck a pod in the machine.

"You used the condom at least, right?"

"Fuck off."

"So I'm thinking pine for the bar you're going to make me, or maybe oak, like from some old whiskey barrels."

Dammit.

"Come on," he scoffed. "You have to give me something. When you guys got out of the car last night, you weren't even speaking."

"We had a good time." I poured some almond milk in my coffee.

"I'm surprised she even let you in, let alone stay over."

"Guess I've got more finesse than you thought." I took my cup and left the kitchen. "I'm going to get dressed. I'll be back down in a minute."

Upstairs, I threw on some jeans and a T-shirt. After combing my fingers through my hair, I stuck a cap on my head and went back down to the kitchen.

"So is this like a romantic getaway?" Xander asked.

"We're going to her dickhead ex-fiancé's apartment to get her clothes. Does that sound romantic to you?"

"No, but once that part is over, why not hang around the city for a couple days?"

"I've got work to do. We'll be in and out."

Xander smirked. "I bet you will."

"Knock, knock." Veronica entered the kitchen, looking fresh

and pretty in denim shorts and a black top. Her hair was up in a ponytail, and her lips were bright red. For a moment, I imagined what it would be like to watch them close around my cock. Would they leave a mark?

There was something about that I liked.

"Good morning, sunshine." Xander was full of cheer. "Isn't it a beautiful day?"

"It is." She smiled at him and at me, a little wistfully. "I wish we didn't have to spend the whole thing in the car. Your dad keeps asking me if I've been for a ride on the old ferry boat yet, and I have to say no every time."

"Sounds like your mean boss should give you more time off," Xander said with a meaningful look in my direction.

I rolled my eyes and rinsed out my coffee mug, placing it in the dishwasher. "Let's get that table loaded so we can hit the road."

• • •

Veronica was quieter than usual on the four-hour drive to Saugatuck, where I delivered the table I'd made to a home owned by Gus's nephew Quentin and his husband, Pierre. They'd seen a table I'd made for Gus and his wife last winter when they'd visited and begged Gus to tell them where he'd found it.

After we'd brought the table into their dining room, they asked me about the wood, and I gave them the details about where I'd salvaged the old cedar planks and how I'd transformed them.

"It's just incredible," Pierre said with a slight French-Canadian accent. "Are you sure you won't make another for us to sell on consignment at the gallery?"

"Gallery?" Veronica piped up.

"We own an art and antiques gallery in town," Quentin explained. "And we think something like this would interest many high-end customers. You'd probably have a dozen orders by the end of the summer. What do you think, Austin?"

"I don't really have that kind of time." I felt Veronica's eyes on me, but I didn't meet them. "It's really just a hobby."

"Let us know if you change your mind," said Pierre. "We want to be your first call."

While Quentin wrote me a check, Pierre gave Veronica a quick tour of their home, which was also a bed and breakfast. Her laugh rang out from the front parlor, and we both looked in that direction. Veronica had a great laugh, deep and loud and joyful.

"Your wife is so lovely," Quentin said. "I didn't realize you were married."

"I'm not. Veronica and I are just friends. Actually, she's the nanny—I'm a single dad."

"Oh, you have children! But you didn't bring them?"

"No, they're visiting their mom in California for a week. I just brought Veronica along to—to—" I groped for a word to appropriately finish the sentence, and Quentin took pity on me, patting my shoulder.

"I understand completely," he said.

• • •

After we delivered the table, we stopped into a small sandwich shop for lunch. I ordered a meatball sub, and Veronica ordered a B.L.T. Seated across from each other in a booth, I watched her take a bite or two, then lose interest.

"Do you want something else?" I asked.

"No." She wrapped up what was left and pushed it away from her. "It's just my stomach is a little weird."

I took another bite and observed her sip her iced tea. "You nervous about running into him?"

"Yes."

"You don't have to be." My protective instincts were sharp

today. "I'll be there the whole time. He won't come anywhere near you."

"I'm not afraid of him like that. It's just, he might—he might *say* things that hurt me. Or embarrass me." She scratched at a chip in the tabletop with her thumbnail. "I don't want you to hear them."

I finished my sandwich in one bite and balled up the wrapper, wondering how mad she'd be if I punched this guy on sight just for fun. "You've got nothing to worry about."

She smiled, but it was half-hearted.

"I mean it. The only one who should be worried is your dipshit ex. If he so much as looks at you wrong, I'll cold-cock him in the jaw."

"No!" She shook her head. "Do *not* get rough with him, Austin. He'd probably call security. Just...no. Leave him to me."

I sighed and sat back. "And you guys call *me* a party pooper. I was looking forward to the chance to drop that asshole like a bag of dirt."

"I'm sorry, but *no*," she said firmly. "It's bad enough I'm dragging you down there, taking up your whole day. I don't want you thrown in jail on top of it. Then who'd drive me home?"

I laughed. "*Now* she tells it like it is."

She smiled, and it looked real this time. "Seriously. I do appreciate this. I hope you know that."

"I do."

"I just want to handle him on my own, okay?"

"Okay."

"Promise?"

"I promise."

• • •

But first we had to deal with the uncooperative doorman. Neil had, of course, given instructions that Veronica was not allowed on the premises. My contempt for her ex grew as I watched her argue and plead.

"I'm sorry, Ms. Sutton," the doorman said. "I can't let you in. Mr. Vanderhoof expressly forbid it."

"Tony, come on," she begged. "You know me. I lived here for a year. My clothes are still here. That's all I want."

"I'm sorry," he repeated, and he did look apologetic. "But I have my orders from management." He lowered his voice. "It's my job."

"I understand," said Veronica. "But isn't there anything you can do?"

"If I let you into the lobby, you could ask the concierge to call him," Tony suggested. "Maybe he'd give the okay."

Veronica exhaled. "I doubt it, but I suppose it's worth a try."

Tony opened the door to the building, and we went inside. My first impression was that the place was fucking freezing. The thermostat had to be set at fifty-five—I couldn't imagine how expensive it was to keep a place this size so cold. And it wasn't just the air conditioning. The place *looked* cold too. Lots of glossy white tables and white marble surfaces and frosted lighting. There was something almost antiseptic or institutional about its cool, curated perfection. Even the white flowers in silver vases looked fake. Nothing about this place said home to me.

Not that I could afford it.

My second impression was that it must cost a fuck-ton of money to live here. This place probably had a rooftop swimming pool and an underground wine cellar. The parking garage was probably full of Land Rovers and Porsches. My pickup, proudly stating its affiliation with TWO BUCKLEYS HOME IMPROVEMENT, was parked in a garage up the street for an astronomical hourly rate. How anyone whose last name wasn't Vanderhoof could afford to live like this was beyond me. I remembered what Veronica had said about wanting this kind of fairy tale life and wondered if she missed it.

She approached the older gentleman at the concierge desk while I hung back, and although he appeared to recognize her, he didn't seem hopeful. "Mr. Vanderhoof's instructions were very clear," he said, "but I can make the call."

He picked up a phone and spoke too quietly for me to hear, then held the phone slightly away from his ear. "Of course, Mr. Vanderhoof. Sorry to disturb you. I'll be sure to—what's that?" He looked at Veronica. "Well, yes, she's right here in the lobby. Would you like to—very well. I'll let her know."

"Can I go up?" she asked hopefully.

"I'm afraid not," he said as he replaced the receiver. "But Mr. Vanderhoof has agreed to come down and speak with you."

Her shoulders slumped. "I don't want to talk to him. I just want my clothes."

"It's the best I can do," the concierge said, his tone regretful. "I'm sorry."

"Thanks for trying, Walter." Veronica turned toward me, her expression crestfallen. "He's coming down."

"I heard." I wanted to put my arms around her, but I didn't. Instead, I shoved my hands in my pockets.

"I'm just going to be rational and polite," she said, more to herself than me. "I'm going to stay calm and be nice. My mom always said you catch more flies with honey than vinegar."

"I'll stay out of your way," I told her. "But I'm here if you need me."

"Thanks." She smiled at me. "If we didn't have to get back tonight, I'd take you to my favorite steakhouse and treat you to dinner."

It sounded so good, I was about to say I could call my dad and tell him I wouldn't be at work tomorrow when the elevator opened and a trim, athletic-looking guy strode out, rudely elbowing other people aside. He had windblown blond hair, a chin that looked too big for his face, and an impressive suntan. He wore all white—white shorts, white Lacoste shirt, white socks, white tennis shoes, white sweatbands around both wrists and his head. The only thing missing was the racket. I might have laughed if I hadn't been filled with so much animosity. He looked like a Saturday Night Live skit.

"Well, well, well." He stood spraddle-legged, hands on his hips, and rocked back on his heels. "If it isn't my little teacup. Change your mind, did you?"

The hell she did, I thought.

"Hello, Neil," Veronica said evenly. "How are you?"

He tossed his head back and laughed too loud. "Me? Fantastic. Just played three sets at the club and won them all. My kick serve was practically unreturnable today. I had ten aces."

"Right. Well, that sounds nice. I was wondering if—"

"I knew you'd be back." Neil's eyes gleamed with arrogance. "Miss me, did you?"

Veronica took a breath. "I'm only back for my things."

"What things?"

"My clothes and the—"

"The clothes I bought?" He laughed derisively. "Those don't belong to you."

"Neil, come on. You didn't buy *all* my clothes."

"The things worth wearing, I did. The rest was garbage. I already threw it out."

Her jaw dropped. "You threw out my clothes?"

"You don't live here anymore."

"Everything?" Her voice cracked.

"They were taking up space. I just ordered some new bespoke suits, so I'll need that second bedroom closet."

Veronica lowered her face into her hands, and I took a step

toward her, torn between wanting to let her handle this, like she asked me to, or step in and mess up this guy's tennis whites. But a second later, she picked up her head, and there were no tears. "Neil, how could you? I had things my mom gave me."

"Your mom, who thought you'd be happily married right now? How do you think she would feel if she were here? Disappointed, that's how!" He shook a finger in her face, like he was scolding a disobedient schoolgirl.

I pushed off the column I was leaning against and almost moved in, but that's when Veronica dropped the nice act and glared up at him, batting his hand out of her face.

"You're crazy!" she snapped. "She'd be glad I didn't marry you! You never loved me one bit. You just wanted to control me. You'd have made me miserable all my life."

Neil's face assumed a fake, overdramatic sad expression. "Oh, poor little Roni in her penthouse apartment with her closet full of Chanel and her Mercedes-Benz! I feel so sorry for you." He smirked again. "Tell the truth. You miss it all now, don't you?"

"Not one little bit," she said venomously. "You don't know the first goddamn thing about me if you think I care about any of that bullshit."

I leaned back again and folded my arms. She had this.

"Then what are you doing here? You honestly expect me to believe you showed up looking for your ratty old clothes?" He raised his voice. "Admit it—you're here because you know you made a mistake, and now you want me back."

"The only mistake I made was saying yes to you in the first place! I wouldn't want you back if you were the last person on earth."

"Suit yourself, Veronica," he said with a haughty sniff. "But you'll never find anyone better."

I burst out laughing—I couldn't help it.

Neil turned toward me. "And just who are you?" he demanded. His eyes narrowed in judgment as they took in my work boots and jeans, the lazy way I leaned against the column.

"I'm someone better," I informed him.

He moved closer and parked his hands on his hips. "Excuse me?"

"Asshole, I met her three weeks ago, and I'll tell you right now, I *know* her better than you do, I *treat* her better than you do, and you can be damn sure I *fuck* her better."

A collective gasp circled the lobby. I imagined women clutching their pearls, but I didn't take my eyes off Neil's furious face. Once the shock wore off, he cocked his right arm back and took the most obvious, inexperienced swing at me you've ever seen. He might as well have announced he was going to hit me and warned me to duck.

I easily blocked it, and before I could stop myself, I landed a blow to his nose with my right fist. It knocked him backward onto his ass, and he sat there, stunned. Blood trickled from his nostril. Gingerly, he reached up and touched his upper lip, then looked at his finger. "I'm bleeding!" he yelled, in the same panicked way someone else might scream, "I've been shot!"

"I didn't even hit you that hard," I snarled, my hand still curled into a fist. "Consider yourself lucky."

"Someone call the police!" he howled, looking like a belligerent toddler on the floor. "And an ambulance! A surgeon! I think he broke my nose!"

Veronica grabbed me by the bicep and pulled me toward the door. "Let's go. Now."

We raced for the door, pushing our way out into the sunshine and then hurrying up the block. Neither of us said anything as we darted through groups of people on the sidewalk, but at one point I glanced back and didn't see her. I stopped moving, and when she caught up, I took her by the hand and we hustled side by side all the way to the garage, up two flights of stairs, and down the row of cars until we reached the truck. I opened the passenger door for her, and she climbed in. By the time I rounded the truck and slid behind the wheel, she was sobbing.

I felt like shit. "I'm sorry, Roni. I fucked up."

"It's ok-kay," she managed between shuddering breaths.

"No, it isn't. I promised you I'd let you handle it, and then I let my temper get the better of me. I should have kept my fucking mouth shut."

"I'm glad you didn't," she wept. "He h-had it c-coming. I just w-wish I'd stood up to him s-sooner."

"Me too. But I was so proud of you today. And your mom would have been, too."

She cried harder.

Slinging an arm around her, I pulled her close. "Come here."

She wept into my shoulder for a minute or two while I stroked her back. I was used to holding Owen or Adelaide while they cried, but comforting a grown woman was something else entirely. There was no scraped knee to bandage or banged-up elbow to rub. I wouldn't be able to distract her with a cookie or a bike ride. For a second, I thought about offering to go down on her in the back seat, but just then she straightened up and wiped her nose with the back of her wrist.

"God, I don't even know why I'm so upset. It's not like this is surprising. Neil's a jerk."

"Well, now he's a jerk with a broken nose."

She laughed ruefully. "I'm a mess. And your shirt's a mess."

"I don't care."

"Do you, by any chance, have any tissues in your glove box?"

"Hmm. I might have something." I leaned across her and opened it up, grateful to see I'd stashed some fast food napkins in there. "How's this?"

"Perfect. Thanks." She grabbed one and blew her nose, then another and wiped her eyes. Then she balled them up in her hands and took a few shaky breaths.

"You okay?"

She nodded. Her nose was red, her eyes were puffy, and her mascara had left some black smudges, but her breathing was calmer. "I'm okay."

"Do you think he's telling the truth about throwing out your things?" I asked. "Maybe that was a bullshit flex."

"No. I think he really did it. He's vindictive and spiteful."

I rubbed the back of my neck. "When you said that thing about stuff your mom gave you, I wanted to kill him."

"Honestly, it wasn't that much. A few pieces of clothing. The stuff of hers that really mattered to me wasn't there—I left a box in Morgan's storage unit when I moved to Chicago. Photo albums from when I was young, letters she wrote to me, some books."

I exhaled in relief. "Thank god."

"It's funny," she said thoughtfully, staring out the front windshield. "I didn't even consider bringing that box to Neil's with me. At the time, I told Morgan that I just hadn't had a chance to sort through it all and the grief was too fresh to handle it, but that was a lie. I just didn't want to share any of it with Neil. It was too personal. Too precious to me."

"Maybe deep down, you knew."

She nodded sadly and dropped her eyes to her hands, which rested in her lap, still clutching the napkins. "Maybe I did."

I started the truck and buckled my seatbelt. "Well, what do you say we leave this place behind and head home?"

"Sounds good." She looked over at me, her expression sorrowful. "I'm sorry I dragged you all the way down here for nothing. I'll pay you back for the gas."

"Listen, I'd have driven another six hundred miles to punch that guy in the face. And you're going to need all your money for new clothes."

"Still." She leaned over and kissed my cheek, then tipped her head onto my shoulder, hugging my upper arm. "Thank you. I'm so glad you're here."

My chest grew warm, and my heart beat faster. "Me too."

She picked up my right hand and looked at it. "Does it hurt?"

I flexed my fingers. "Not a bit."

"That was a hard punch you threw."

"Eh. I've hit Xander harder than that. But Xander fights back."

She laughed. "I bet."

I was about to put the truck in gear when she did the craziest thing—she lifted my rough hand to her soft mouth and kissed the back of each finger. Then she studied it. "I like your hands. I like them even better when they're on me."

My dick jumped, and I threw the truck in reverse. "Then let's get the fuck out of here."

Chapter 16

Veronica

"Tell me more about growing up with five siblings," I said once we were heading east on the interstate out of Illinois. I wanted to know more about him, and family seemed like his first priority.

"We were close, when we didn't want to kill each other."

"Did you share bedrooms?" I asked, remembering how quiet the house was growing up an only child.

He nodded. "Xander and I shared, Devlin and Dash shared. Mabel was the princess who had her own room."

"She grew up with four brothers," I said with a laugh. "She needed space. But she doesn't strike me as the princess type."

"I guess she wasn't, not in the spoiled brat sense of the word. And she wasn't super girly. She was more of a tomboy if anything. She was always trying to keep up with us."

"So other than you and Xander, did all of you get along?"

"Yeah. And I think Xander and I only fought so much because we're closest in age, and both of us were competitive. He had sports as an outlet, but I didn't have time for sports in high school. I always worked."

Sympathy squeezed my heart—he really had been forced to grow up fast. "What's Devlin like?"

"Now? I'd say he's driven. Successful. Focused. As a kid, he was a handful, but he quit being so rebellious once he got to high school. He wanted a college degree and knew he'd need decent grades."

"So he was a good student?"

"He was definitely the best student of the boys. But he was motivated—he wanted to run his own business, make a lot of money, drive a nice car, all that."

"And does he?"

"He's on his way," Austin said, a touch of pride in his voice. "He works his ass off. An office job would not be for me, but he seems to love corporate life."

"And he's how old?"

"He's twenty-eight. Lives in Boston."

"What about Dash?"

"Dash is twenty-six. He was wild as a kid, tons of energy, always breaking the rules. But he was always such a ham, he got out of trouble pretty easily. He could sweet talk anyone."

I smiled. "Did he always want to be an actor?"

"Yeah. Have you seen Malibu Splash?"

"No," I admitted. "But the twins told me it's good."

Austin laughed. "That's because they're the target audience. Sometimes I feel bad for Dash because he wants to be a more serious actor, but he got popular on this show, and now he's kind of trapped by his contract. Other times, I see his photos online attending a party or premiere, and I think, you know what? That asshole's doing just fine."

I smiled. "Does he have a girlfriend?"

"Not that I know of. Dash says dating is too hard in Hollywood. Everyone seems fake." He was silent a moment. "I'd never want to be famous."

"No?"

He shook his head. "Nah. I mean, the money would be nice, but it seems like it comes with some pretty big downsides. No privacy, no freedom to do normal things without people in your face, no way to know for sure who you can trust. And you always have to be *on*, you know? Fuck that."

"Yeah."

He glanced at me. "What about you? You've got all kinds of talent. Did you want to be famous?"

I laughed. "I have *one* kind of talent, and it's not really the kind that takes you to Hollywood, not these days anyway. I missed the golden age of the Hollywood musical by about eighty years. But I like the stage better than the camera, anyway."

"Yeah?"

"It feels more immediate, more exciting. I love a big audience, the applause, the energy in the air. Honestly, being a Rockette was my dream from a really early age. My mom cleaned for a wealthy family that gave her two tickets to see the Christmas show when I was young, and she scraped together train fare and took me—I had stars in my eyes from the moment the curtain went up. I knew what I wanted to do with my life."

He glanced at me. "Do you miss dancing?"

"Yes," I said without hesitation. "Without dance, it's like a huge part of me is just dead—my soul or something. It's always been my escape, my passion, my happiest place."

"How old were you when you started?"

"Two. And it was pure luck that got me started. My mom took

a job cleaning a local dance studio on Sundays when it was closed, and she had to bring me along. I used to spend hours twirling and jumping and dancing to music only I could hear in front of all those mirrors. One day, the studio owner was there doing paperwork or something, and she saw me and thought I had potential. She invited me to take a class for free, even though I wasn't even technically old enough."

"And you loved it?"

"More than anything." The childhood joy of arriving at the studio before class hit me all over again. "Growing up, I was never happier than when I was dancing. Not just because I got attention for it, although the attention was nice. But I was home alone a lot, and the studio was always so busy and noisy and welcoming. It was a second home. My teachers and friends were like family."

"I bet you were the best one there."

I laughed. "You know what? I was good, but I wasn't always the best. I just worked my ass off, and it was obvious I loved being there and wanted to learn. I was determined—eyes on the prize." I smiled at him. "What was *your* prize when you were young? Did you always want to run the family business?"

"Not really." He was silent a moment, eyes on the road. "I wanted to go to college to study architecture."

"Why didn't you?"

"My family needed me at home."

I waited for him to go on, but he didn't, and I realized that for Austin, it was as simple as that—his family needed him, and he wasn't going to let them down. He'd set aside his own goals, stayed home, helped raise his siblings, and worked with his father. Then he watched every single one of his siblings leave the nest to chase *their* dreams. It made even more sense to me now that he'd insisted on raising the twins on his own rather than give them up. He'd never put his own needs or wants first.

It was honorable—and undeniably sexy—but it also had to result in a lot of pent-up frustration, didn't it? Did he ever feel angry? Did he ever resent being the one left behind? The one who never got to go after what he wanted? Even now, he refused to abandon the family business and treated his furniture business more like a passion project.

What about personal needs? He was an amazing son, father, and brother, but he was still a man. I glanced over at his handsome profile, then let my gaze wander down his chest to the apex of his thighs. Memories from last night flooded my mind, and the flutter from my stomach moved between my legs.

I wanted him in my bed again tonight, but more than that, I wanted to do something for him that made him feel like the center of the universe. Like only his needs mattered.

He could have delivered that table this morning and had the rest of the day to spend in his workshop, doing what he loved. This was his first full day without the kids. Instead, he spent most of the day hauling me to Chicago just because he didn't want me to face my ex alone. And he'd stood up for me too. He would have taken a punch for me if Neil hadn't taken such a ridiculously slow and obvious swing.

I felt like he'd put *me* first. Besides my mom, had anyone else ever done that?

He hooked his left hand over his right shoulder and kneaded the muscle.

"Is that still bothering you?" I asked. "Here, let me." Shifting sideways on the seat, I reached over and began to massage his neck and shoulder. "God, you're so tight. We need to stretch you out."

"That sounds really fucking painful. I'm picturing a rack."

I giggled. "No torture devices. We'll do some yoga together."

"No. Fucking. Way."

"Why not? The kids love it."

"The kids have seven-year-old bodies. And besides, there's no way I could concentrate on stretching while you do those yoga poses. I almost lost my mind the first morning I saw you out in the backyard."

"Oh yeah? Were you watching me?" I asked coyly.

"I couldn't look away—I felt like the world's biggest pervert."

"It was just a few yoga poses."

"Not in my mind, it wasn't."

"Okay, then how about a real massage?"

"No, thanks. I don't like other people's hands all over my body."

"I meant from me, silly." I leaned closer to whisper in his ear. "Complete with happy ending."

He groaned. "You're making my pants tight."

"I can take care of that right now, if you want." I moved my hand to his crotch and stroked him through the denim. "With my hand, or with my mouth."

"Jesus Christ. You have to stop that or I won't be able to drive. And I'll have a hell of a time explaining to the state trooper behind us why I'm all over the road."

"That's fine. You can save it all up for me until we get home." I leaned close again, tugging at his earlobe with my teeth. "I'll be very thirsty by then."

His jaw clenched. "Fuck."

"And Austin—we should probably stop and get some more condoms. A giant box of them."

Despite the state trooper behind us, he pushed a little harder on the gas.

• • •

We didn't get home until almost eleven. As we pulled into the driveway, Austin said he wanted to call the kids really quick.

"That's fine," I said. "I'd like to take a shower anyway."

"I'm going to grab one too. I'll leave the back door open. Come over when you're ready?"

"You want me to come to the house?" I asked, surprised.

"Is that okay?"

"Yes, I just…" I struggled to explain why it felt like a big deal. "The house is like your family space. I don't want to intrude on it."

He cocked his head. "Veronica, for the past six hours, all I've done is think about all the ways I'm going to intrude on your body. For fuck's sake, you can spend the night in my room."

I laughed. "Okay, I'll be over in a few."

Up in my apartment, I jumped in the shower, delighting in the butterflies in my belly. I couldn't remember the last time I felt them. When I got out, I rubbed my vanilla body lotion all over my skin, remembering how Austin had liked the way it smelled on me. Feeling naughty, I skipped panties, but tugged the white T-shirt over my head and pulled out my ponytail, fluffing my hair. Pulse racing, I hurried down the stairs and across the yard.

As promised, the back door was open. The kitchen was dark and silent, and I locked the door behind me before heading upstairs.

In Austin's bedroom, one lamp was on, and the bathroom door was closed. On the nightstand was the jumbo box of condoms we'd purchased on the way home, and just seeing it made my core muscles clench. I inhaled—the room smelled like him. Manly but clean, like a new leather belt.

Behind me, the bathroom door opened, and I turned around. "Hi," I said, my heart beating like crazy, as if I hadn't just seen him fifteen minutes ago.

Plus, he was naked.

My breaths turned to pants as he came toward me, hair wet and messy, skin damp and slightly flushed, eyes dark and hungry.

My gaze traveled over his broad chest, down his rippling abs, to the thick, heavy cock between his thighs.

I licked my lips. "How are the kids?"

"Fine. But I don't want to talk about the kids right now." He moved close enough to bury his face in my neck and slip his hands beneath my shirt. "Fuck, you smell good."

"Thanks."

His hands moved over my butt. "You came here without panties on?"

"I didn't think they'd last long anyway." I shivered as his lips and tongue worked down my throat.

"You were right." He steered me backward toward the bed. "It's bad enough you're still wearing this shirt. You've been here at least thirty seconds."

"Take it off me. It belonged to Neil anyway, and—"

"What?" His body immediately went tense. He picked up his head and stared at me, fury ablaze in his eyes.

"This T-shirt. It was Neil's, but I—"

Before I could finish my sentence, Austin grabbed two fistfuls of cotton at my chest and fucking *ripped it apart*. He kept tearing until the shirt was split completely down the front, then he shoved it from my arms and threw it to the floor. It was as if the grizzly inked on his shoulder had taken control.

"Nothing of his will ever touch your skin again," he fumed.

I didn't know whether to be turned on or terrified at this display of possessive rage. But my heart was galloping like a racehorse, and my breath was coming in short, quick bursts. Between my legs, I felt the flutter of arousal, and my nipples were hard and tingling.

Turned on, it was.

"Fuck. I'm sorry." The cords in Austin's neck tightened, and his eyes closed for a moment. "I keep losing my shit today. I don't know what it is. I just can't fucking stand the thought of him near you, not even his shirt."

I smiled coyly. "You'll have to give me one of your shirts to replace it."

"Deal." He kissed me ravenously, his tongue sliding between my lips. His cock sprang to life between us, and I took it in one fist, wrapping my fingers around him, working my hand up and down the thickening shaft.

He slipped his hand between my legs. "You're already wet," he growled, his fingers easily gliding inside me.

"It's your body. It does something to me." Then I rose up on my toes to put my lips to his ear. "And now I'm going to do something to you." I dropped to my knees, enjoying the sharp intake of his breath as I wrapped his swelling cock with both hands. "Something I've been thinking about all day."

"All day, huh?" His voice was low and thick with desire.

"Maybe even all week." I moved my fists up and down the hard length of his shaft, teased the soft, smooth tip with my tongue.

He groaned, his hands flexing into fists at his sides.

"Don't tell me you haven't." I slid one hand between his thighs, cradling his balls in my palm.

"Haven't what?"

I looked up at him coquettishly as I swirled my tongue around his crown. "Thought about this."

"Only every other minute since I met you."

I laughed and licked him root to tip, the skin hot and firm and ridged with veins. "Good." I circled the ridge at the top and pumped my hand up and down his length, gratified by his deep, tortured moan when my lips hovered, wet and open, over the sensitive head. I tipped my head up and met his eyes again. "But before I do this, I want to make something clear."

"I'll give you a warning."

"That's not what I meant." I stroked my lips with the tip like it was my lipstick, coating them with his salty taste. "I meant, I want it clear that you are not allowed to hold back."

His hands moved into my hair. "Jesus."

"I'm on my knees for you," I whispered. "I want to make you feel good. Tell me what to do."

An agonized growl rumbled from his chest. "I want your mouth on me."

"Come on, you can do better than that." I rubbed my lips up and down the underside of his erection. "Let me hear what you're really thinking."

"I want you to suck my cock."

I smiled and took just the tip in my mouth, gave him a few playful little tugs.

His fists tightened in my hair. "I want to fuck your mouth so deep and hard, you choke when I come."

And then I couldn't talk anymore, because he was using his grip on my hair to hold my head steady while he pushed the full length of his cock between my lips, right up until the tip hit the back of my throat. He stopped there for a second, going completely still, so still I felt him thicken and pulse once inside my mouth. With an anguished groan, he began to rock his hips—slow, rhythmic thrusts that slid along my tongue, never quite withdrawing entirely, but always hitting the deepest reaches of my mouth. My eyes watered. My scalp stung. I struggled for breath, managing to grab a little air each time he pulled back.

But it was exactly what I wanted. There was a sense of power in knowing he was willing to let go with me, to say what he was thinking, to do what he wanted to do without hesitation. This was a man unused to putting his pleasure first.

I wanted to provide that pleasure, *embody* that pleasure. I wanted him to be selfish with me. Rough with me. Real with me.

He started to move faster and harder, his hips driving forward in deep, sharp jabs. His fingers loosened in my hair and cradled my head, holding it in place. I could feel the orgasm building in both my hands—the one wrapped around the base of his cock and the one between his legs, every part of him growing harder as his body barreled toward release. I could taste him, and I moaned reflexively. My nipples were tingling, my core muscles tight. My thighs were trembling and slick with heat. I wanted his hands on me. I wanted to fuck him. I imagined how good it would feel to push him down to the floor and ride him until I came. I promised myself I would do it later.

Right now, it was all about him.

"Fuck—Roni—so good—"

I sucked harder, gripped his shaft tighter, and just for fun, slid the tip of one finger farther back between his legs, penetrating him just slightly, since I wasn't sure if he would like it.

A second later, I had my answer, because he lost control with one final thrust. His body stopped moving, except for the throbbing pulse in my mouth, which coated the back of my throat in thick, hot bursts.

As soon as he recovered, he pulled back and I dropped my butt to my heels, gasping for breath.

"Christ. Are you okay?" Austin let go of my hair and crouched down in front of me.

I nodded. "Yes. Just needed some air. You weren't kidding about that whole choking thing."

"I'm sorry, baby."

"Don't be. I asked for it, didn't I?"

He gave me a sexy grin. "You did. Now I get to ask you for some things."

"Like what?"

"Well." He slid one hand up my thigh. "How about you hop up on this bed and sit on my face so I can fuck you with my tongue?"

I smiled seductively. "I only want to please you."

"Then we're going to leave the light on too." Rising to his feet, he scooped me up off the rug and set me on the mattress.

"It's like you own the electric company," I teased.

"If it means I can watch you come, I'll fucking buy it."

A minute later, his head was between my thighs as I held onto the wooden headboard and slowly rocked my hips above his face. His hands were on my breasts, his thumbs teasing the humming peaks of my nipples before he pinched them hard enough to make me gasp. But it was sublime, the sting from his fingers and the stroke of his tongue at the same time. He licked and sucked and kissed and tasted, teased and flicked and fluttered. He slipped his tongue inside me and swept it up the seam at my center in one long, glorious caress. He devoured me slowly, like I was a decadent dessert he was trying to make last all night. Sometimes he moaned like he couldn't get enough.

For a minute, I watched him, his dark eyes locked on mine. But eventually, I had to look away or I was going to finish too quickly. It was so hot, seeing him beneath me, hearing the sounds he made, feeling his scruffy jaw on my thighs. I'd actually never done this before—Neil was not the type to request that I sit anywhere near his face, nor was he particularly talented with his tongue or knowledgeable about female anatomy.

And sex with the lights on? Never. Which was fine with me, because being in the dark made it easier to pretend I was with someone different. Someone who actually cared about me. Someone who might hold me close afterward and tell me how good I'd made him feel or kiss my tattoo or punch a big jerk in the face for me. Someone who stood up for me instead of cutting me down.

And if his tongue happened to be a magic wand, well, lucky me.

"God, Austin," I breathed, my hips undulating faster as the tension in my body wound tighter. "You're fucking incredible. That feels *so good*..." Then my words were gone and the stars collided and my body exploded in wild, rippling waves of bliss that made my legs tremble and my clit beat a rhythm on his tongue. I cried out with every single pulse as it moved through me.

When I could breathe again, I shimmied down his body and collapsed on his chest, babbling incoherently. "Oh my god. You're amazing. This job is amazing. If I'd known orgasms were a perk of being your nanny, I might have tried harder at the first interview. Or lied and said I could cook."

Laughter rumbled in his chest. "Yeah?"

"Yes. Actually, I really should learn how. Maybe I can do it while the kids are gone."

"Don't bother. Your pussy is my new favorite meal."

My lady parts experienced an aftershock. "Then you will be well-fed while they're away."

"Good." He put his arms around me and stroked my back, his fingers trailing up and down my spine.

I sighed contentedly, my eyes drifting closed, surprised at how comfortable and easy this felt. Wasn't this kind of intimacy supposed to take more time? It was hard to believe we were the same two people who'd met on his porch that day.

I picked up my head and looked down at him. "What did you think of me the day we met?"

"I thought you were missing a few marbles."

I laughed and swatted his chest. "Be serious."

"I am. Veronica, you knocked on my front door wearing a wedding dress."

"I know, but...did you at least think I was cute?"

He smiled and tucked my hair behind my ear. "I thought you were gorgeous. But that wasn't enough to make me want to hire you. In fact, that made your chances worse."

"Why?"

"Because the last thing I wanted to do was hire someone I was attracted to."

"You were attracted to me? That very first day?" I was giddy at the thought. "But you were so grouchy during the interview! You looked at me like I was a stain on the carpet."

"Because I didn't want you around all the time. I didn't trust myself."

I gave him a slow, sly grin. "Then I seduced you in the dark and it was all over."

"Actually, I think it was the yoga shorts the next day."

I laughed. "That's right. You were spying on me."

"I wasn't spying!" He flipped me onto my back and pinned my wrists to the mattress. "You were right there on my back lawn, and I *happened* to see you out the window. Was that a strategic move on your part?"

"No." I giggled. "Although now that I know you like my yoga clothes, maybe I'll walk around in them all the time."

His eyes narrowed. "Don't you dare. I'll never get anything done."

"I might have to," I said seriously. "It's not like I have a lot of options in my closet."

He was silent a moment. "I'm sorry again about today."

"Don't be. Maybe getting new clothes is part of starting over."

"I still feel bad."

"I bet you can find a way to make it up to me."

He buried his face in my neck and inhaled. "Mmm. I'm thinking of several."

"How about shopping?"

"No." He kissed his way down my chest. "My ways don't involve clothing at all. But they do involve you screaming my name some more."

Against my leg, I felt his cock jumping to life again. "Already?"

"Listen, I already warned you that I don't plan on wasting any time," he said, circling my nipple with his tongue. "So am I still the boss this week even though the kids are gone and you're not technically the nanny?"

"Definitely." I wrapped my legs around him. "What can I do for you, sir?"

"I have a list," he said.

I laughed as he tickled my ribs with his chin. "I bet you do."

Chapter 17

AUSTIN

*T*he last thing I wanted to do Monday morning was get out of bed and go to work.

Not only had I been up until almost two a.m., but Veronica was still asleep beside me, warm and beautiful and smelling like cupcakes fresh from the oven. I hoped that scent would stay on me all day.

I opened my eyes a few minutes before seven, which was the time my alarm normally buzzed, and quickly switched it off so it wouldn't wake her. Then I curled my body around hers like a question mark, pulling the covers up to our shoulders, slipping my arm around her waist.

"Mmmm." She hugged my arms closer to her. "This is nice."

"I know." I tucked my knees behind hers and pressed my morning hard-on against her ass. "So nice I'm thinking about calling in sick."

"Do it."

"I can't."

"Why not?"

"Because my dad needs me. We have to finish the cabinetry in someone's kitchen by this afternoon, and it's not something he can do alone." I kissed her shoulder. "What will you do today?"

"I've decided I'm going to learn to cook while the kids are gone. Maybe I'll do that today."

I laughed. "That might be more than a one-day project."

"I'm a fast learner. When you come home tonight, there might be a rack of lamb waiting for you. Or beef bourguignon. Or coq au vin!"

"I don't even know what that is," I confessed.

"Me neither. But it sounds impressive." She tapped my arm. "I want to impress you."

"Believe me. You have."

"Really?" She sounded surprised. "Like how?"

"Well, for one thing, you're awesome with the kids and they love you. I was thinking last week how everything you said at your interview turned out to be true—you memorize routines fast, you work hard, you make everything fun, and you're teaching the kids things that I could never teach them."

"Thank you," she said, like she was surprised by the compliments.

"And you're brave," I went on. "Kicking that asshole to the curb when you knew it would mean losing everything? Confronting him the way you did yesterday? Standing up for yourself? A lot of people in your situation might have broken down and begged. You stood your ground. I was fucking blown away."

"You were?"

"Yes." Unable to help myself, I slid my hand down between her legs, finding her warm and wet. "Also, you are unbelievably hot. And have I mentioned your spectacular blow job skills?"

"No." She moaned softly as I rubbed her clit.

"Unrivaled in the history of all blow jobs," I told her. "I. Saw. God."

She slung one leg back over my hip, opening her thighs wider. "Think your dad will mind if you're a little late this morning?"

"I've given him a lot of years. He can give me twenty extra minutes."

"This won't even take twenty minutes," she said breathlessly. "You know how to make me come so fast... I don't know what kind of magic you've got in those hands, but I like it."

I got her off with my fingers, and it was so hot watching her pale skin flush with color and hearing her desperate cries and feeling her grow hotter and wetter that I nearly came too, my aching cock pressed against her perfect round ass.

While she caught her breath, I rolled away from her just long enough to grab a condom and tear open the packet. "So you know that yoga pose you do where you're on your hands and knees and you sort of arch your back and stick your butt out?"

She laughed, watching me roll on the condom. "Yes..."

"Could you please do that right now and I'll show you what I think about doing every fucking time I see you out there in the yard?"

Grinning, she flipped onto her stomach, popped onto her hands and knees, and arched her back. Then she looked over at me, her expression coy and seductive. "Is this the one?"

"Yes. Fuck, that's hot." Quickly, I got to my knees behind her and eased my cock into her tight, wet pussy. After only a few slow thrusts, I felt the climax beginning to build. I grabbed a fistful of her hair with one hand and gripped her hip with the other. "Jesus Christ. You know what? I might not even be late today. In fact, I might be early."

The last thing I heard before I lost control was her deep, sexy laugh.

I couldn't remember when I'd felt so good.

. . .

When I got home from work that evening, three things greeted me at the back door. First was the sound of Latin music playing, which I heard through the screens as I approached the house and grew louder as I entered the kitchen.

Second was the delectable aroma of barbecue sauce, which made my stomach growl with hungry anticipation the moment I stepped into the kitchen.

Third was the sight of Veronica dancing with her back to me as she chopped lettuce at the counter, her bare feet moving in a rhythmic pattern, her hips swiveling to the beat. She wore denim shorts and that halter top she'd removed in the window, and her hair was tucked up in a messy knot on the top of her head. The music was so loud, she hadn't heard me come in, and I stood there for a moment, undetected, in a sort of mesmerized stupor.

My senses were overwhelmed. My mouth watered. I might have moaned.

Veronica set the knife aside and scooped up the lettuce with her hands, dumping it into two wide, shallow bowls. Once I could tear my eyes from her, I noticed two large chicken breasts, smothered in glistening barbecue sauce, resting on a foil-lined baking sheet near the stove. They didn't appear burnt or undercooked. Next to the bowls was a cutting board with a pile of halved cherry tomatoes and a clump of chopped herbs.

Veronica turned around and shrieked. "Oh! You scared me!"

"Sorry," I said with a grin, setting my keys and wallet aside. "Didn't mean to sneak up on you. It smells fantastic."

"Good." She turned down the music. "How was your day?"

"The usual." I took off my work boots and left them on the rug.

"Talk to the kids at all? How are they?"

"They're great. Dad and I FaceTimed with them." I gave her a quick kiss and went over to the sink to wash my hands. "What's for dinner?"

"Barbecue chicken salad. It's not coq au vin," she said. "But Pioneer Woman calls it one of her go-to summer recipes."

"Pioneer Woman?" As I dried my hands, I checked out what was on the stove. On one gas burner was a large skillet full of black beans and corn. A small saucepan, empty now, looked like it might have contained the barbecue sauce.

"Yes. I went to the library and asked Noreen, the librarian, if she had any recommendations for cookbooks, but she pointed me in the direction of some YouTube tutorials and websites instead. She said Pioneer Woman is her favorite, so I started there." She shrugged, palms up. "I think I did okay! I found a meat thermometer in one of your drawers, and that helped me know when the chicken was done. I'd never used one of those before."

I laughed. "It's good to have tools. Do I have time for a quick shower?"

"Yes," she said. "I still have to slice the chicken off the bone and finish putting the salads together."

"Perfect."

"I have to confess, I didn't make the sauce from scratch—it's just from a jar," she said, her expression guilty. "Same with the apricot preserves I added to it. But," she went on, brightening up, "Noreen told me that the Cherry Tree Harbor farmers' market is on Tuesdays, so tomorrow I'm going to go check it out, and maybe get some local ingredients to make something fully from scratch. She said everything tastes better when it's direct from farm to table."

"I'm sure whatever you made tonight will taste as good as it smells. I appreciate you making dinner—you didn't have to."

Pink roses bloomed in her cheeks. "I wanted to."

I dropped another kiss near her temple. "I'll be right down."

Taking the steps two at a time, I started stripping my clothes off before I even reached my room.

• • •

"It's official," I told her, setting my fork down. "This is the best meal you've made yet. Ten out of ten. Highly recommend."

"Thank you," she said, bowing her head. "I appreciate that."

"I'll do the dishes."

"I don't mind doing them. With the kids gone, I don't have much else to do, and you're still paying me." She took a sip of her wine. "Don't you want to work tonight?"

The only thing I wanted to do tonight was get inside her again. It was my new favorite place. "I don't really have anything I'm working on right now. I have to find the wood for Xander's bar. That's my next project."

"Oh right—the bet."

"He texted me like fifty times today asking when it's going to be ready." I picked up my beer and took a long swallow. "Pain in the ass."

"I don't blame him for wanting you to make it." She brushed the tabletop with her fingertips. "Your work is so beautiful."

"Thanks."

"That was cool about Quentin and Pierre wanting to sell your tables at their gallery," she said. "Think you'll take them up on the offer?"

"I doubt it."

"Why not?"

"If orders started coming in, I'd have to devote serious time to keeping up with them, and I just don't have it."

She propped her elbows on the table and rested her chin in one hand. "In all these years, you've *never* thought of leaving Two Buckleys? Of doing your own thing?"

"Actually, I have."

"Tell me."

"When I was twenty-five, and Mabel was sixteen and pretty self-sufficient, I wanted to move out to California. A friend of mine from high school had opened up a surf shop in Santa Cruz and had this idea about making custom paddle boards. He invited me to go into business with him, so I went out for a visit. That's where I met Sansa."

"Ah. I feel like I know how this ends."

"Exactly." I finished off my beer and set the empty bottle down. "Back at home, I spent a few weeks working up the nerve to tell my dad that I wanted to quit Two Buckleys and move across the country, but before I could do it—literally the very day I'd planned to have the talk with him—I got the phone call that changed everything."

"*Wow*, the timing. Were you devastated?"

I shrugged. "I just figured it wasn't meant to be. And I wouldn't trade my kids for anything."

"I know you wouldn't. But you're also *really* talented at something you love to do. It doesn't seem fair that you can't do it."

"I *can* do it," I argued.

"I meant make a living with it."

I frowned. "Look, I've had this argument with Xander and Mabel a thousand times. I won't quit on my dad."

"So you've never told him you'd like to start your own business?"

"There's no point."

"Don't you think he'd want you to do what you love?"

"It doesn't matter what I love," I said, anger working its way up my spine. "Last year, he had a heart attack and fell off a ladder. Fractured his arm and some ribs. If I hadn't been there, he wouldn't have been found for hours."

"Oh no!" Veronica gasped, her elbows coming off the table. "Owen mentioned something about a heart attack. Poor George!"

"He's okay," I said. "But I don't trust him not to climb ladders or lift things he shouldn't or exert himself too much. I make sure he's safe. It's what he'd have done for *his* father."

"Is it the thing you'd want Owen or Adelaide to do for you?"

I thought for a second. Would I want them to set aside their dreams for my sake? "No. But it's different."

"How so?"

"It just is," I snapped. "And it's my family and my business so leave it alone." I stood up and grabbed both our empty bowls, carrying them to the sink.

A few minutes later, I was still at the sink doing dishes when she came up behind me and wrapped her arms around my torso. "I'm sorry, Austin," she said, laying her cheek on my back.

The tension in my back eased. "I'm sorry too. It's a touchy subject between me and my siblings, but I didn't mean to get short with you."

"I was out of line to push you. I just wish there was a way for you to do what you really love."

I shook my head. "Me too, but there isn't. It comes down to a choice between what's best for my family and what I want for myself. And I won't be the kind of guy who chooses himself."

"I understand." She pressed a kiss to my spine. "And I admire that. Your family is lucky to have you."

Turning off the faucet, I rotated to face her. Lowered my lips to hers, warmth flooding my body. "Thanks. Want to go upstairs and let me untie your top with my teeth?"

She laughed. "That's why I wore it."

• • •

The next morning, I woke up to multiple texts from Xander.

Dude. Lumber yard. Today.

I'll be at your house at four. We can drive together.

No excuses. YOU LOST.

My groan must have awakened Veronica, because she rolled to her side and faced me. "What's wrong?"

"My brother is bugging me to knock off work early and take him to the lumber yard to find some wood for his bar."

"And you can't?"

I exhaled and scratched my stomach. "I don't like leaving my dad alone on the job."

"Hmm." She snuggled closer. "What if I invited your dad to come with me to the farmers' market this afternoon?"

"Would you?"

"Of course! I'd love his company. But will he say yes?"

"I think he would." I thought for a second. "Would you be willing to come ask him in person? I don't think he'd be able to resist you."

"Like father, like son." She giggled, dropped a quick kiss on my chest and hopped out of bed. "I'm going to work out, and then I'll clean up and pop over to the job site. Can you text me the address?"

"Yes." I watched her pulling on her clothes and wished I could yank her right back into bed.

I could practically hear the clock ticking down on our time together.

• • •

She showed up at lunch time, while my dad and I were eating sandwiches in the shade of our client's side porch.

"Hi there," she called, strolling up the driveway. "How's it going?"

"Veronica!" My dad, as expected, was delighted to see her. He rose to his feet and smoothed his Two Buckleys work shirt over his ample belly. "What are you doing here? Did you come to see me?"

"As a matter of fact, I did!" She beamed at him in full cherry-lipped glory, then gave me a smaller, more secret smile. "Hi, Austin."

"Hi." I took another bite of my sandwich, wishing I could eat her for lunch instead. How many hours was it until bedtime?

"So George, Noreen at the library told me about the farmers' market, and I'm planning to head there this afternoon. I wondered if you and Xander might like any fresh produce."

"Well, sure! Isn't that nice of you?" My dad slipped his thumbs beneath his suspenders. "I haven't been to the market in years."

"Why don't you come with me?" she suggested. "I'm all by myself with the kids gone, and I'd love the company."

"I'd love to, honey, but I've got work to do."

"Go on, Dad," I said. "We're about done here. I'll finish up."

"You sure?"

"Positive. And since I picked you up this morning, why not just go with Veronica now?"

"I guess I could," he said. "Long as you're okay without me."

"I'm fine." Behind his back, I gave Veronica a thumbs up.

"Are you ready?" she asked him.

"I guess I am," he said, stuffing the trash from his lunch back into his reusable bag. "And maybe if we have time, we can stop into the barber shop. Gus always gets a proper shave on Tuesday afternoons, and we can see if he or Larry need anything from the market."

I was one hundred percent sure his motive for stopping into

the barber shop was more about Gus and Larry seeing him with Veronica than offering to pick up beans and squash for them. Hiding a smile, I waved goodbye as they headed back down the driveway, and Veronica lifted her sunglasses and winked at me over one shoulder.

My heart stumbled over its next few beats.

• • •

"So?" Xander said as soon as we hit the road. He'd left his SUV at my house so we could make the thirty-mile drive in my truck, which meant I was stuck with him for the next half hour.

"So what?"

"So how's it going with Veronica?"

"Fine."

"That's it? Fine?"

"Yep."

"Does that mean it's still on?"

"It means what it means."

He thumped my shoulder. "Don't be a dick. How'd it go in Chicago? She get her stuff?"

"No. But I did get to punch her ex in the face."

"Nice." Xander sounded impressed. "So now what?"

"Now she has to buy some new clothes."

"I mean, now what for her? Will she stay in Cherry Tree Harbor?"

"Just for the summer," I told him. "In the fall, she's going back to New York." As I said it, I realized how much I hated thinking about it.

"Why?"

"She misses her life there."

"You can't convince her to stay?"

I frowned. "Why would I do that?"

"I don't know. Because you're into her?"

"I've known her for less than a month, Xander. I shouldn't even be messing around with her."

"But you are. She's the first woman I've seen get under your skin."

"We're just friends." I rolled my shoulders, wishing he wasn't right. "We have a good time together. But when the kids come home on Sunday, it has to stop."

"Why?"

"Are you serious?" I shot him a look. "Because it's not okay to fuck the nanny—or anyone else—with the kids in the house."

"Is that what she thinks too?"

"Yes."

He shook his head. "I don't get it."

Of course he didn't. When Xander saw something he wanted, he always went for it. "Look, if I'd met her under different circumstances, maybe I'd go down that road, see where it led, but as it is, things between us end when the kids get back."

He was silent for a moment, the hum of the tires on the highway filling the cab. Then he asked, "You really think that?"

"Think what?"

"That if you'd met Veronica under different circumstances, like maybe if she'd just been a girl you saw one night at The Broken Spoke, you'd have gone down that road? Because I don't believe it."

"Why not?"

"I don't know. I just don't. Somehow you always have a reason why you can't ultimately do the thing that would make you happy."

I scowled. "Right now I can't think of a single fucking reason not to throw you out of my truck right here on the highway, and that would make me very happy."

Xander exhaled. "Never mind. Sorry I brought it up."

• • •

I was annoyed for the rest of the trip, giving short, dickish answers when Xander asked my opinion on anything at the lumber yard and barely nodding my approval at the gorgeous barn wood he chose for the bar, even though I was excited about working with it.

What he'd said had hit a nerve.

Of course I wanted to be happy. But you couldn't just go around doing whatever you wanted without thinking about the fallout—at least I couldn't. The one time I'd acted selfishly, carelessly, I'd gotten Sansa pregnant.

At the same time, I hated thinking about what it would be like not to have Veronica in my bed at night. See her naked. Touch her when I wanted to. I felt like a kid who'd just opened the best Christmas gift ever only to hear that he couldn't keep it.

By the time we loaded the lumber in my truck, my mood had soured to the point that Xander didn't even bother talking to me on the drive back to the house. We unloaded the wood in silence, and he uttered a quick thanks before he left.

I closed the garage door and headed for the house, wondering if I had time for a run before dinner. I felt like I needed to work off some of this tension or else I was going to take it out on Veronica.

She could tell something was up the moment I walked into the kitchen, which smelled so good my stomach growled.

"Uh oh," she said, wiping her hands on a dish towel. "What's wrong?"

"Nothing." I ditched my work boots by the back door and tossed my keys on the counter.

"Are you hungry? Dinner is ready."

"I was thinking about taking a run before dinner if I have time. Is that okay?"

"Sure." She glanced behind her at a pot on the stove, and I felt guilty.

"You can eat without me if you want."

"That's okay, I'll wait." She looked at me again and bit her lip. "Do you want company on your run, or would you rather be alone?"

"I'll run alone." I headed out of the room, but only made it as far as the stairs before stopping. Fucking Xander's voice was in my head again. Making me question things.

When I re-entered the kitchen, she was putting the lid back on the pot. "I changed my mind about company," I told her. "Do you still want to run with me?"

She turned around, her expression surprised. "Sure. But I'm not super fast or anything."

"I don't care. Come with me."

A smile lit up her face. "Give me five minutes to change."

• • •

She met me out front wearing her black yoga shorts and a Two Buckleys Home Improvement T-shirt, knotted at the waist.

I laughed when I saw it, my bad mood evaporating further. "Where'd that come from?"

"Your dresser," she said, giving me an impish grin. "I stole it yesterday morning, so I didn't have to walk back to the garage naked."

"Looks good on you."

She curtseyed. "Thank you."

"Ready to run?"

"Yes, but don't kill me, okay? My legs aren't as long as yours."

I eyed them with appreciation. "They're pretty damn close."

We jogged in silence, side by side, winding our way through hilly neighborhood streets and ending up down at the harbor.

After catching our breath at the crosswalk, we hurried across the street and without saying a word, we both headed for the seawall.

I took her hand as we carefully stepped across the rocks to the same big, flat boulders we'd sat on the day I hired her. The sun was low on the horizon, painting the sky with streaks of pink and orange. Seagulls swooped above us as I leaned back on my elbows and inhaled the lake air. The breeze cooled my hot skin.

"How was your afternoon with my dad?" I asked.

Veronica leaned back on her hands, her legs stretching out in front of her. "Lovely. He's so sweet."

"Did he show you off at the barber shop?"

She laughed. "Yes. Told all his friends he was on his first date in twenty years. We spent two hours at the farmers' market, then he insisted on taking me for a ride on the ferry. He told me all about growing up in Cherry Tree Harbor, all the changes he's seen, and how some things never change."

"Thanks for spending the afternoon with him. I know you didn't hire on to be an old man's nanny."

"It was honestly my pleasure. And you're paying me for this week even though the kids are gone, so I want to help you out."

"I appreciate it."

"We made a date to go back again next Tuesday—I want to bring the kids too. And did I tell you he wants to come to my dance class tomorrow night?"

I laughed. "No. I've been trying to get him to go to that senior mixer for years. He says no to me every time, but naturally, since *you'll* be there, he'll go."

She smiled. "Naturally."

We rested there for a couple more minutes, listening to the gulls overhead and the water splashing against the seawall. From the nearby Pier Inn restaurant, I smelled something cooking, and hunger began to gnaw at me. I was about to suggest we head back and eat dinner when she spoke up.

"So what was your bad mood about earlier?"

"Something Xander said that pissed me off."

"What did he say?"

I watched a sailboat glide into the harbor. "That I always seem to have a reason for not doing the thing that would make me happy."

She digested that for a moment. "Do you disagree?"

"Yes," I said, slightly irritated by the question. "I'm not unhappy. I mean, is my life perfect? No. But I'm doing the best I can with the cards I've been dealt."

She studied me for a moment, then looked out at the water. "Xander is really different than you. He's not as right as he thinks he is."

"What do you mean?"

"I mean, if he sees your sense of duty to people you love as a flaw in your character, he's wrong. It's part of what makes you, you. It's what makes you such a great dad and son and brother and friend. You put others first, and *that* makes you happy."

I looked over at her, wondering how she could know me so well in such a short time. "Thanks."

"But it also means you ignore a lot of your own needs, and I think that's why you get so uptight. It wouldn't kill you to put yourself first every now and again, even with family," she said. "Love isn't an obligation. It's a gift."

"Excuse me. Did you just call me uptight?" I leaned over and poked her shoulder.

"Yes, I did." She laughed. "But I'm doing my best to loosen up all your tight spots. Maybe I'll give you that massage this week."

"Maybe I'll let you."

She stood up and brushed off her butt. "I'm hungry. Should we go home and eat? I made orecchiette with bacon and summer squash that I got at the market."

I looked up at her from where I sat on the rock. "You should wear my shirt every day."

She beamed. "Yeah?"

"Yeah. I like it on you."

It made her look like mine.

Chapter 18

*T*he following morning, I was sitting in one of the Adirondack chairs in the yard with a cup of coffee when a text popped up from Austin.

My dad will not shut up about you.

Haha. What's he saying?

Just going on about how sweet you are, how pretty you are, how lucky it was that you showed up when you did. Basically he's in love.

It's mutual.

He told me I should take you out to a fancy restaurant while the kids are gone.

Oh really? And what did you say?

I told him I was already fucking you at home for free.

JERK.

Kidding. If you'd like to go out, we can. I just like being alone with you. I don't want to share.

I also don't want people talking.

It's fine. I don't need fancy restaurants. What I need are clothes. Any suggestions?

Lots of skimpy things. Maybe something see-through. Or those panties without a crotch. Might be tough to find in Cherry Tree Harbor.

That's not what I meant. What SHOPS should I go to? I want to buy local.

Oh. I have no idea. Ask Mabel?

Good idea.

I didn't expect Mabel to answer, so I was surprised when she picked up. "Hey, Veronica!"

"Hi!"

"I was just thinking about you. How are things going?"

"Great," I told her. "Really great. How's the dig?"

"Fantastic," she bubbled. "Are the kids in California?"

"Yes. They left on Saturday."

"Has my brother been a bear ever since? He's extra hard to live with when he's away from them."

"He's been okay," I said casually, although *extra hard* was accurate too, just not in the way she meant.

"So you're getting along?"

"Yes."

"Good. Austin can come off prickly, but once you get to know him, he really is sweet. He'd do anything for people he cares about."

"I can see that about him."

"I don't know how much he's told you, but he practically raised me and my brothers."

"He's told me a little," I said. "Sounds like he had to grow up fast after your mom died."

"Totally. Austin basically took over as a second parent back then, because my dad had to work so much to support us all. But my dad sort of returned the favor when the twins arrived."

"That's what it sounds like. I know you guys have been through some really hard times, but it's nice how close you all are."

"It is," Mabel said, emotion in her voice. "And Austin has been so strong and so supportive of every single one of us. I hope one day he does something for himself."

"Me too. I was asking him about starting his own furniture business."

"Good luck. I'm always on him about that, but he thinks my dad would be upset."

"Would he?"

"I mean, maybe. But he's a grown man. And he's a great father. I think he'd want to know Austin's true feelings." She sighed. "But my brother is not good at sharing his true feelings, which is probably why he's still single."

"He mentioned he doesn't date."

"Nope, the man lives like a monk."

Not this week, I thought.

"He says he doesn't have the time," Mabel went on, "and it's true he doesn't have much to spare. But sometimes I think that's just an excuse."

"An excuse for what?"

"He would *never* admit this, but I think he avoids relationships so he won't have to be real with someone."

"Maybe," I said, thinking that he'd actually been fairly real with me. "Has he always been that way?"

"As far as I can remember. Xander told me that even when our mom died, Austin never broke down. Ever. Our dad even told the boys it was okay to cry, but Austin refused."

A lump was swelling in my throat as I pictured a twelve-year-old boy with dark hair and big brown eyes holding his sadness inside because he didn't want anyone to see it. Did he feel like he'd have been letting someone down? His dad? His mom? Himself? "That hurts my heart," I said to Mabel.

"I know. Mine too." She exhaled. "And what sucks is that Austin would be a great boyfriend or husband, you know? He's so giving. And when he lets himself relax, he's a lot of fun."

Can confirm, I thought.

"But no woman I know wants to be with someone who keeps his feelings under lock and key."

"He does seem to keep some things bottled up," I said, recalling his words. *Certain emotions are kind of pointless.* "But once he warms up to you, he lets down his guard. I've seen it."

"See if you can get him to leave the house," Mabel encouraged with a laugh. "Take him on a play date. Go to dinner at The Pier Inn. It's my favorite restaurant in town. The food is great, and the view is amazing."

"I'll try," I said. "I was actually calling to see if you had any suggestions about where to go for some cute clothes. I can order some things online, but I'd like to shop local too."

She named several stores she liked in town, and I made notes in my phone. "Thank you," I said. "I appreciate it."

"No problem. Hey, don't tell Austin what I said about feelings, okay? He gets mad when I bug him about that stuff."

"No problem. I won't say a word."

After hanging up with her, I texted Austin again.

> Hey. I just talked to Mabel and she said I need to have dinner at The Pier Inn. Want to go with me?

> Meh.

> Don't be a stick in the mud. I'll make a reservation.

> But people will be there. I don't like people.

> I'll be there. You like me, don't you?

> Only when you're not trying to get me to do shit I don't want to do.

> Come on. Please?

> Fine. But you have to let me eat you for dessert.

> Deal.
> OMG
> Your dad better not be standing there reading your texts.

> I made him take an early lunch. He wasn't doing any work anyway. Just singing your praises.

> Are you sick of hearing about me?

> No. But I'm not productive when all I can think about is how you taste.
> And all the places on my body I want those red lips.
> And what I want to do to you when I get home.

My nipples tightened. I crossed my legs.

You're turning me on.

I'm turning myself on.

I think you should come home for lunch.

Fuck, I want to…

I'll serve your favorite meal.

Be right there.

• • •

When he arrived twenty minutes later, I was stretched out on my side on the dining room table, wearing just a black lace bra and matching panties.

He unlocked the back door and came striding through the kitchen, probably on his way upstairs. Spotting me, he stopped and stared. "Holy shit," he said. "I thought you'd be up in bed."

"Want me to move?"

"Don't you dare." He came toward me, and my heart began to pound. "I'm hot and sweaty."

"You're gorgeous."

"Come here." Standing at one end of the table, he grabbed one ankle and tugged me closer to him.

I rolled onto my back and let him pull my underwear off, then I propped myself up on my elbows and watched him push my knees apart. "Goddamn," he said, his eyes on fire.

"Hungry?" I teased.

"Starving. I'm going to devour everything on my plate and lick it clean." He bent down and stroked me with his tongue, one long, decadent sweep.

My stomach muscles tightened, and my legs began to tremble as I watched his head move between my thighs, his mouth slanting this way and that, his hands spread on the edge of the table. When he'd gotten his fill and had me arching and crying out so loud I would never be able to face the neighbors again, he yanked me to my feet, spun me around, and bent me forward over the table.

He placed a hand on my back. "Don't. Move."

I stayed right where I was as he hurried upstairs. He was back in less than fifteen seconds, and stood behind me once more.

I heard his belt buckle coming undone and rose up on my tiptoes, spreading my legs wider. I imagined him freeing his cock from his jeans and rolling on the condom, my core muscles clenching in anticipation.

Both of us moaned as he penetrated my body and began to move. I was already soaking wet, still sensitive from the orgasm he'd just given me. His hands gripped both my hips as he drove his thick, hard length inside me again and again. He was rough with me, the force of his thrusts rattling my bones, and I cried out with every powerful stroke. He was hitting some hidden spot deep within me, and my body tightened around him like a vise. My eyes watered. My legs hummed. I wished I had something to grab onto, but the table was wide, so all I could do was flatten my palms on its warm, wooden surface. Behind me, Austin's breaths grew more ragged, his pace more frantic, his fingers digging hard into my flesh until finally he stopped moving and buried himself deep, his cock throbbing rhythmically as my second climax ripped through me.

When it was over, Austin braced his hands on the table and kissed my back. "Thanks for lunch. What time is dinner?"

I laughed. "You have a *very* healthy appetite."

He pulled out and kissed my tailbone. "I hope that wasn't too rough."

"It wasn't. I liked it." I let him help me up and turned to face him. "Neil used to call me his teacup, and it always drove me nuts. I'm not some fragile, breakable thing."

"Teacup!" he scoffed. "Fuck that. You're more like…a beer mug."

I laughed. "A beer mug?"

"Yeah." He disappeared into the bathroom for a moment but kept talking. "Something sturdy and durable. I mean, you're pretty and all, but you can take a pounding."

"Is that a compliment?" Spying my underwear on the floor, I snagged it and tugged it on. When I turned around, Austin was standing there, ready to pull me into his arms.

"It was a compliment," he said, holding me close. "You know I think you're strong in every possible way. But I hope I didn't hurt you."

"You didn't." I looped my arms around his waist and tucked my head beneath his chin. His body was warm and smelled sweaty, but it was a good sweat—hard-work-in-the-sunshine sweat.

"I never want to hurt you." His voice was quiet but strong.

I closed my eyes. "You won't."

• • •

That afternoon, Austin texted me that Xander needed his help at the bar tearing out the old bathrooms and told me not to worry about making dinner—they were just going to grab sandwiches. He said he'd message me when he got home.

Since I had a little extra time, I walked down to the senior mixer, taught my dance class, and stayed around afterward chatting with some of people who'd attended. After arriving back at home, I made myself some boxed mac and cheese for dinner, but I ate it with a salad using veggies from the farmers' market, so I figured it all evened out. When I was done eating, I cleaned up the kitchen and went back to my apartment.

Around ten p.m., I took a shower and got ready for bed. In the bathroom mirror, I examined the bruises he'd left on my hips, surprised to find myself aroused by them.

But maybe I shouldn't have been surprised. Maybe it made perfect sense that I would like wearing the evidence of Austin's powerful desire for me, that they made me feel strong and sexy. Maybe it was part of reclaiming my body as my own—I could decide when pain felt good. I could decide that bruises were beautiful. I could decide to be a canvas for my own pleasure—and for his.

I checked my phone one last time before crawling into bed, trying not to feel disappointed that he hadn't texted or called. A glance out the window told me his truck wasn't in the driveway.

Get over it, I scolded myself. *It's just one night. It's just sex. Okay, maybe it's earth-shaking, mind-blowing, soul-shattering sex, but you went without it for twenty-nine years, so you can certainly handle going without it tonight.*

But we only had three nights left. What was I going to do when our time was up and I had to go without it forever?

Don't think about it.

I slammed my eyes shut, but I was still awake when I heard my phone vibrate. My hand shot out to grab it off the nightstand.

Hey. Sorry to text so late. Xander was fucking everything up and I had to fix things. You still awake?

Yes.

I'm getting in the shower. Want to keep me company?

Yes.

I'll leave the back door open.

Okay.

Hurry.
I've been hard for you all day.

• • •

The shower was running when I slipped inside the bathroom, the marble tiles cool beneath my bare feet. The shower door was steamed up, but the blurry shape of him behind it made my breath come faster. Eagerly, I stripped off my clothes.

He pushed the door open, and my heart careened at the sight of him—wet and muscular and, as promised, already hard.

"Hi," I said breathlessly.

"Hi, baby." He looked me over head to toe, then studied my hips. "Are those marks from me?"

"Yes."

"Fuck." His hands skimmed over them. "Do they hurt?"

"No."

His dark eyes smoldered. "Will you think I'm a dick if I tell you I like the way they look?"

I shook my head. "Will you think I'm crazy if I ask for more?"

"I think you're fucking perfect." Wrapping his arms around me, he sealed his mouth to mine as the hot water streamed down our bodies. His hands roamed freely, gliding easily over my wet skin, while his tongue stroked mine with possessive fervor. I worked my hands up and down the solid length of his erection as the steam rose around us.

He turned me to face the wall and pressed up tightly behind me, reaching between my legs with one hand and covering my breast with the other. I braced my hands on the tiles, which were rectangular, charcoal gray, and laid in a herringbone pattern. It was so cool, I was momentarily distracted. "Wow, this shower is gorgeous. Did you remodel this bathroom yourself?"

"Yes."

"I *love* it."

He slipped a finger inside me. "Can we please talk about that later?"

"Sorry—yes." But *god,* it turned me on that he was so talented. So good with his hands.

His lips moved down the side of my throat as his fingers rubbed my clit. He sucked hard on the spot where my neck sloped toward my shoulder. "I want to leave a mark right here," he told me, his voice low and gravelly.

"Yes," I whispered, even though I knew it would be visible in most of my tops. "I want it where I can see it."

With his mouth and tongue working on my neck, he used his hands to deliver an orgasm that turned my bones to jelly. His name was still echoing off the tiles when he turned me to face him. He fisted his cock with one hand while he pinned me back against the wall with his other hand on my throat, his thumb stroking the bruise he'd left with his mouth.

"Fuck," he rasped, his eyes traveling over my skin. "You're so damn beautiful."

Held immobile against the wall, I watched with wide eyes and heavy breaths as he pumped his hand up and down his shaft, the muscles in his arm working, his abs flexing. His chest rose and fell rapidly, and his jaw was clenched. "I could come just looking at you."

"Do it," I whispered. "Let me watch. Put it on me."

"Is that what you want?" he growled. "My cum on your skin?"

"Yes," I panted. "You can mark me like no one else ever has."

Within seconds, he was ejaculating onto my stomach in quick, hot bursts. Then he took his hand and rubbed it into my skin— over my breasts, down my ribcage, and over the bruises on one hip.

Finally, he let go of my neck and pulled me toward him, wrapping me in his arms. He didn't say anything right away, and it took a minute for his breathing to slow. I felt his heartbeat against my chest.

"There's something about you that brings out the caveman in me," he said.

"You're not always like this?" I asked.

"Never."

"Good." I smiled, pleased that this was a side of him he'd never shared with anyone else. "Neither am I."

"Let me do something nice for you."

"Like what?"

"Like…wash your hair."

I leaned back and looked up at him in surprise. "You want to wash my hair?"

"Yes. I fucking love your hair. I remember the day we met, when you came back after taking your hair down, I couldn't stop staring at you."

"I believe you were *scowling* at me."

"That was only because I was mad at you for being so beautiful. For making me want you." He let me go and reached for his shampoo bottle. "But I won't hold a grudge if you let me wash your hair."

"With your man shampoo? Is my hair going to smell like wood chips and baseball glove?"

"It's all I have," he said apologetically. "But I am very good at washing hair. I won't get soap in your eyes."

I laughed. "Okay. Then it's a deal."

. . .

Later, when the lights were off and I was tucked against his side in bed, he told me he'd made a dinner reservation for Saturday night at The Pier Inn.

"You did?" I asked, surprised.

"Yes. There was no way we were going to get in so soon without a little help. My cousin Delilah is a manager there. She reserved a table for us at eight."

"That's so nice," I said. "Will I get to meet her?"

"If she's there, I can introduce you."

I smiled. "I'm excited. I want to get something new to wear."

"It's not fancy or anything."

"Hush." I swatted his bare chest. "I want something new for our date night." As soon as I said it, I was sorry. "I didn't mean date night like *date* date," I said quickly. "I know it's not a date. We're not dating. It's just dinner with a friend."

"Relax," he said. "It doesn't matter what we call it. People are going to see us and make up stories anyway."

"Really?"

"Definitely. By Sunday morning, everyone will know Austin Buckley took his runaway bride nanny to dinner, and there will be half a dozen rumors about what it *means*."

I giggled. "What will they think it means?"

"Well, someone will swear to god they saw a ring on your finger, so it probably means we're secretly engaged. Someone else will say they saw us sitting at the seawall at sunset, so you're definitely pregnant. And someone else will say they heard from their sister's best friend's cousin's ex's dog groomer, who lives in Chicago, that I attacked your former fiancé with an axe right on Michigan Avenue."

"Those are some *serious* rumors."

"Yeah, well, Cherry Tree Harbor is a small town with two specialties: fudge and gossip."

"But it's so charming! Everyone I've met has been so kind. It must have been a wonderful place to grow up. And it's a great place to raise a family."

"It is." He was quiet for a moment. "Do you want kids?"

"Yes. I've always had this dream about belonging to a big family. I was so lonely growing up, so envious of kids at school who had lots of brothers and sisters and cousins around."

His hand began to stroke my shoulder, soothing and sweet.

"But pursuing that dream wasn't as easy as pursuing dance. It would have meant handing over a part of me I was used to keeping to myself. My mom always said, *Guard your heart like it's your home. Be careful who you let in.* I did a good job of that."

Austin didn't say anything, but his hand continued to caress me.

"I think that's part of why I agreed to marry Neil. I had this idea that being part of a family like his would fulfill that yearning I'd had as a child." My fingers played with the hair on his chest. "But it backfired. His family was awful. I didn't fit in, they never accepted me, and I ended up feeling unwanted all over again."

"What do you mean all over again?" Austin asked quietly. "Who didn't want you before?"

"Well—my father," I said. "And my grandparents. The only other family I had besides my mom."

His hand stilled for a moment.

"That probably sounds stupid," I said quickly. "Because it's not like they *knew* me and rejected me. It wasn't personal. They just didn't want me in the first place. But it...it *felt* personal. I always wondered what was wrong with me."

"There is nothing wrong with you." He pulled me in a little tighter and kissed my head. "There never was."

"Except that I can't seem to get a relationship right, which is eventually a problem if you want a family."

"And yet somehow I managed it," he said wryly.

I smiled. "You did. But I'd like to share a life with someone. I just need to get better at trusting people not to hurt me. Or at least better at choosing who to put my trust in." I picked up my head and looked at him. "I can't depend on you to punch every guy that hurts me."

"I would," he said seriously, tucking my damp hair behind my ear. "Honestly, I fucking would."

My heart liked that a little too much.

"God, I didn't mean to dump all this on you." I put my head down again. "I'm sorry."

"It's okay. I'm glad you did. I like knowing things about you."

"I like knowing things about you too. You just don't talk as much as I do."

"*No one* talks as much as you do. Not even Mabel."

"Okay, but tell me *one thing* about yourself."

"Like what?"

I thought for a moment. "Who did you admire most growing up?"

"My dad," he said without missing a beat. "He was always the strongest person I ever knew. I wanted to be like him."

"You are," I said softly.

He kissed my head again and sniffed. "You're right—your hair totally smells like wood chips and baseball glove."

Laughing, I put my arms across his chest and held him tight.

But my smile faded when I remembered that we only had three more nights together.

I didn't want this to end.

Chapter 19

AUSTIN

*L*ate Thursday afternoon, Xander sent me a text asking if I'd come help him paint at the bar. Before I answered him, I messaged Veronica.

> Hey. My brother is asking for help again at the bar after work. Should I tell him to piss off?

> No! Why would you do that?

> Because I'd rather be with you.

> Aww. How about I come up and help? I could bring snacks.

> You don't have to.

> I don't mind! What are you working on?

Painting.

Perfect! I've got lots of experience painting NYC apartments. Got any old shirts lying around I could wear?

Bottom left side dresser drawer. Take anything you want.

Okay. See you soon!

Given the haphazard way Veronica slapped color on the walls, I wasn't sure how true her statement about experience was, but she looked adorable in one of my old shirts and ball caps, her blond ponytail sticking out the back. We had music on, and she was definitely doing more dancing than painting, but just having her there put me in a good mood.

At one point, we ran out of tape, and she volunteered to run to the hardware store to pick some up.

"How are the kids doing?" Xander asked when we were alone.

"Good," I said, rolling on the navy blue paint. "We FaceTimed yesterday. They're having a ball."

"Back Sunday?"

"Yep." I was torn every time I thought about their return. I missed them like crazy and couldn't wait to have them home again, but I would miss being able to spend time with Veronica too, and we only had three nights left. "Hey, can I borrow your SUV Saturday night?"

"Sure. What for?"

"I'm taking Veronica to dinner at The Pier Inn. I thought it might be nice not to drive the truck."

"Ooooh. A date."

I frowned. "It's not a date."

"Oh, sorry, I must have misheard. I thought you said you were taking Veronica to dinner at The Pier Inn—because that's a date."

I ignored his attempt to pick a fight. "I'll return it on Sunday."

"No rush," he said. "So I take it things are good with you guys?"

Things were better than good. I was having more fun with Veronica than I'd ever had with anyone. "Yeah."

"Definitely seems cozy between you."

"What do you mean?"

"I mean you guys just seem really comfortable together. This is the most I've heard you laugh in years."

I put the roller in the paint tray and worked it back and forth.

"And you're definitely more relaxed, but I'm going to assume it's not because you're getting more sleep."

"Safe assumption."

"You give her that hickey on her neck?"

"Fuck off."

He burst out laughing. "Don't let Dad see it. I think he might be in love with her."

I cracked a smile. "I know."

"He said her fiancé must have been a complete idiot to let her go."

"He was."

"Still planning on ending it when the kids get back?"

I kept my mouth shut.

My brother shook his head as he rolled paint onto the wall. "I'm not even gonna say it."

• • •

We ended up staying at the bar later than I wanted to, and by the time we got home, we were starving.

"I'll just make us something really quick," I said to Veronica.

"I've got it," she told me. "Why don't you go take your shower and when you come down it will be ready?"

"Sounds good." Even though I was dirty from work and probably smelled like sweat and primer, I couldn't resist wrapping my arms around her. "Thanks for everything you're doing this week. It's above and beyond what I deserve."

"Not true." She locked her arms around my waist and looked up at me. "If it weren't for you, I'd be singing for my supper on some street corner, and let me tell you, *no one* wants that."

I dropped a kiss on her lips. "I wish there was more I could do for you."

"I can't imagine what that would be," she said. "You've given me a job, a place to live, a little taste of family life. I feel like I've been adopted at age twenty-nine! I've got a dad, a brother, a sister…"

"You should just change your name to Buckley," I teased.

"Veronica Buckley." She laughed. "It has a nice ring to it!"

"Veronica Buckley." As I said the name, I realized that's what her name would be if we were married. "Wait a minute. Did I just accidentally propose?"

She tilted her head. "You know what? I think you did. But since I am not currently interested in matrimony, I will have to respectfully decline. I mean, why buy the cow when you can get the milk for free?"

Laughing, I let go of her and headed for the stairs, the name *Veronica Buckley* still lingering in my head.

It was official. I was losing my mind.

• • •

"I made my specialty," she said, setting two plates on the table. "Fried bologna sandwiches."

I half-groaned, half-laughed. "You didn't."

"I did." She brought in two cold beers, then sat down across from me and picked up her sandwich. "I haven't had one of these in ages. And this is *much* better than the ones I used to make as a kid. This is *artisanal bologna*, the butcher told me, *premium meat* from Yale, Michigan with a cult following. This bologna has its own festival!"

"Oh yeah?" I picked up my sandwich and took a bite.

"Yes. And I got fresh buns from the bakery, and that's lettuce and tomato and homemade mustard from the farmers' market. Nothing but the best for you." She took a bite too, chewing with exaggerated relish.

I was amazed by how good it actually tasted. "Fuck. It's delicious."

"Told ya." She took another bite. "Did you talk to the kids today?"

"Yeah, I called them earlier. They said to tell you hello." I grinned. "Apparently, they snuck their new tap shoes into their suitcases. They've been showing off their dancing."

Her face lit up. "I love that. So there's no dance studio around here anymore? Someone told me there used to be one. I think the kids would enjoy a real tap class in a studio."

"But they wouldn't have you for a teacher."

"That's true."

"Have you ever thought about owning your own studio?"

"Here and there. I do like teaching. But I'm actually waiting to hear back about a job this fall."

"Are you?" Tension crept into my neck and shoulders. "With the Rockettes?"

"No. As an assistant to the lead choreographer for a show that's opening on Broadway."

"So you wouldn't be performing?"

"Well, no, but it would be a fantastic opportunity. It would see me through the next six months until I can re-audition for the Rockettes. Those auditions aren't until March, and if I don't have to bartend or waitress in the meantime, I'd be thankful."

While she talked, I finished my sandwich without really tasting it.

"I don't have a lot of details yet, but my friend Morgan passed my new number along to the choreographer. He's actually someone I used to know pretty well, so I think I'd have a good chance of getting the job."

"Did you date him?" The words were out before I could stop myself, but I hated how they made me sound. Even worse? I hated the idea that she'd been intimate with someone else. Anyone else.

She looked surprised. "No. He's a teacher, and I took his class a lot. He's gay, actually."

"Oh." I exhaled, shaking my head. "Sorry. That question was out of line."

"It's okay."

"No, it isn't. It's not my business who you date." I got up and took my empty plate to the sink, but instead of putting it in the dishwasher, I left it there and stared out the kitchen window into the dark, my hands on the edge of the counter.

This was fucking stupid. I had no right to be angry that she would leave here and go on with her life—her bright, exciting life in the big city with its stages and applause and guys in fancy suits that lived in penthouse apartments. If she wanted that, that's what she should have.

Veronica joined me in the kitchen a moment later. She placed her dishes on the counter and leaned back against it. "Hey."

"Hey."

"Did you know that when you get jealous, two little lines appear between your eyes?"

"I'm not jealous." Damn those lines. I tried to relax my face.

"Yes, you are." She bumped her hip against mine. "But I like it."

I looked over at her. She was so fucking cute in my shirt and hat. "You gonna give my clothes back when you go to New York?"

She tugged the bill of the cap down. "Nope. You want your stuff back, you'll have to fight me for it."

"Deal." I grabbed her and tossed her over my shoulder, heading for the stairs. She kicked and squealed and squirmed, batting my ass with her hands and calling me a brute.

Up in my bedroom, I tossed her onto the mattress before snatching the hat off her head and tossing it aside. "You just gonna let me win?"

Giggling, she rolled over and tried to scramble off the bed, but I had her pinned to the mattress in three seconds flat, my body sprawled over hers. "Let me up," she begged. "This was *not* a fair fight. I needed a head start."

"I never said I fought fair." I pushed her hair aside from her neck and tugged down the back of the shirt she wore, sealing my mouth to her skin.

Was it unfair of me to leave another mark that could be seen so easily? Probably.

But I didn't care.

And she didn't stop me.

Chapter 20

VERONICA

*O*n Friday, I decided to follow through on the threat to give Austin a massage.

You. Tonight. My place. No argument.

Are you going to have whips and chains?

No. I'm going to have candles and massage oil.

I think I'd prefer the whips and chains.

Tough. I've listened to you gripe about sore muscles for weeks now, and I want to help.

Will you be naked?

If I say yes, will you agree to let me do it?

It would definitely sway me in that direction.

Then yes. I'll be naked.

Look for me about 7.

I'll be waiting.

And I get to be the boss tonight.

We'll see about that.

• • •

That afternoon, I gave Morgan a call.

"I thought you were coming to visit me," she whined. "You said the kids were going somewhere and you'd have days off."

"I said *maybe* I would come to visit you," I corrected with a laugh. I put her on speaker and set the phone aside so I could fold my laundry. "But the tickets were expensive, and I really need to save my money."

"So what have you been doing while they're gone?" she asked.

"Oh, this and that," I said airily, pulling Austin's TWO BUCKLEYS T-shirt from the basket. It made me smile.

"Does 'this and that' include your hot boss?"

"It might."

She gasped. "Details!"

"We're having fun."

"But like how *much* fun?"

"*All* the fun," I confessed.

"Every night?"

"Every night, every room of the house, every which way you can imagine." I folded my yoga shorts.

Morgan groaned loudly. "God, I'm so jealous. I remember those days. So is he good?"

"So good I can't describe it."

"Body?"

I closed my eyes, picturing him. "Ten out of ten."

"Package?"

"Long, strong, and he knows how to use it."

"Thank god. Nothing worse than a guy who's hung but helpless."

I snorted, matching a pair of socks. "For real."

"So are you guys dating or just messing around?"

"Just messing around," I said. "It has to end when the kids come back."

"When is that?"

"Sunday." I tried to sound cool and casual, which was how I wanted to feel.

"In *two days*? Jeez. No wonder you guys are going at it like rabbits. That stinks."

"No, I think it's better."

"Why?"

"Because I like that we both know the score. It feels even." I folded my sports bra. "No one will be blindsided by the end."

"If you guys have such good chemistry, why let it end?"

"That would get awkward, because of the kids. I've still got another month here, and I need this job. If something went wrong with Austin—"

"But what if something goes *right*?"

"He's not really a dater," I said, avoiding the question. "He's told me several times he likes being single. He's one of those guys who doesn't do feelings. Not in an asshole way, just in a sort of businesslike way. Like, he's here to deliver the orgasms, get the signature, and get back in the truck."

She laughed. "Okay, but what if—"

"There are no what ifs, Morgan," I said, getting up from the couch and wandering over to the window. "The boundaries were established from the start. I flat out told him I was not looking for a relationship. It's casual. Temporary. Just for fun."

"If you say so."

"I say so," I told her, wishing I *felt* so. "I'm just going a little wild because I was all cooped up for a year. I'm enjoying my freedom. And my orgasms."

She laughed. "Sounds like it. Well, good for you."

"And besides, no use in carrying on when I'm leaving in a month anyway. It would just be delaying the inevitable. Better now than later."

"That's true, I suppose. Hey, did Scott Blackstone reach out yet?"

"No, is he going to?"

"He told Jake he was. Jake said he was super excited to hear you were interested in the job."

"Oh, that's awesome. Please thank Jake for me."

"I will, and let me know as soon as you hear from Scott. Next, we need to find you a place to live! Let me ask around—I'm still close with a lot of the current Rockettes and maybe someone is looking to sublet or share a two-bedroom or something."

"Thanks, Morgan. I appreciate it."

We hung up, and I put my clean clothes away, trying to get excited about moving back to Manhattan.

But all I could think of was leaving here. Leaving him. Somehow New York City was losing its appeal.

I repeated the words I'd said to Morgan.

It's not like that with us. It's casual. Temporary. Just for fun. We are not dating, and there are no feelings involved.

And when my heart tried to argue, I repeated them again.

And again.

And again.

• • •

When he knocked on my door about quarter after seven, I was ready. The shades were drawn, the lights were out, and a dozen candles flickered in the dark. Dreamy spa music played on my phone in the bedroom, and I'd covered the bed with towels. On the nightstand was the fancy massage oil I'd splurged on at a high-end Main Street boutique, which offset the dollar-store candles.

I opened the door wearing a sundress, and he immediately frowned. "You said—"

"Relax," I said, bringing him inside. He wore only his sweatpants, and his hair was damp from the shower. I could smell his man shampoo. "Come here."

Leading him into the bedroom, I gestured toward the bed. "Okay, take off your pants and lie down."

He gamely doffed his sweats and climbed onto the bed, stretching out on his back, hands behind his head. "My body is ready."

"Turn over. Lie on your stomach."

"But my fun bits are on the front."

"Do it, please." I gave him a stern look.

"Take off the dress first."

Sighing, I pulled the dress over my head and tossed it aside, then shimmied out of my underwear. "There."

"Well, now I don't want to turn over. I want to look at you." His eyes swept over my skin, which bore fading marks from the last two nights, and his cock began to swell.

I put my hands on my hips. "Don't make me get rough with you, Buckley."

He groaned and flopped over onto his stomach. "I'm giving you five minutes. And then *I'm* getting rough with *you*."

"Shhhh. Just relax." Grabbing the bottle of massage oil from the nightstand, I straddled his hips, sitting on his ass.

He moaned. "This is just cruel."

"Hush. Put your hands by your head." I rubbed some oil into my hands and started with light strokes up and down either side of his spine, between his shoulder blades, and on the back of his neck.

"That actually feels pretty good," he said. "Much better than the revenge massage."

"This is just the warm-up," I informed him. "I'm about to get mean."

Increasing the pressure, I worked all the muscles of his back and shoulders and neck, then moved on to his arms. He groaned and cursed me out a few times, especially when I used my elbows, but I could feel the knots loosening up. I scooted down and massaged his legs and feet, admiring the solid thighs and calves. I let my hands glide up his inner thighs and get close to his fun bits, but I was careful not to touch them. I didn't want him to get turned on and take over—I had a plan.

I saved his butt for last and had a good time kneading the firm flesh with my hands, enjoying the string of curses he muttered. "Okay, now you can turn over," I told him.

He rolled onto his back. "Are you going to straddle me again?"

"In a minute." I started with his legs, moving from ankle to thigh. His cock was hard, and it jumped when my hands came near it. Finally, I knelt with a leg on either side of his thighs and took it in my hands, which were warm and slick with the oil.

"Fuck, yeah," he said, reaching for my breasts.

I pushed his hands away. "No touching, sir."

"You didn't mention that rule before."

"Just lie back, please. You're going to like this." I moved up, straddling his torso to rub his pecs and deltoids and biceps. "Doesn't that feel good?"

"Yes," he said, scowling. "It does, but I'm dying to get my

hands on you."

"I know. You love your hands on me. And your mouth. Look at the marks you've made."

Once more, he admired the bruises lingering on my skin. "I fucking love them."

"Now it's my turn." I crawled over to the nightstand, set the massage oil down and grabbed my red lipstick. Then I straddled his hips, trapping his cock between us.

He watched as I applied the lipstick, slowly painting my mouth with my favorite shade of red.

"Fuck me," he growled, gripping my thighs.

"Eventually," I said. "We should discuss consent."

"Like permission?"

"Yes. Do I have your permission to leave marks on your skin?"

"You have my permission to do any fucking thing you want."

"Good." I started with his neck and worked my way down, leaving a kiss print on his throat, his collarbone, his shoulder, his tattooed bicep, his nipple, which I licked and sucked, aroused by the way it hardened against my tongue. I teased the other one with my fingertips, and his breathing grew heavy and hard.

Moving down his legs, I left kiss marks on his ridged abs, his hip bones, both sides of his V lines, which I traced with my tongue. Then I took a moment to reapply, gliding the color on and rubbing my lips together. His body already had the power to turn me on, but those kiss marks on his skin had my blood running *hot*.

I lowered my head and pressed my lips to either side of his cock, getting just close enough to torture him. Then lower, on his thighs. Then just above the spot where the tip rested, glistening and smooth.

"Veronica." A plea. A rebuke. A prayer.

I smiled and gave him what he wanted, taking his erection in my hand and positioning it in front of my mouth. Then I slid my lips down his rigid length, taking him as deep as I could. When I couldn't fit another inch of him in my mouth, I contracted my lips as well as I could, then slowly lifted my head, squeezing his shaft along the way, wanting to leave rings of Don't F*ck With Me red in my wake. He grunted and cursed, his hands fisting in the towels on the bed.

When I got to the top, I pressed a kiss to the tip and looked at what I'd done. "A masterpiece," I said. "A work of art."

"I need to fuck you. Right now."

But I bent my head and took him deep once more, bobbing my head in a steady rhythm, rubbing my painted lips up and down his cock. He pulsed once in my mouth, and I tasted him on my tongue.

"That's it." Bolting upright, he hooked me beneath the arms and dragged me up his body. "I want you to ride it. Now."

"So much for me getting to be the boss." But I reached into the nightstand drawer for a condom.

"I'll let you be on top. That's the compromise."

He watched as I rolled the condom on, his entire body radiating impatience. When I positioned him between my legs, he gripped my hips, moaning as I sank down, inch by inch. When he was sheathed inside me, I went still for a moment, my hands on his chest, my eyes closing, giving my body a moment to adjust to being invaded so deeply and fully.

Then I started to move—slow, languorous rocking motions in time to a lazy beat. He fastened his mouth to one breast, each pull resonating deep within me. Cradling his head in my hands, I circled my hips a little faster, feeling him grow harder inside me, my need for release spiraling higher. But even as all my muscles tightened, my body felt free and easy and loose. I was heat, I was golden, I was liquid, I was passion. I was motion, I was friction, I was rhythm, I was desire.

And I was the object of *his* desire. I was wanted. I was craved.

Beneath his hands, my skin caught fire. Beneath his mouth, my body begged for more. I rode him with shameless abandon, tugging his hair, scratching his back, clutching his shoulders. I took what I wanted, what I needed, reveling in the way my core was tightening around him, in the way he drove into me, in the way our bodies moved in perfect harmony.

"Come for me," he growled, barely taking his mouth from my breast. "I want to feel your pussy come on all those marks you left."

His words pushed me over the edge, and my climax tore through me, my body clenching around him again and again. He came immediately after I did, his cock throbbing within my fluttering walls. It was heavenly perfection, as if we'd been made for each other. How was anyone else ever going to measure up?

Don't think about that, I warned myself as I caught my breath.

Austin fell back and took me with him, so my head rested on his chest. His arms came around me and his heart thundered in my ear. I closed my eyes and listened to its rhythm slow.

"So was the massage just an excuse to put those kiss marks all over me?"

"No. But I can't say I didn't enjoy it. Did you?"

"Yes. But you can never put on lipstick in front of me again, because I will immediately get a hard-on."

I smiled. "Good to know."

• • •

We slept at my apartment. Saturday morning, Austin was gone when I woke up. I reached for my phone and saw he'd texted.

> Didn't want to wake you. Working with my dad today, then running a few errands. I'll call you later.

> My shoulder and neck feel better than they have in months, so thank you for that.

And thank you for this.

The next thing he'd sent was a photo of his chest—his collarbone still wore the kiss mark I'd put there last night. It made me smile.

I washed the rest of them off in the shower this morning. DAMN that stuff is hard to remove. But I couldn't resist leaving this one alone.

I'm glad. I like thinking about it.

And about you.

Must be why I'm always doing it.

After I hit send, I wondered if that was too much. We didn't really message mushy stuff to each other, just logistics and sometimes dirty things. Maybe I was overthinking it.

But I couldn't help comparing the experience of receiving his photo to the last time a guy had sent me one—Neil's wedding-day dick pic. I shook my head. That one made my stomach turn. This one made my heart flutter.

I lay back in bed, draping an arm over my forehead. If I'd met Austin at another time in my life, or in his life, could things have been different between us? I couldn't imagine when that might have been, since I was only twenty-two when he'd become a father.

We'd never really stood a chance.

• • •

That afternoon, I ran into Ari at the salon, where I'd lucked out with an appointment to get my nails done last-minute. She'd just gotten a haircut and highlights.

"You look fabulous," I told her as we left the salon together. "I hope you have a hot date tonight."

"I do—with my Kindle." She laughed. "We get hot and steamy on my couch every Saturday night. I light a candle, open some wine…book boyfriends never let me down. Hey, you want to grab coffee or something?" She tossed her mahogany waves over one shoulder. "I don't want to waste this hair entirely."

"Sure," I said. "I have some time."

We headed up the block toward a place called L'Arbre Croche Café. "What are you up to tonight?" she asked.

"Austin and I are going to dinner at The Pier Inn."

Her eyebrows shot up. "Austin Buckley?"

I laughed. "Yes."

"So are you two…" She trailed off dramatically.

"We're just friends."

"Austin's never taken any other friends to dinner at The Pier Inn," she said, elbowing me.

"I'm sure he has."

She shook her head. "This is a small town. And Austin is one of its most eligible bachelors. Trust me—I'd have heard about it. The man doesn't date."

"He's mentioned that a few times."

We reached the café, and she pulled the door open. "Mabel is always giving him shit about it."

After placing orders at the counter, we moved toward the pickup station. "You and Mabel have been friends a long time, huh?"

"Oh, yeah. For as long as I can remember. If we weren't at her house, we were at my house. My mom was really close to her mom," she explained. "So my parents were always trying to help out. Mr. Buckley had his hands full—although Austin did a lot too."

"That's what I hear." We picked up our drinks and moved to a table by the window.

"When he wasn't working, he was doing something for one of the other kids. It had to be frustrating to see all his friends goofing off or going out when he had responsibilities."

"Yeah."

"He'd take it out on Xander. Those two used to beat the crap out of each other." Ari shook her head. "But if anyone *else* messed with Xander, Austin would be the first to defend him, and vice versa."

I nodded and sipped my cold brew. "They're such a close family. I hope I get a chance to meet the other siblings."

"Devlin doesn't get home too often. Dash usually honors everyone with his presence around the holidays." She rolled her eyes.

"Not a fan?" I asked.

"He just gets on my nerves," she said with a shrug. But the way her cheeks were suddenly painted raspberry-pink told me there was probably history there.

"Do I sense a crush?"

The raspberry turned to crimson. "No," she said emphatically. "He's like an older brother to me. And he treats me like another little sister. He always has."

Oh, there was a crush all right. But I let it go for now. "So let me ask you this. When you guys were all growing up, did Austin ever have a serious girlfriend?"

She exhaled and looked out the window for a moment, like she had to think hard. "Not that I recall. But Mabel and I were a lot younger. When he was in high school, we were still pretty little. I do know that once the twins arrived, he never dated anyone around here. The town biddies are always trying to set him up— my mother has tried to get him to take every single one of my cousins out—but he just doesn't do it. If he didn't have those kids, I might think he wasn't that into women."

"He's definitely into women," I confirmed without thinking.

Her eyes met mine and widened like full moons. "You sound very certain of that. Almost like you had inside information."

Heat crept up my neck and into my face.

"And now you're blushing," she pointed out. She sipped on her straw, waiting for me to say more.

"Uh…" I tried to think of a way to cover for myself, but the truth was that I was dying to talk about this with someone who knew Austin. Could I trust Ari? "So this is a bit delicate."

"I am the soul of discretion. You can ask Mabel—I was one thousand percent the better secret-keeper between the two of us."

I hesitated. Was this okay? I mean, Xander knew, right? And Ari was like family. "Okay, but this really needs to stay between us."

She crossed her heart.

"So ever since I met Austin, there's been this…"

"Tension between you," Ari said with a nod. "I saw it the day you came in for breakfast. And *everyone* saw it at The Broken Spoke."

"Were you there that night?" I couldn't remember seeing her.

She shook her head. "I didn't need to be. Small town. Go on."

"Okay. So we sort of agreed that it would be inappropriate to act on it once he hired me, but that line grew a little fuzzy once the kids left for California."

"And by fuzzy you mean it disappeared entirely."

I snapped my fingers. "Like *that.*"

"So?" Her eyes danced. "How was it?"

"So good you wouldn't believe me if I told you." I took a breath. "So good I don't want it to stop."

"Why would it stop?"

"Because the kids are coming home. And we agreed from the

get-go that was the finish line."

Ari tilted her head. "Have you talked about it since?"

"Not really." I shook the ice around in my cup. "I can't bring myself to ask him what he's thinking."

"Why not?"

My fear of rejection seemed like a lot to get into right now. "I'm just worried that the answer won't be what I want it to be."

"I get that," she said. "It's scary to put yourself out there, especially if you laid out the parameters beforehand."

"We did. That's exactly it—we did. I'm afraid that he might get upset with me for trying to change the rules. And we'd have to sneak around behind the kids' backs. And I'm leaving in a month anyway, you know?"

Ari thought for a moment. "Do you *have* to leave in a month?"

"Yes. The nanny job is over mid-August. I'm going back to New York."

"You have a job lined up already?"

"I'm working on it."

"I'm just wondering if there was a way you could stay here. Find a different job."

"And live where?"

She shrugged. "Over Austin's garage."

I shook my head. "No. I can't suggest that. It's way too much." And I would rather die than see the look on Austin's face as he tried to let me down easy, or worse, agreed to let me stay even though he didn't really want me to because he thought it was the right thing to do. What if he said yes because of his sense of duty? What if he felt obligated to say yes because he promised he'd never hurt me, but he didn't really want me to stick around?

My skin started to prickle. My heart began to pound. Suddenly I felt like I couldn't breathe, and little gray dots began to swim before my eyes. A siren went off in my head.

"Hey, are you okay?" Ari asked.

I refocused on her concerned face. "What?"

"You suddenly turned white."

"Oh, sorry." Closing my eyes, I inhaled and exhaled. "Just a little panic attack."

"Need some air? Want to go outside?"

"Yeah, maybe."

"Come on." We got up from the table and she took my arm, leading me back out into the sunshine.

I gulped several breaths of fresh summer air—fudge. The lake. The baskets of fragrant flowers hanging off each streetlamp on Main Street. Gradually, my pulse decelerated, and my skin stopped tingling.

"Better?" she asked.

"Better."

"I'm sorry for upsetting you. I didn't mean to."

I shook my head. "It's not you. Believe me, it's nothing I haven't thought about, I just can't face my fears enough to do it. We've only known each other for a few weeks. It seems ludicrous to suggest that what we have might be worth upending our lives for."

"Well, I don't know." She smiled. "Have you ever heard the story about Mr. and Mrs. Buckley?"

"Yes. Austin told me."

"So it *can* happen quickly. And a man can swear up and down he's never going to fall in love, but the right woman comes along, and boom—he burns down a city for her."

I laughed ruefully. "I think you've been out with too many book boyfriends."

She sighed heavily. "I know. It's a problem."

• • •

Back at home, I got ready for our not-a-date, telling myself just to relax and have a good time tonight. Not to think about tomorrow. Not to think about leaving him. Not to think about loving him.

One final, glorious night before the curtain came down.

Chapter 21

*A*t quarter to eight Saturday night, I walked up the garage stairs to knock on Veronica's door.

While I waited for her to answer, I straightened my tie and smoothed my freshly cut hair. The suit might have been overkill, but I couldn't help wanting to impress her. Every day, she saw me in dirty jeans and sweaty work shirts. Maybe I didn't have a closet full of bespoke suits, but I wanted to show her I could clean up nice.

She pulled the door open and I lost my breath.

My eyes wandered from the blond hair piled on top of her head to the diamonds twinkling in her ears to the blue strapless dress to the high-heeled shoes. The scent of her perfume hit me, and my knees nearly buckled. "Wow. You look gorgeous."

She smiled, and my heart skipped a few beats. "Thank you. I bought a new dress." She twirled around. "Do you like it?"

"I love it. The color matches your eyes."

"You look very handsome. That suit on you is…" She kissed her fingertips like a chef. "Perfection."

"Thank you."

"But you didn't have to come up and get me, silly," she chided. "You could have just texted. I'd have come down."

"I didn't mind. Are you ready?"

"I am." She pulled the door shut behind her. "Let's go."

I took her arm as we went down the steps. "Are those new earrings? I've never seen you wear them before."

She stopped halfway down the stairs and looked at me, her expression worried. "I wasn't sure if I should wear them. They were a birthday gift from Neil. But I literally have no jewelry that wasn't from him, and I wanted to look pretty tonight."

"You don't need diamonds to be the most beautiful woman in the room."

Her smile returned. "Thank you. Want me to take them off?"

"No." What I wanted was to be the one that could give her that kind of gift. I hadn't even thought to bring her flowers. "It's okay."

"You know what? Give me a minute. I want to take them off."

I shook my head. "You don't have to do it for me."

"It's for me." She kissed my cheek, then hurried up the stairs and disappeared into the apartment. When she came out of the door again, the earrings were gone. "There. I feel better without them."

We started down the stairs again. "Is Xander coming with us?" she asked, spying his SUV in the drive.

"No, I just traded the truck for his car tonight—it's nicer." I opened the passenger door for her.

"Austin, you didn't have to go to any trouble."

"No trouble," I said, eyeing her legs as she got in the car.

But there *was* trouble.

As I drove toward the harbor, I couldn't stop thinking about the fact that I would never have the chance to give her a birthday gift, watch her unwrap something I'd chosen for her, and see her wearing it.

As we walked into the restaurant, I put my hand on the small of her back and realized I'd never take her on another Saturday night date, be seated across from her at a table by the window, watch the light of the setting sun reflect in her hair, in her eyes, on her skin.

I'd never get to see her get ready beforehand, zip up her dress, fasten her necklace, catch the scent of her perfume in a room we shared.

I wouldn't get to take her home afterward, pay the babysitter, check in on the kids, then unzip that dress and take her to bed, where we'd have to be quiet so the twins didn't hear us, but we'd whisper and laugh about the times we'd been noisy and wild. I'd keep my voice low as I talked dirty to her. She'd cover her face with a pillow as I made her come with my tongue. I'd try not to be so rough the bed thumped against the bedroom wall.

Just rough enough to leave a mark.

I fucking loved seeing them on her, and when she asked for them, it felt like a gift. But I was about to lose it all.

"Hey. You okay?"

I realized I'd zoned out. "Yes."

She set her fork down and picked up her wine glass. "You're a little out of it tonight."

"Sorry. A client just walked in, and I got distracted thinking about work," I lied. "We're really busy next week, and I'm trying to get Xander's bar top done, and Quentin called again asking about a table for his gallery. I want to say yes, but I need more hours in the day."

"I wish you'd talk to your dad," she said.

I picked up my whiskey and took a sip. "I wish a lot of things."

• • •

We spent our final night together in my bedroom, and in some ways, it seemed like the opposite of our first night together in hers. The chemistry was just as hot, the build-up just as intense, the release just as satisfying, but in place of the playful banter, there was silence. Where the mood had been light, it felt heavy. If last weekend there had been a sense that things were just getting started between us, last night had the inescapable weight of an ending.

Afterward, as we lay in each other's arms, neither of us spoke. Which was normal for me, but Veronica's uncharacteristic silence was unnerving. I wondered what she was thinking about, but I didn't ask. I racked my brain, trying to come up with a way this could continue, but I came up empty. I wished I had the words—and the nerve—to tell her how I felt, but I didn't.

And maybe it would have been a mistake anyway. What good would it do her to hear that I didn't want to lose her, that this week had been more to me than just sex, that she made me feel things I didn't want to feel, couldn't explain, and had no idea what to do about?

I knew exactly what she'd say.

What things, Austin? What do you feel?

So I held her for one more night and stayed silent.

• • •

"Daddy!" The twins rushed off the plane and wrapped their arms around me.

"Hey!" My throat closed up as I hugged them back, and my eyes grew a little misty. "I missed you two."

"We missed you too." Owen's tan had grown deeper, and he wore a shirt I'd never seen that said California Dreamin' with palm trees and a surfboard on it.

"Where's Veronica?" Adelaide asked. Her hair looked even lighter, bleached by the sun, and freckles were dusted across the bridge of her nose.

"She's at home making dinner." She hadn't offered to come with me this time.

"I hope it's tacos," Adelaide said a little warily. "That's my favorite thing she makes."

"Actually, while you were gone, she learned how to cook more things. In fact, she found a slow cooker in the basement I forgot I had, and she's making brown sugar barbecue chicken sandwiches for us."

"We told her barbecue was your favorite," Owen said. "That's probably why she's making it."

It probably was, which didn't help.

I changed the subject. "So you had a good time on your trip?"

"Yes! I took surfing lessons," said Owen proudly as we headed for luggage claim.

"Me too," Adelaide chimed in. "And we went hiking, and slept in a tent, and had our fortunes told!"

"You did?"

"Yes. My fortune is very good. I'm going to be rich and famous."

"She didn't say that, she just said you were going to be on TV," argued Owen. "You could be, like, a weather person or something boring like that."

"And what'd she say to you?" I elbowed my son gently.

"I'm going to travel the world," he announced. "Maybe as a pilot."

"That's fine, you can fly me around in my plane," said Adelaide.

I grinned. "I'm so glad to have you guys back."

Maybe with the twins home again, I'd be so distracted with

dad stuff, I wouldn't even have time to miss Veronica.

At least, that's what I was hoping.

When we got back, she was there in the kitchen, ready with huge smiles and hugs for the kids. "Wow, look at you guys! I'm jealous of your suntans! Wash your hands, then come sit at the table and tell me everything. I hear you showed off your tap dancing while you were there."

But she barely looked in my direction. It had been like that all day.

This morning, she'd slipped out of bed early, leaving me lonely and disappointed. When I went down to make coffee, she was nowhere to be found, but about twenty minutes later, she jogged up the driveway and began stretching in the yard.

I thought about going out there, making sure we were okay— it wasn't like her at all to ghost me in bed—but then figured she probably needed her space. I'd ask her how she was doing when she came in for coffee.

But she hadn't come in. Instead, she'd gone straight up to her apartment.

After returning Xander's car and getting my truck back, I headed into the garage to work. Eventually she appeared in the garage door, looking so sweet and pretty my arms physically ached to hold her.

"Question," she said. "I found a slow cooker in the basement. Can I use it to make dinner tonight?"

"Of course. You can use anything you want. What's mine is yours."

"Okay. Thanks. I'll have dinner all ready by the time you get home from the airport." She'd smiled at me before walking back to the house, but it seemed oddly impersonal. Like what had happened between us meant nothing to her.

Now I watched her move around in the kitchen, much more

confident than she used to be, piling pulled chicken on bakery buns, spooning coleslaw onto plates, laughing and talking with the kids, shining all her light in their direction.

And I was jealous—of my own damn kids!

Angry with myself, I took their suitcases up to their rooms, dumped all their dirty laundry into their hampers, put their shoes in their closets and their toothbrushes back in the bathroom. Then I studied myself in the mirror, dismayed to see those two lines between my beetled brows.

I tried to force my forehead muscles to relax, but those lines refused to go away.

"Dad!" Adelaide called up the stairs. "Dinner!"

"Coming." But before I went downstairs, I entered my bedroom and hurried over to the bed. Picked up the pillow she'd used. Held it up to my face and inhaled.

She was not, by any means, out of my system.

• • •

It went on like that all week.

On Monday, she and the kids were back in their routine— camp, chores, activities, leisure time. I watched them come and go, heard all about their adventures together when I put the kids to bed at night, suffered silently through meals during which the three of them talked and laughed.

We were never alone together. I wasn't sure if she was avoiding me on purpose or what, but somehow she and I were never in the house when the kids weren't home. She didn't pop into the garage to chat. If she passed me on the driveway or in the hall and the kids were out of sight, she didn't make eye contact, and she certainly didn't get close enough to brush my sleeve as she went by. I never saw her wear my shirts or my hat again.

She seemed fine without me, and I was losing my mind.

On Friday night, she went out, wearing that fucking red miniskirt. I was like a stupid jealous husband or nervous father all night, watching for her headlights out the front window. When I finally saw them around eleven p.m., I quickly grabbed my beer and ran out to sit by the fire pit, as if I'd been out there relaxing all night.

She walked up the driveway and headed for the garage stairs without seeing me.

"Hey," I called.

Startled, she looked over at me. "Oh! Oh. Hey. I didn't see you there."

"Did you have fun?"

"Yes."

"Who were you with?" I asked, knowing it was none of my business.

"Ari."

Relief washed over me. "Where'd you go?"

"A wine bar called Lush."

"Never been there."

"It's nice. You should go sometime." She glanced up at her apartment, like she couldn't wait to get away from me.

"Was it just the two of you?"

"Yes."

"See anyone you knew?" *Like fucking Daniel?* I still hadn't forgotten the guy she'd danced with at The Broken Spoke.

"A few people. Bubba and Willene Fleck. Your aunt Faye and a friend. And Ari introduced me to some people."

Men or women? I wanted to ask, but knew I couldn't. My gaze wandered over her blond waves, those scarlet lips, the long legs beneath that little red skirt. I gripped my beer bottle tight. The need to touch her was nearly unbearable.

Say something, you idiot. Don't let her leave.

But I couldn't think of anything, and after a moment of crickets chirping in the dark, she said goodnight and went up to her apartment.

I watched the light come on and saw her come over to the window. She stood there for a moment, looking down at me. I took a long pull on my beer. Then she pulled down the shade, disappearing behind it.

I felt like smashing the bottle on the concrete.

Rising to my feet, I went inside, angry at myself, at her, at the world. I went to bed mad, refusing to even look at her side of the bed. I'd changed the sheets but not her pillowcase, but I didn't sniff it tonight. I didn't jerk off either, which I'd done several times this week, the angriest self-serve hand jobs imaginable.

Saturday morning, the first thing I did was shove that pillowcase in the washing machine, as if that would punish her.

I wanted to punish myself for getting close to her.

Why hadn't I known better?

Chapter 22

Veronica

I'd been miserable all week and trying not to show it.

Each day that passed, Austin and I exchanged fewer and fewer words, until we barely nodded when we crossed paths. I'd gotten used to how it was when it was just the two of us—he'd been so open and warm—and I hated the weird silence. He worked long hours, and he seemed to spend even more time in the garage than he had before.

One day this week, while he'd been at work, I wandered in there just to feel close to him, and I saw a stunning dining table. Closing my eyes, I ran my fingers across the surface, reveling in the knowledge that his hands had been on this wood too. I yearned for those hands to touch me again.

By Friday afternoon, I gave up trying to pretend everything was fine and called Morgan. "Help," I said. "I did something bad."

"What happened, honey?" Just the sound of her voice had tears spilling from my eyes.

"I caught feelings, that's what happened."

"For your boss? The handyman?"

"Yes."

"You said it was just sex! Temporary and casual."

"That's what it was supposed to be." Grabbing the tissue box, I sank down on the couch. "But my stupid heart got involved and ran away with the plan."

"Are you sure it's not just a rebound thing? Like a reaction to being with someone so opposite Neil?"

"I thought that, at the beginning. I came up with all kinds of logical reasons why he seemed to have this effect on me." I blew my nose. "But they were all just excuses. The truth is, I think I'm falling for him."

"Maybe you should quit and come back to New York now, before you get in any deeper," she suggested.

"I can't leave them. They need me."

She sighed. "How does *he* feel?"

"I don't really know. He doesn't talk to me."

"Can you ask him?"

"No!" I shuddered. "No. I can't."

"Then just try to be strong, Roni. And don't let him con you into sex while no one's looking. You deserve the real fucking thing."

"Thanks." I grabbed a new tissue and blew my nose again.

"You should get out and about. Do you have any friends there other than his family?"

"Yeah. I have one friend—Ari—and she's trying to drag me to a wine bar tonight."

"Go! Get dressed up and put on your favorite red lipstick and just have a girls' night. Forget about men."

I smiled weakly. "I'll try."

And I *had* tried—I wore something I felt good in, I curled my hair, I painted my lips cherry red, and Ari was good at making me laugh.

But Austin was on my mind the entire time.

It was obvious he'd been waiting up for me to get home, and I could hear the jealousy in his voice when he asked me about my evening. *You idiot!* I wanted to shout. *I don't want anyone but you!* I even thought he might show up at my door like he had the first time, shirtless and angry, unable to stay away.

Obviously, things had changed. He was able to resist me now. He didn't feel what I felt.

And I needed to stop hoping he would.

• • •

Saturday afternoon, I got a text from Ari.

> Broken Spoke tonight. I'll pick you up at nine.

> I don't know if I feel like it.

> I didn't ask if you felt like it, I just told you what time I'll be there.

I allowed myself a tiny smile. Ari was good for me. And maybe a little music and dancing would be good for me too. The kids were sleeping at George's tonight, so they wouldn't need me until they got home tomorrow afternoon.

> Okay. I'll be ready.

I set my phone aside and curled up in my bed again. It wasn't like me to nap, but I just didn't have the energy to do anything else. Xander had taken Austin, George, and the kids out on the boat this afternoon, and they'd asked me to come along, but I'd declined. It was hard enough seeing Austin fully clothed at the breakfast and dinner table every day—seeing him shirtless wasn't going to help me stop thinking about him. My throat closed up, and the tears I'd been holding in all day insisted on being shed.

Allowing myself the cry, I sobbed into my pillow. When the wave of sadness had passed, I got up, went over to the dresser, and took out the two shirts of his I'd stolen. Then I grabbed his cap from a hook on the wall.

Knowing the house was empty, I walked up to Austin's bedroom and placed the items on the bed.

I cried it out again when I got home.

· · ·

"Oh god," I said to Ari over the loud wail of the guitar. We were standing at the bar, waiting for drinks.

"What?"

"Austin and Xander just walked in."

She glanced over her shoulder toward the door.

"Don't *look*!" I said, horrified.

"Sorry." She stared straight ahead. "But they spotted us. And judging from the look on Austin's face, he is not happy."

"Ladies." Xander came up and clapped us on the shoulders. "How are we tonight?"

"Good," Ari answered.

I said nothing. But in the mirror over the bar, I could see Austin's dark hair right behind me. His wide shoulders. His angry expression.

The bartender set two beers in front of us.

"Can we get this round?" Xander asked.

"Actually, someone already offered," said Ari.

Austin's arm shot out so fast and spanked his credit card on the bar, it was a blur. "I'm getting it."

For some reason, it really bothered me. I looked back at him, eyes narrowed. "Gee, thanks."

"Two more," he ordered over Xander's shoulder.

Ari sighed.

"Should we get a table?" Xander asked, looking around. "Might be tough. Crowded in here."

"We actually promised those guys over there we'd be back in a minute," I said, sliding away from the bar. I tried not to let my body touch Austin's, but there were so many people, my ass brushed his crotch.

I thought I heard him growl.

"Come on, Ari." I grabbed her arm and tugged her back toward the table of guys I couldn't care less about. But if Austin wanted something to be jealous about, I could put on a show. I'd been putting on a show all week, pretending everything was fine.

So I sat a little too close to a ginger-haired guy whose name I forgot immediately. I laughed too hard at his jokes. I smiled a lot in his direction. I hoped Austin was watching.

After I finished my beer, I excused myself to use the ladies' room. Ari offered to go with me, but I assured her I was fine. Following the signs, I made my way to the back hall and was just about to enter the restroom when someone grabbed my arm.

"Hey."

I spun around, totally unsurprised to see Austin there with a frown on his face. "Do you mind?" I shook my arm free. "I'm going to the bathroom."

"I'll wait." He folded his arms over his chest.

"Why?"

"You shouldn't be alone in this place."

"That's why you're waiting?"

"Yes."

"Don't bother. I told you once before, I don't need to be

rescued." I turned away from him and went to push the bathroom door open, but found myself being dragged out the back door and hauled around the side of the place—exactly where we'd stood two weeks ago. "Austin, what the hell?"

He didn't answer. Instead, he caged me against the side of the old barn and crushed his lips to mine.

I wanted to resist, I really did. But I couldn't—all week long, I'd ached for this kiss, this closeness with him. My arms circled his neck instinctively. My mouth opened wide. My defenses slipped.

He broke it off, breathing hard, his lips hovering over mine. "You gave my stuff back."

"It wasn't mine to keep."

His mouth claimed mine again, his tongue hot and possessive, demanding mine answer in kind. I gave myself over to him, rising up on my toes, pressing my chest against his, frustrating noises coming from my throat. What *was* this?

"The kids are gone tonight." His voice was low and urgent. "Come home with me."

Oh god, I wanted to. I wanted him. But then what? Were we just going to sneak around, jumping into bed when the kids were out of the house? Exchanging hot text messages? Stealing kisses when no one was looking?

That wasn't going to work—I couldn't guard my heart that way.

But his kiss was draining all my defenses.

I needed air. I needed sense. I needed space between us. Placing my hands on his pecs, I pushed him back. "Wait. Wait. I can't do this. We've hardly talked all week."

"Because you ignored me. You acted like nothing mattered."

"I'm a good actress."

"But *why*?"

"I'm protecting myself, Austin!"

His jaw clenched. "You don't need to protect yourself from me."

"You don't understand," I told him, fighting tears. "I can't fall for you."

That seemed to get through. "Fall for me?"

"Yes. Actually, you know what? The problem isn't that I can't fall for you—it's that I *could*. And if we keep doing this, I'm afraid that's what's going to happen."

He swallowed. "I don't want you to be afraid."

"I know you don't. But you have to trust that I'm doing the right thing for both of us." I took a deep breath, trying to stay calm.

"You said you weren't looking for a relationship." He said it softly, no accusatory bite.

"I wasn't, Austin. But things between us got intense, and I…" I shook my head. "Look, I'm sorry I returned your clothes like that. It was childish."

He exhaled, his shoulders slumping. "I'm sorry for getting jealous and acting like I own you. I know I don't."

"I think—I think our timing was just bad, you know?" I tried hard to smile. To be brave. "Maybe if we'd met some other time, in some other place, we could have been something more. But the way things are, it's just not meant to be."

He nodded slowly.

"I wouldn't trade the time we had together for anything, Austin. You were so good for me. You don't even know." I felt tears spring to my eyes. "But I think walking away now is best."

"It will be hard," he said quietly.

"I know." A lump was trying to form in my throat. "But I'll be gone soon, and your life can go back to normal. Mine will too."

He opened his mouth, and I thought maybe he'd argue with me—I wanted him to argue with me—but he didn't. He kissed my forehead, took my hand, and led me back inside.

"I need a minute," I said at the ladies' room door. "You don't have to wait for me."

Then I went into the bathroom, locked myself into a stall, and cried.

When I came out, he was gone.

Chapter 23

AUSTIN

*S*tanding over to one side of the dance floor, I watched her come out of the bathroom and made sure she got back to her table. Then I stood nearby like a sentry, making sure no one laid a finger on her or Ari.

Xander told me I was being stupid, then gave up talking to me completely and went to find someone to flirt with.

I stayed right where I was until Veronica and Ari left, then I stealthily followed them outside, making sure they made it to their car okay. It was only when I saw them drive away that I went back inside and ordered a beer.

Xander found me at the bar. "Dude," he said. "That was the most obvious tail I've ever seen. They totally saw you following them out."

"I don't care," I said stubbornly.

"I don't fucking get it."

I tipped up the bottle. "You wouldn't."

"Why don't you go after her?"

"I can't."

"Because…"

"Because she's afraid that if we keep messing around, she'll end up hurt when she has to leave."

"And she has to leave?"

"She has to leave. She *wants* to leave. This isn't her home."

Xander cocked his head. "You sure about that?"

• • •

The following week was better—and worse.

Better because Veronica didn't ignore me, I made an effort to include myself in conversations, and if we happened to find ourselves alone in a room, we didn't run in the other direction.

But it was torture that I couldn't touch her. Every time she got close to me, I battled the urge to take her in my arms.

Better because Tuesday night, she and the kids came out to the garage and invited me to watch a movie with them, and instead of staying out there alone, I said yes and joined them.

Worse because I could hear her laugh, but I couldn't put my arm around her in the dark.

Better because Thursday was my dad's birthday, and we all went out for dinner at The Pier Inn. More than once I saw her glancing over to the table by the window we'd shared.

Worse because I was doing the same and wishing I could have that night alone with her all over again.

Better because Friday evening, she went out with Ari, and this time I forced myself to tell her to have a good time and go to bed early. My bedroom window was open, and I was relieved when I heard her come home around ten and go up the stairs to her apartment.

Worse because I so desperately wanted to go knock on her door and kiss her goodnight, but I couldn't.

Better because Saturday morning was their 5K, and I tagged along, signed up to run it at the last minute, and waited for them at the finish line, pretending to be asleep. The four of us had such a good time together. That night I thought she might hit The Broken Spoke again with Ari, but she didn't, choosing instead to spend her evening in the backyard with me and my dad and Xander and the kids, roasting marshmallows on the grill, sipping a beer, and watching the twins and some other neighborhood imps dance around with sparklers.

Worse because I wanted to pull her aside where no one could see and put a hickey on her neck, so I'd still feel like she was mine.

I wanted it so badly that when we found ourselves alone, I lost control.

She was just coming out of the bathroom off the kitchen—I'd watched her go into the house and followed her a minute later—and as soon as the door opened, I barreled in and shut it behind me.

"Austin, what—"

But I didn't let her finish the question. I took her roughly in my arms and put my mouth on hers, kissing her hard and deep. She fought me for less than two seconds, then gave in, her hands skating over my back and down my ass, pulling me against her. Sliding one hand into her hair, I used it to tilt her head to one side and moved my mouth down her throat.

"Stop," she begged. "No more."

Grudgingly, I tore my mouth from her skin and rested my forehead against hers, breathing hard.

"You can't keep doing this," she said. "It's not fair."

"I know."

Placing her hands on my shoulders, she pushed me away. "I

should leave."

I nodded. "You go out first. I'll wait a minute."

She shook her head, her blue eyes shining with tears. "No, I mean leave your house. My living here is making this really hard."

"No!" It killed me to think of her gone. "Don't leave, Roni. The kids would be devastated. They adore you."

"I adore them too. I don't *want* to go."

"Then stay. I won't do this again. I promise."

She put her hand on her stomach and took a deep breath. "Okay. I'll go out first."

I watched her leave and pulled the door shut again. Then I stared at myself in the mirror over the sink, furious that I'd upset her.

What the fuck was wrong with me?

• • •

Sunday morning, we went to Moe's for breakfast. After I handed the kids a bunch of quarters, all I could do was stare across the table at the woman whose existence I hadn't even known of two months ago, but whose departure in two weeks was tearing me apart. What if I never saw her again?

Ari came and poured coffee, and the two women chatted for a moment. When Ari turned to leave, Veronica caught her arm. "Hey, can you bring some almond milk?"

"Of course." Ari smiled at me. "Sorry I forgot. Be right back."

When we were alone again, Veronica smiled hesitantly at me. "So I got the job," she said.

"The job?"

"The assistant choreographer's position." She lifted her coffee mug to her lips.

"Oh." My heart sank. "That's—that's good."

"Yeah. I was getting nervous."

"And you have a place to live?" My eyes fastened onto the beginnings of the bruise I'd left on her neck last night. She'd worn her hair down this morning, which hid it fairly well, but I knew where to look. I knew so many things about her body.

"I think so. Morgan connected me with someone looking to sublet their studio apartment in Little Italy. I just have to confirm what I'll earn before I say yes. Then book my ticket." She set the mug down.

"You're probably excited to get back to New York."

"Yeah." Her eyes dropped. "Although I'll miss it here. It will be hard to leave. In some ways, I wish I had a reason to stay."

Maybe it was her words that made me do what I did next.

Or maybe it was the red lipstick mark on her white coffee cup.

• • •

Later that afternoon, I took the kids over to see my dad. While they ran around in his backyard, which still had the playscape we'd built them when they were younger, we sat on his patio under the shade of an umbrella.

"Where's Veronica?" he asked.

"She's at home. She had some things to do." The truth was that I hadn't asked her to come along.

"Boy, that was lucky, finding her. Wasn't it?" My dad chuckled. "Someone like that doesn't knock on your door every day."

"That's true."

"Too bad she's got to leave," he mused. "Kids are crazy about her."

"So I've been thinking about that." I leaned forward in my chair, elbows on my knees. "I was thinking I'd ask her to stay."

"Oh?"

"Yes. I was thinking that it might be nice to have her around this fall, and—and beyond. For childcare, while I work."

"Won't the kids be in school?"

"They will, but they're getting older, and they'll need help with homework and rides to activities. I might be too busy to handle it all."

"Why's that?"

"There's something I'd like to talk to you about." I took a breath. "I'd like to cut back at Two Buckleys and go into business for myself."

"Oh yeah?" He rubbed his chin. "Making those tables? I was looking at your work in the garage last night. It's beautiful. You've got a gift."

"Thanks." I felt proud that my dad liked my work. "I can make a lot of things. But yes, there's a lot of interest in tables. I have orders I'd like to fill. I just need time to do it."

My dad looked away from me, his eyes shifting to the twins chasing each other around the playscape. When Owen caught his sister, he tackled her and threw her to the ground. She quickly flipped him over and sat on him.

My dad laughed. "Looks like you and Xander out there."

"I wouldn't need to leave Two Buckleys completely," I told him, impatient for him to comment on what I'd just said. "I could still help you out."

He continued to watch the kids, a nostalgic kind of smile on his face. "I didn't get to do this all that much when you guys were young—just watch you kids run around and have fun. It's nice. And going out on the boat last week—that was nice too."

I shifted in my chair, rubbing my hands on my knees.

"Course, you didn't get to do much of that once your mom was gone. You always had to work. Then when Harry died, you stepped into his shoes. Kept us in business."

"Right. But maybe now, I could go part-time. Maybe work for Two Buckleys in the mornings, and then work for myself in the afternoons. What do you think? Would that be okay?"

He didn't answer right away. Then he simply said, "No."

Closing my eyes, I leaned back in my chair. "Okay. Forget I asked."

"You need to go full-time for yourself."

"Huh?"

"I know Two Buckleys isn't your dream. You know what? It's not even my dream anymore." He pointed to the kids, who were now elbowing each other out of the way to get down the slide first. "That is. Being with my grandkids. Going fishing with my friends. Sleeping in a little. Taking an afternoon nap. I think I'd like that."

I stared at him. "You mean it?"

"I mean it. Two Buckleys has provided a good living for three generations, but I think maybe it's time to let it go. History is important, but so is the future." He looked at me. "Sometimes, change is good."

My pulse had started to race. "So what will happen to the business?"

"Well, we'll hang on to it until you're sure this furniture thing takes off, and then we'll sell it. I'll keep some to live on, and we'll invest the rest in your business." He held my gaze. "You've invested a lot in me over the years. It's about time you invested in yourself."

"Thanks, Dad." I could hardly get the words out, my throat and chest felt like someone was standing on them.

He looked out at the kids again. "So what about Veronica?"

My heart skipped a few beats just hearing her name. "I'm going to ask her if she'll stay on as the kids' nanny."

My father nodded slowly. "And will she?"

"I hope so." Truth be told, I was nervous about it. "But she'd have to walk away from a pretty cool job she just got offered in New York."

"Well, then, I guess you'll just have to make her a better offer."

"Right," I said, starting to sweat. "A better offer."

Chapter 24

Veronica

"Two more weeks," I moaned to Morgan over the phone after getting home from Moe's. "Honestly, I'm not sure I'm going to make it."

"It's that bad?"

"It's just *hard*." I perched on the foot of my bed and flopped onto my back. "How do you get over someone when you have to see them every day? And you practically live together? And you feel like part of the family?"

"It's funny, you didn't talk this way about Neil and the Vanderhoofs," she said. "And you saw him every day, you definitely lived with him, and you nearly took his family name."

"I never felt this way about Neil. Or anyone else."

"I've never heard you *talk* this way about anyone else." She sighed. "Is it possible Austin feels the same as you do but he's just being all closed-off man about it?"

"Yes. But don't tell me to confront him about his feelings. I'd rather die."

"But if you—"

"I want him to come to me, Morgan," I said quietly. "I *need* him to come to me and say the words."

"And if he doesn't?"

"Then I'll see you in two weeks."

· · ·

I didn't go over to the house for dinner that night. Instead, I went to the grocery store and picked up some ready-made pasta salad and a bottle of wine, and ate by myself in front of the TV.

I was finishing my second glass of wine and third episode of *Ted Lasso* when I heard a knock on the door. Hitting pause on the remote, I set my wine glass aside and went to answer it. My heart was beating fast, but I told myself not to get my hopes up.

It was Austin.

"Hey," he said, wiping his palms on his jeans. "You're here."

"I'm here."

"When you texted you weren't coming over for dinner, I thought maybe you were going out."

"No, I just...had a headache," I lied. "But I'm fine now."

"Can I come in?"

I stood back as he entered, closing the door behind him.

"I wanted to tell you something," he said.

"What?"

"I talked to my dad," he said, a hint of a grin appearing. "About my business."

My jaw fell open. "You did?"

"Yes. And you were right. He wants me to do what I love."

"Oh, Austin, I'm so happy for you." I smiled at him. "That's great news."

"It is." He rushed toward me, placing his hands on my shoulders. "And it means you have a reason to stay, if you want to."

I looked up at him, confused. "Huh?"

"I'll need a nanny to help me out with the kids even after they go back to school. Starting my own business will take a lot of time and energy, and Two Buckleys can't just close up shop without warning. We have a lot of jobs on the books."

"You want me to stay...as your nanny?"

"Yes. It's perfect." He dropped his hands and began pacing back and forth in front of the TV. "The kids adore you, and you're so great with them. You learned the summer routine so quickly, I'm positive the school routine will be a piece of cake. You can stay here over the garage—I'll insulate and heat it for you. Of course, if you want to get a different place, that's cool too. I can—"

"Hold on." I held up both palms. "Stop a minute. I just want to be clear. You're asking me to stay because you want me to continue being your nanny?"

He looked uncomfortable. "Well...yeah."

I took a breath and forced myself to be brave. "What happens with us?"

"Well, we could be like before. I mean, not out in the open, since you'd still be working for me, but it's better than nothing, right?"

I closed my eyes, disappointment washing over me like heavy rain. "It's better than nothing. But it's not enough."

"What do you mean?" His tone had an edge to it.

"I mean, I love the kids, and I love it here, but I'm not interested in staying because you need a nanny, Austin." I didn't want to cry, but a sob was working its way up to my throat.

"But this is what I can offer you right now," he said angrily. "And I don't understand why you won't take it. You said you wanted a reason to stay. I'm giving you one."

"I didn't want to be Neil's trophy, and I don't want to be your secret." The tears started to fall.

"What do you want?" he demanded.

"I want to be chosen!" I cried. "I want to be enough for someone—just me. As I am."

He looked dumbstruck. His mouth opened, and once again, my foolish heart filled with hope—maybe he'd say the words.

But instead, he stepped back and held up his hands. "You know what? Never mind. This was a mistake." Shouldering past me, he stormed out the door, slamming it shut behind him.

I jumped at the noise.

Then I ran into the bedroom, threw myself facedown, and sobbed.

Chapter 25

I stomped down the stairs so heavily I thought my boots might snap the steps in half.

What the hell? I'd done exactly what she wanted me to do. I'd talked to my dad, been honest about my feelings, came to her with a *good* offer—just like my dad said!—that meant she could stay in Cherry Tree Harbor and we could still see each other.

Okay, maybe I hadn't given much thought to how she'd take the whole keeping it secret thing, but dammit! I'd practically come right from my dad's house to her door. I hadn't had a chance to think everything through. It's not like I was embarrassed of her—I just needed to figure out the best way forward.

But she'd shot me down, so that was that.

"Fucking hell," I grumbled as I crossed the yard. "I should never have hired her."

Because now I loved her.

And I couldn't fire my fucking feelings.

• • •

The following week was utter torture.

Veronica and I weren't speaking. The kids caught colds and were tired and cranky. Xander was on my ass about installing the bar top. The truck blew a tire. On Friday morning, my dad complained about chest pains at work, and I called an ambulance, then followed it to the hospital in the truck. On the way I called Xander, and he met me there.

We were sitting in the waiting room drinking cardboard cups of terrible coffee and awaiting test results when Veronica arrived. As soon as the elevator doors opened, she flew over to us, her expression tormented. "Is he okay?"

"He's fine right now," I said. "They're running some tests."

"Oh, thank god." She put a hand on her chest. "I was panicked."

"How did you know?" I asked.

"Xander texted me."

I glared at my brother. "You didn't have to do that."

"I'm glad he did," said Veronica. "What can I do? I don't have to pick up the kids from camp for another couple hours. Are you guys hungry? Can I bring you some food?"

"No," I said.

"Yes," my brother replied, looking at his coffee cup. "This coffee sucks. I'd give my right arm for a good dark roast right now."

"You got it," she said. "Austin?"

"I'm fine." I continued to brood into my shitty coffee.

She stood there for a moment, then turned around and went to the elevator. From the corner of my eye, I watched her hit the button, get on, and disappear behind the doors.

My leg began to twitch, waiting for my brother to start in on me. His silence was driving me crazy. Finally, I broke down.

"Just say it," I snapped.

"Say what?"

"That I'm a fucking idiot. I know it's what you're thinking."

"Seems like I don't need to say it."

"Well, you're wrong. I asked her to stay, and she turned me down."

He looked at me. "You asked her to stay?"

"Yes," I snapped.

"And she said *no*?" Xander's surprise was evident.

"Exactly. So you can stop being so smug—you were wrong."

"What did you say?"

"I said that since I'm starting my own business, I'd need a nanny during the school year."

Xander dropped his head. "Jesus. Of course you did."

"Look, she said she was looking for a reason to stay, I gave her one, it wasn't good enough." I took another sip of the watery garbage in my cup and winced. "Fuck. This is so bad."

"Should have told her to get you something better."

"I don't want to ask her for anything, okay? She rejected me."

"She didn't reject *you*. She rejected your stupid job offer."

"Fine with me," I said bitterly.

"No, it isn't. You're just too stubborn to say the thing you should say to change her mind." He shook his head. "As usual, you're standing in your own way of being happy. So what's the excuse this time?"

I didn't answer. Instead, I got up and went over to the trash can to throw away my coffee. When I returned to my seat, he started up again.

"I'm not saying it's easy. I have no idea what it's like to be in love."

"It's some bullshit," I said. "Remember when I got hit in the face with that line drive you hit, and my eye was black and blue and swollen shut and my cheek blew up and I couldn't eat or talk or sleep or even breathe right?"

"Yeah."

"This is worse. I can't fucking wait for it to end."

"And you think it will end when she leaves?"

"It fucking better." But I knew, even when I couldn't see her every day, that I'd only be more miserable.

At that moment, Veronica came out of the elevator again, a drinks carrier holding two large coffees in one hand and a white bag in the other. Xander and I both stood up as she approached.

"I got you both large dark roasts," she said. "Austin, this one labeled with the A is yours—it has a little almond milk in it. And in this bag are a couple egg sandwiches. That's all they had at the coffee shop downstairs."

"Perfect," Xander said, taking the cup with the X on it and the sandwich bag before sitting down again. "You're a saint."

She handed me the other cup.

"Thanks," I muttered stiffly.

"You're welcome. You'll let me know about George?"

"Yes."

"Okay." She turned to leave, then suddenly spun around and threw her arms around me. "It will be okay," she whispered.

I closed my eyes and held her close, breathing in the sweet scent of her hair. She let go too soon, and without saying anything else, hurried over to the elevator and got in. As the doors closed, I could see her wiping her eyes.

I stood there for a moment, my heart telling me to run after her, my feet refusing to budge.

"I just have one more thing to say," Xander said.

I sank down beside him, figuring he was just going to insult me again. "If you're going to call me names, fuck off."

"I wasn't going to call you anything. I was just going to remind you of what Dad would say if he was here—it only happens once."

...

They kept my dad overnight for observation and released him on Saturday with a couple new medications and instructions to take it easy. Xander and I took turns staying with him over the next few days, and on Thursday evening, Veronica and the kids came to stay with him for a bit while Xander and I brought the new bar top over to his bar.

After installing it, we stood back and admired the way it looked. I had to admit, Xander had been right—it was perfect.

"Thanks, brother." He clapped me on the shoulder. "It's exactly what I wanted. I swear I'll pay you for your time as soon as I can."

I shrugged. "Don't worry about it."

He glanced at me. "How are you?"

"This week has been rough," I admitted.

"When does she leave?"

"Saturday morning."

"And you're going to let her go?"

"It's her choice," I said, rubbing my stiff neck.

"But to be fair, she's not making an informed decision. She doesn't know how you feel about her. You need to get over yourself and tell her."

I clenched my jaw. "What's the point? These things never work out anyway. What if I tell her and she stays and then later, she's sorry? What if she gives up everything to stay here with me and she realizes it was a mistake? What if I just keep fucking things up and saying the wrong things and failing her?"

"Aha," Xander said knowingly. "There it is."

"There what is?"

"The reason not to do the thing that would make you happy—fear. Only in this case, you'd make her happy too. And my guess is the kids as well. But…" He thumped my back again. "You do you."

. . .

On Friday night, I took the kids out for dinner. I thought about inviting Veronica, but I wasn't sure I could handle seeing her across the table from me. We hadn't spoken more than a few words to each other all week, and when we did, it was only about the kids or my father. There was a text from her on my phone that I couldn't even bring myself to read. The first few words were *You don't have to drive me…*

She probably thought she was doing me a favor by getting another ride to the airport. Maybe she was. It's not like I was looking forward to goodbye. Or maybe she just didn't want to see me again. Fine. Good. Great.

She just needs to go, I kept telling myself. Once she was across the country, I'd work on getting over her.

At dinner, both kids were quiet and withdrawn. I'd given them some quarters to play video games, but neither of them had gotten too excited about it. When we got home, the lights in the garage apartment were off, and I wondered if Veronica had already gone to sleep. I pictured her sleeping, and the fierce longing to hold her struck me in the chest.

I would never hold her again. Never kiss her. Never touch her. Never be the one to keep her warm or safe, or make her laugh, or put a mark on her skin.

The realization hit me so hard, I nearly doubled over on my way up the stairs to put the kids to bed. Someone else was going to do all those things. Veronica was gorgeous and sweet and sexy.

And maybe she guarded her heart, but she'd let me in, hadn't she? She could let in someone else, and that someone else might fucking hurt her.

My brother was right—I was a total fucking idiot. And as soon as I got the kids in bed, I was going to go over and talk to her.

When I was tucking Owen in, I noticed a new stuffed toy under his arm—a green apple with a face on it. "What's this?"

"It's from Veronica. Because she's moving to the Big Apple. She said this will remind us of her, and if we miss her, we can hug it."

"That was nice of her."

"I'm sad about her leaving," he said. "I don't want her to go."

"Me neither, buddy."

"She told us she wished she didn't have to leave," he said. "Can you make her come back?"

"I'll try."

In Adelaide's room, it was more of the same, this time with tears. "I'm going to miss Veronica so much," she said, hugging her apple—a red one. "It was so sad to say goodbye."

"Well, she's not gone yet." I tapped her nose. "Maybe we can convince her not to go."

"But she *is* gone. She left."

My heart stopped. "What?"

"That's why I'm so sad."

"Her flight is tomorrow," I said, my entire body suddenly on high alert. "I was supposed to drive her to the airport."

"This morning, she said Ari was driving her. And she was leaving tonight."

What the fuck?

I jumped off Adelaide's bed and raced out of the room.

"Daddy! You forgot to give me a kiss!"

"Fuck," I muttered, halfway down the stairs. I took them up

two at a time and ran back into her room, dropped a kiss on her forehead, then bolted down the steps again.

Locating my phone on the kitchen counter, I read Veronica's full text.

> You don't have to drive me to the airport. I changed my flight, and it leaves late tonight, so Ari is going to drive me. The kids will be in bed.
>
> I just want to say that I'm sorry for the way things ended with us. I never intended to make a mess here. I just wanted a fresh start. But I had so much fun with you and the kids and your family that I got a little carried away.
>
> It felt like home, like a dream come true. But I'm awake now, and I know it wasn't real. At least you all showed me what's possible.
>
> Take care of each other. I will never forget you. And I'll always wonder.
>
> I love you, Austin.

"FUCK!" I roared. "No!"

I called her. No answer.

I found Ari's number and dialed. No answer.

I texted Veronica.

Please don't go. I have to talk to you.

Holding my breath, I waited for her reply. Nothing.

"Dammit!"

I dialed Xander. "Hey," I said when he picked up. "Did Veronica say anything to you about leaving tonight?"

"No." He paused. "But come to think of it, she was a little clingy and emotional when she said goodbye to me and Dad last night. She doesn't usually hug me."

"Dammit!" I yelled, bringing a hand to my head.

"What's wrong?"

"She changed her flight and snuck off to the airport tonight without telling me!"

"Shit. Why?"

"Because I'm an asshole!"

"Okay. Stop yelling. I'm on my way over. I'll stay with the kids. You can go get her."

"What if I'm too late?"

"You can't be that far behind her. When was the last time you saw her?"

I heard Xander's car start, and his phone switched to Bluetooth. "When I got home from work. Around six or so. Then I took the kids out for dinner, and I think she was gone when we got back."

"How'd she get to the airport?"

"Ari."

"Did you—"

"No answer."

"Shoot Ari a text and explain that you need to talk to Veronica, and *anything* she can do would help."

"Okay."

"And Austin—figure out what you're going to say to Veronica if you get the chance."

"I know what to say," I told him. "I just need the chance to say it."

With shaking fingers, I texted Ari.

> Where is she? PLEASE tell me.
>
> I fucked up and I need to talk to her before she leaves.
>
> Ari I'm begging you.
>
> If I have ever been like a brother to you, please tell her to call me.

"Daddy?"

I turned around to see the twins standing there in their pajamas, both hugging their stuffed apples.

"We heard yelling," Owen said, his expression worried.

"I'm sorry, guys. I just realized I made a huge mistake, and I'm—"

My phone buzzed. It was a message from Ari.

> Hey. She's here at Moe's. But she

I didn't even bother reading the rest of it. I grabbed my keys and told the kids to get in the car.

"So here's the thing," I told them as I sped toward Main Street. "I'm in love with Veronica."

"You are?" Owen asked. "Like you want to kiss her?"

"Yes."

"Gross!"

"I don't think it's gross," Adelaide said. "I think you *should* be in love with her. I think you should marry her and she should live with us."

I started to choke. "One thing at a time."

Chapter 26

VERONICA

"I don't understand why you're leaving," Larry said, scratching his head. "Tell us again."

Sighing, I looked down at the burger and fries on my plate. Ari had talked me into coming to Moe's before taking me to the airport since we had so much extra time—I'd wanted to be out of the house by the time Austin came home with the kids. I was seated at the counter in the same spot I'd sat in the day I ran out on my wedding. The day I met Austin.

"Because I don't have a reason to stay," I said again.

"But I heard Austin is starting his own business," put in Gus from the other side of Larry. "Won't he still need you?"

"He needs a nanny, yes," I said, my chest tight. "But I don't think he needs *me*."

"Hogwash!" said Larry, his face scrunched up like a fist. "I saw the way he looked at you all summer—everybody did."

"I agree," said Willene Fleck, whose date night had mostly been spent listening to me weep about leaving Cherry Tree Harbor. "He's head over heels for you, and we all know it. He just doesn't want to do the work—it's tenth grade history class all over again. He's lazy."

Despite everything, I jumped to his defense. "No, he's not. He works harder than anyone I've ever known," I said. "He'd do anything for anyone."

"Hmph." Willene wasn't sold. "Then where is he?"

"He's with his children," I said. "Family is what matters most to Austin and always will."

"That's right," said a deep voice behind me. "And my family includes you."

Gooseflesh swept down my arms. Slowly, I spun around on the stool.

When I saw Austin standing there, the kids at his side— wearing pajamas with sneakers and hugging the stuffed toys I'd given them—my heart started to pound.

"Sorry, Roni." Next to me, Ari reached over and squeezed my hand. "He texted me a few minutes ago, begging to talk to you. He played the big brother card. I had to tell him where you were." Then she pointed at Austin. "Don't make me sorry, Austin. This better be a good grovel."

I felt like I was having an out-of-body experience. The entire place had gone silent. Every eye seemed to be on us. "Austin, what is this?"

"It's me being selfish," he said, his dark eyes serious. "It's me asking you to stay when you have every reason to go. It's me admitting my mistake, thinking I could let you go without a fight. It's me doing the thing that would make me happy, and hoping it will make you happy too." He moved closer to me, close enough to take my hands and pull me to my feet. "It's me choosing you—just you. As you are."

My eyes filled with tears as I recognized my own words.

He smiled. "Because you're not just enough—you're everything."

The bell over the door rang, and Xander busted in. "Did I miss it?"

"It's still happening," said Gus. "We're waiting for the big dummy to tell her he loves her."

"Oh, god." Panicked, I shook my head. "Austin, you don't have to do this here."

"I love you, Veronica Sutton," he said, his eyes locked on mine like we were the only two in the place. "I probably loved you the minute I saw you at my door in that ridiculous wedding dress. I love your grit and your resilience and your light and your heart. I love the way you embraced my family. I love the way you embraced this town. I love the way you make me better. I wish I had said this all sooner."

"Even his best assignments were late," Willene whispered loudly.

"Hush," said Ari. "Don't interrupt the grovel."

"So what do you think?" Austin glanced at each of the kids, who were grinning like crazy and jumping up and down. "Does this look anything like the family you always dreamed about?"

I nodded as tears splashed down my cheeks. "Yes."

"Good, because someone once told me a love like this only happens once." With that, he took my face in his hands and lowered his lips to mine. The entire place erupted with cheers and whistles and applause. I threw my arms around Austin's neck, and he lifted me right off my feet. "Thank god," he said in my ear. "Thank god I got here in time."

"My heart was always going to be yours, Austin," I whispered back.

"I'll take good care of it. I promise you."

The kids tugged at my clothes, and I gave them each a hug. "I'm so happy to see you guys," I said.

"Are you really staying with us?" Owen asked.

"I'm really staying."

"Yay!" Adelaide wrapped her arms around me again.

Xander came over and thumped Austin on the back. "There. Was that so hard?"

"Yes," Austin admitted, tugging at his collar. "I was running on adrenaline before, but now I'm starting to sweat. Did I say the right things?"

"You did." I slipped my arm around his waist. "It was everything I wanted to hear. I can't believe you did it in front of all these people!"

He kissed the top of my head. "I only saw you."

Ari wiped her eyes. "This is better than a book," she said. She hugged me and then Austin.

"So was it a good grovel?" he asked, moving behind me and wrapping his arms around my shoulders.

"It was an excellent grovel," she said with a laugh. "Five stars."

• • •

Back at home, we put the kids to bed, and he walked me up to my apartment. "You have no idea how badly I want to throw you over my shoulder and take you to my bed," he said as we ascended the stairs hand in hand.

"I have some idea." I squeezed his hand. "Trust me. But let's go slow where that kind of thing is concerned. This is a lot all at once, and I want to give them time to adjust to the idea of us."

"I think they're going to be just fine." At the landing, he wrapped his arms around me and kissed me, sweetly at first, but then his hands started to move and his mouth opened wider and his hips began to move against me.

"Do you think they'd be fine for a few minutes in the house?" I asked breathlessly.

"Maybe I could run down to the garage and get the monitor," he said, his lips working their way down my throat.

"Go." I gave him a gentle push. "I want you, even if it's quick."

It was *very* quick—so quick we barely made it to the bed. So quick we didn't even undress all the way. So quick we didn't stop to think about protection.

"I'm okay with it if you are," I said as he hovered over me in the dark. "I'm on birth control shots."

He paused, looking down at me. "You know what? I'm okay with it too."

"Are you sure?" My heart was racing with excitement.

"Yes. I never thought I would be okay with this." He eased inside me, one delicious inch at a time. "But then, I never thought I'd fall in love."

"I never thought I would either."

"I love you," he whispered as he began to move. "Say you're mine."

"I'm yours," I promised, wrapping my legs, my arms, my heart around him. "I'm yours."

Epilogue

THE FOLLOWING JUNE

*a*ustin's alarm went off, yanking me from a deep, contented sleep. He reached over and hit snooze, but before he could get out of bed, I looped an arm around his torso. "No. Stay."

He laughed gently. "I have to get on the road soon."

"But it's our anniversary."

"Anniversary?"

"Yes! It's the third Saturday in June. One year ago today, I came knocking on your door looking for a job."

He settled back on his pillow and put his arms around me. "Huh. I guess you're right. It has been a year. Feels like longer."

"Is that a good thing?"

"Yes." He gave me a squeeze. "It feels like you've always been here. Always belonged here."

I smiled. "It does. So I will forgive you for not remembering this *very* important anniversary. The day I found the life I was looking for."

He kissed the top of my head. "I found the same thing."

"What time will you be back tonight?"

"Pretty late. The client is in Ann Arbor. And they have a photo shoot scheduled on Monday for Architectural Digest, so I have to get it down there today to give them time to stage the dining room."

I gasped and picked up my head. "I didn't know about the photo shoot!"

"I just found out about it."

"That's amazing!" Excitement overshadowed my disappointment that he'd gone all day.

Over the last nine months, demand for a custom Austin Buckley table had exploded—he had more orders than he could possibly fulfill. His tables were in shops and galleries in five different cities, including Chicago and Detroit, and this summer he was moving from the garage into a real workshop, one that had a showroom up front.

He'd have done that already, but he'd been busy last fall rehabbing Miss Edna's School of Dance into Sutton Dance Academy. The building, just outside of town, had actually been in pretty good shape, but had needed new floors and barres, a new sound system, and a lobby remodel.

I'd started teaching classes in October, enrollment had grown steadily all year, and my summer workshops were jam-packed—I actually had waitlists. I'd hired a college student to help me out over the next couple months, and I was planning to hire one more full-time instructor in the fall.

"I'm so proud of you," I said, my eyes misting over. "You work so hard."

"I'm proud of you too." He tucked my hair behind my ear. "And I'm sorry I won't be around today to celebrate us. But you'll be right here when I get home, right?"

I smiled. "Absolutely."

I'd moved in last fall before it got cold enough that Austin would have had to heat the garage. We'd been discussing it for a couple weeks—it seemed silly to go through all that trouble when I was spending nights in his room anyway. And even though I tried my best to sneak out at the crack of dawn so the kids wouldn't see me, they'd totally caught me in the hallway like three times. We were trying to think of the best way to approach it with the kids when they sat us down one night and announced they thought I should move in. They even helped bring over all my stuff.

Sometimes they asked if we were going to get married, and we always said the same thing—maybe, when the time is right. But we'd been too busy getting our new businesses up and running to really give it serious thought.

When it happened, it happened. What I had now was everything I'd ever wanted.

Love. Family. Home.

I was right where I belonged.

· · ·

"Owen! Adelaide! Let's go!" I shouted up the stairs just before nine. "The teacher can't be late!"

"Coming!" Adelaide came rushing down the steps dressed in her dance clothes, holding up a few hairpins. "Can you help me with my bun?"

"Yes. Where's your brother?" I asked, taking the pins from her hand and sliding them into her hair.

"In the bathroom. Ouch—that one hurts."

I readjusted the hairpin. "Shake your head. Everything secure?"

She shook her head and jumped up and down. "Yes."

"Good. Grab your dance bag and get in the car." I called up

the stairs one last time to tell Owen to get a move on, then wrote Austin a quick text.

> I miss you already. Drive safely and let me know when you get there, okay?

I added the red kiss mark emoji like I always did and hit send.

"I'm ready," Owen said as he came down the stairs. He jumped from about the fifth one.

"Nice," I said, ruffling his hair. "Good plié on the landing."

Both kids had a lot of talent—Adelaide was progressing beautifully in jazz and ballet, and Owen was fantastic at hip hop and tap. I loved that I was their first dance teacher.

"Where's Dad again today?" Adelaide asked once we were on our way to the studio.

"Delivering furniture."

I heard giggling in the backseat and checked on them in the rearview. "What's so funny?"

"Nothing," said Owen. "I, uh, made a funny face."

But the look they exchanged had me wondering if they were up to something.

• • •

Later that afternoon, I was cooking dinner when the doorbell rang. I heard the twins' feet clatter down the stairs and then giggling.

"Kids? Who's at the door?" I set my spatula down on the spoon rest and turned off the heat under the pot.

"It's a delivery man!" Adelaide shouted. "He needs you to sign something."

I smiled. Maybe he'd sent anniversary flowers? Austin was good at surprising me and he loved doing it—small things like bringing me coffee or fudge during the day, thoughtful things like shoveling the snow at the studio or salting the parking lot, sweet things like roses for no reason, dirty things like a hot text message in the middle of the day, and big things like an October weekend in New York City so I could pick up the box of items I'd saved from my mother and see Morgan and her family.

I tried to be just as thoughtful—bringing him lunch while he was working, checking in on his dad, massaging his sore muscles (although that usually led to other things), and when I saw him getting too wound up, reminding him to take a break every once in a while. Go easier on himself.

When Morgan saw us together, she told me she knew instantly he was the one.

"I've never seen you so happy," she said, hugging me tight. "This is right. I feel it."

As I made my way to the front door, I remembered I owed her a phone call. We were trying to—

My feet stopped moving. My heart began to race.

Through the screen door, I saw Austin standing on the front porch, wearing a black tuxedo and a grin.

I covered my mouth with my hands. "Oh my god."

"Hi," he said, holding up a ring box. "I'm here about a bride."

"Oh my *god*." Tears sprang to my eyes as a thousand butterflies took flight in my belly.

Next to me, the twins were giggling. "Go out there," one of them said.

I pushed open the door and stepped out onto the porch. My legs trembled, and my head spun.

Austin—my gorgeous, strong, beloved Austin—went down on one knee and opened the little ring box. A diamond winked at me. "About a year ago, a woman showed up at my door wearing a wedding dress and sneakers," he said. "She was the most beautiful girl I'd ever seen, so I tried to make her go away, because I didn't want to feel the things she made me feel. I didn't like the idea that she might turn our lives upside down. I didn't want anything to change." His lips tipped up, and his dark eyes twinkled. "But she didn't stay away."

I shook my head, tears splashing down my cheeks. "She couldn't."

"I'll be forever grateful that she came back. And I'd like her to stay forever." He glanced through the screen door, where his children stood side by side, just as they had the first day we met. "Now?"

They nodded, their smiles mile-wide.

Austin focused on me again, melting my heart with his gaze. "Veronica Sutton, will you marry me?"

"Yes!" I tried to shout it, but it came out like a squeak because my throat was so tight. "Yes, I'll marry you!"

The kids cheered as he slid the ring on my finger. He rose to his feet, and I threw my arms around him, crying tears of joy. The twins came out and we opened up our hug to include them. "You guys knew!" I accused, squeezing them tight. "That's why you were giggling this morning!"

"They knew," said Austin. "But they were sworn to secrecy."

"We did a good job," said Adelaide. "Mostly."

"You did a perfect job," I assured her. "This was the best surprise ever."

"Can we be in the wedding?" Owen asked.

"Of course!" I said, filled with joy at the prospect of being able to plan a wedding to the man of my dreams. Absolutely everything was going to be different this time. It would be *real*.

"And can we call you Mom?" Adelaide asked shyly. "We want to. We think it's cool to have two moms."

Austin and I locked eyes—his were shining too.

"That would make me very happy," I said, smiling through tears. "Sometimes I don't know what I did to deserve you all."

"You knocked on the right door," said Owen.

I laughed and pulled them all in close once more. "I certainly did."

BONUS

CONTENT

Austin

Knock, knock, knock. "Dad?"

I'd just pulled a sweatshirt over my head when I heard Owen's voice outside my closed bedroom door. My hair was still damp from a shower. "Yeah?"

"Can I come in?"

"Sure, buddy." I dropped onto the foot of the bed to tug on my socks.

The door opened, and my nine-year-old son appeared. For once, his mop of brown hair was neatly combed. I also noticed that his shirt was tucked in, his shoelaces were tied, and he wore khaki pants instead of his usual blue jeans. "Hey. You look fancy." I looked down at my denim-clad legs. "I thought we were just going to Moe's for dinner."

"We are," he said. "But before we go, Adelaide and I want to have a family meeting."

I cocked my head. "A family meeting? For what?"

"We have something we want to ask you."

"Can't you ask at Moe's?" I stood up and went over to my dresser, where I picked up a brush and ran it through my hair.

"No. It sort of involves, like, a presentation." He skipped over to the bed and began bouncing up and down on the edge of the mattress, clearly excited.

I glanced at him in the mirror. "A presentation?"

"Yes."

"About what?"

"I can't tell you without Addie. I promised."

"Hmmm." I put the brush down and stole some of Veronica's fancy hand cream, rubbing it into my face, even though it made me smell like potpourri. "Can you give me a hint?"

He bounced a couple more times. "Well…it's about something we want."

"Something you want? Your birthday was last month," I teased. "It's already March."

"This isn't a birthday present."

"Is it a trampoline?"

"No. But we do want one of those."

"A trip to Disney World?"

He shook his head. "Uh-uh. We'd rather go to Cedar Point. They have bigger roller coasters."

I turned around and leaned back against the dresser, arms folded across my chest. "Is this thing you want expensive?"

He stopped bouncing and thought for a moment, squinting up at one corner of the room. "I don't know for sure. I think it's free. But you might have to pay to take it home."

I laughed. "Do you have to feed it?"

"Yes."

"Is it a dog?"

"No." Owen grinned. "But you're getting warmer."

. . .

VERONICA

I was sitting at the kitchen table, obsessing over the photo on my phone again, when I heard my name.

"Roni?"

I looked up and saw Adelaide standing in the doorway. Quickly, I flipped my phone down on the table. I didn't want her to see what was on the screen—it would spoil the surprise. "What's up? Oooh, you look so pretty!"

"Thank you." She looked down at her best dress, the one usually reserved for school concerts and holiday parties. Her long, wavy hair had been brushed and was held off her face with a headband. In her hand were sheets of looseleaf paper. "Could you come into the living room, please?"

"Of course." Rising from my chair, I glanced down at my stomach, which was only just starting to get a little round. Pretty soon, I wouldn't be able to hide it.

We were having a baby.

Unable to keep the smile off my face, I followed Adelaide into the living room. We were planning to tell them soon—I was just about at the end of the first trimester, which was when we'd agreed to do it. Not only did that give Austin and me a little time to celebrate privately, but we didn't want to throw too much change at the twins all at once.

We'd gotten engaged in June and married that fall. Austin and I had talked it over and decided we wouldn't try to prevent a pregnancy but we wouldn't stress over when it happened. We weren't in a rush.

I'd tucked the positive pregnancy test in his stocking Christmas

Eve after the kids were in bed. Once we'd placed all the gifts from Santa Claus under the tree, I told him a little elf had left something for him. I'd never forget the way his eyes filled when he saw that plus sign. Or the protective way he gathered me in his arms and rocked me back and forth. He said my name, his voice cracking. He choked back tears.

I cried, too, my emotions all over the place. I was happy, of course—I'd never loved anyone the way I loved Austin, and the twins were the cherries on top—but I also missed my mom during times like this, and I felt sad that she wouldn't be here to experience becoming a grandmother. Austin, of course, understood completely.

He suggested we plant some rosebushes in our backyard in honor of my mother, and then in the fall, when his mom's roses were dormant, we'd transplant some here. That way we'd have something beautiful that made us think of them.

It was pure Austin—trying to come up with things he could *do* to make me happy. Words might not have been his thing, but he took care of the people he loved.

I was so lucky to be his wife.

"Sit here, please," Adelaide instructed, pointing to the couch. Then she went over to the stairs and yelled up. "Owen, come on!"

Three seconds later, her brother came bounding down the stairs, leaping from the middle of the steps down to the landing. Austin descended behind him at a much slower pace.

"You sit there, Dad." Adelaide pointed at the empty cushion next to me.

Austin dropped onto the couch and put his arm around me. I leaned into his side and kissed his cheek. Then I sniffed it. "Did you put my hand cream on your face?"

"Uh…yes."

"Austin, that is not for faces! Why didn't you use the

moisturizer I bought you?"

"I don't know. Because it was in the bathroom, and I was by the dresser." He shrugged. "What difference does it make?"

I sighed. "Never mind."

"Okay, are you ready?" Owen asked. "Can we start?"

"Proceed," said Austin. "The king and queen will hear you now."

Adelaide giggled and handed one sheet of paper to her brother. "Here. This is yours." They stood side by side, facing us. Their expressions were determined. "Okay," she said. "We've asked you here this evening to discuss a very important matter."

"Oh?" I looked back and forth between them. "What matter is that?"

"The matter of family." Owen checked his notes. "You both always say that nothing is more important than family."

"That's true," I said.

"And Dad, you grew up in a very big family with three brothers and a sister," Owen went on. "And you love them."

"Most of the time," Austin joked, which earned him a slap on the leg from me. "I'm kidding—yes, of course I do."

"And Veronica grew up without any siblings, and she was sad about it," said Adelaide.

"Very sad," I agreed. "I always wanted brothers and sisters. I think big families are wonderful—especially this one."

The twins looked at each other. "We do, too," Adelaide went on. "That's why we'd like to formally submit a request that you please have a baby."

My jaw dropped open.

Austin started to laugh. "What?"

"It doesn't have to be twins like us," Owen said quickly. "Just one brother would be fine."

"Or one sister." Adelaide shot her brother a look.

"Or one sister," he mumbled.

"And we have several reasons why you should consider this request." Adelaide studied her paper. "Number one, we have not had a pet since the hamster died."

Owen looked towards the heavens. "Rest in peace, Arlo."

"But when we had the hamster, we were very good at remembering to feed it and give it water," Adelaide went on.

"You were very responsible hamster owners," Austin confirmed.

"But Arlo passed on two years ago, and since then, we have not had anywhere to put our love for something small and cute," Adelaide said eagerly. "A baby would be perfect."

My throat felt tight, and I touched my chest.

Austin squeezed my shoulder. "Go on."

"Next, you said last summer before you got married that you wanted to have more kids, and it's been several months already," Owen pointed out.

"Now, just a minute." Austin's voice held a note of mock defensiveness. "These things take time. You can't just go to the pet store and get a baby like you can get a hamster."

"We *know*, Dad." Adelaide rolled her eyes. "They take nine months to grow."

"And it's only been six months since we got married."

"We know that, too," said Owen. "But you always tell us not to leave things until the last minute."

A laugh escaped me. "That's true, Austin. You're not a fan of procrastination."

"Finally," Adelaide said, standing up taller, "we think we would be great at being an older brother and sister. We each have things that we want to teach the baby. For instance, I could teach it how to sing the 'Fifty Nifty United States' song. I already have it memorized."

Owen bounced around excitedly. "And I could teach it to play the guitar, since I just got one for my birthday."

"You've only had one lesson," Austin said wryly.

"I know, but Mr. Mike said I did *very well* for a first-timer, remember?"

"I remember."

I looked at Austin, eyebrows raised. "What do you think, honey? They've made some really good points."

"They have," he conceded. He tapped his chin. "And do you both promise to help out with a baby? Change diapers and things?"

"Yes!" Adelaide shouted.

Owen shifted his weight from one foot to the other. "Do I have to do the poopy ones?"

"All of them," Austin said seriously. "Even the poopy ones."

"I guess," the poor kid mumbled.

"And you'll be quiet when the baby is sleeping?" I asked, unable to keep a smile off my face. "And take him or her for walks in the stroller?"

They both nodded. "Yes," said Adelaide. "And if it has hair, I'll brush it."

"Well, then I think we've heard enough." I patted Austin's leg. "Should we tell them?"

My husband nodded. "Yes."

I looked at my two hopeful cherries on top and grinned. "Want to see something?"

They exchanged glances. "Yes," Owen said.

Tapping my phone screen a couple of times, I brought up the photo of the eight-week ultrasound. "Look."

The twins eased closer and studied the photo. "What's that?" Adelaide asked.

"It's what you wanted—a baby."

Their expressions grew even more befuddled. "It doesn't look like a baby," said Owen. "It looks sort of like a ghost."

I laughed. "It's still growing. But I promise you—it's a baby." My voice caught. "It's your little brother or sister."

Owen's jaw dropped. "Seriously?"

"That was easy," said Adelaide, blinking in surprise. "Is it really true?"

"It's really true." Austin hugged me closer. "The baby is coming this summer."

The twins jumped up and down, tossing their sheets of notes in the air. I quickly got off the couch and picked them up—I would treasure them forever.

"Is the ghost baby a boy or a girl?" Owen wanted to know.

"We're not sure yet," said Austin, rising to his feet.

"Are we going to find out before it's born?" Adelaide looked at me.

"We can," I said. "Would you like to know?"

"Yes!" She beamed and clapped her hands. "It's like knowing the future!"

I laughed, glancing down at their notes. REASONS FOR BABY, Owen had scrawled at the top. Adelaide's said, FAMILY MEETING ABOUT BABY. Suddenly, my eyes swam with tears, and the lump in my throat expanded. These sweet kids had gone through all this trouble—making the list, dressing up, stating their case so earnestly—because they wanted to love a little brother or sister.

"Come here, you two," I said, my voice wavering. I opened my arms and they came crashing into me for a hug. It wouldn't always be this way, I knew. Someday, they would be teenagers and a hug from their parents would be the last thing they wanted. But today, they let me, and I was overcome with emotion by it all.

"Why are you crying?" Owen asked. "Aren't you happy?"

"Yes," I sobbed. "I'm so happy. I love you all so much, and I just feel so lucky."

Austin came over and wrapped us all into his arms, dropping a kiss on my head. "I'm feeling pretty lucky right now too. I already had the two best kids on earth, somehow I got the most beautiful woman in the world to marry me, and now I'm going to be a dad again."

"*And,* you get to have dinner at Moe's tonight!" Owen reminded him, disengaging from our family hug. "Can we go now?"

"Yes," Austin said. "Family meeting adjourned."

"So about that dog you mentioned," Owen said as we headed out the front door. "Is that a possibility?"

Austin ruffled his son's hair. "One thing at a time, kiddo."

The twins raced each other to the car, and Austin took my arm as we went down the porch steps—the very same porch where I'd shown up so desperate and unhappy almost two years ago. Now I had everything I'd ever wanted.

Life was beautiful.

And it was only the beginning.

Acknowledgments

As always, my appreciation and gratitude go to the following people for their talent, support, wisdom, friendship, and encouragement…

Melissa Gaston, Kristie @read_between.the_wines, Brandi Zelenka, Jenn Watson, Hang Le, Corinne Michaels, Anthony Colletti, Rebecca Friedman, Flavia Viotti & Meire Dias at Bookcase Literary, Nancy Smay at Evident Ink, Julia Griffis at The Romance Bibliophile, Michele Ficht, One Night Stand Studios, the Shop Talkers, the Sisterhood, the Harlots and the Harlot ARC Team, bloggers and event organizers, my readers all over the world…

To Cori Callahan, for telling me all her Rockette stories!

And once again, to my family. You're everything.

Runaway Love is a heartwarming small town romance about a single dad and the runaway bride he hires to be the nanny. However, the story includes elements that might not be suitable for all readers. Death of a parent, and an emotionally abusive ex are mentioned, referenced, and discussed in the novel. In addition, a few of the intimate scenes, while entirely consensual, may be construed as rough. Readers who may be sensitive to these elements, please take note.

*Don't miss the exciting new books
Entangled has to offer.*

Follow us!

 @EntangledPublishing

 @Entangled_Publishing

 @EntangledPub

AMARA
an imprint of Entangled Publishing LLC